THE NØKK AND THE JOCK

LESLIE MCADAM

BOOK 1

TABLE OF CONTENTS

About this Book

You're formally admitted to Creelin University—known locally as "Creepin U." The only things wilder than the monster shifters prowling around campus are the spicy male-male love stories unfolding between classes. *The Nøkk and the Jock* is book one, starring an emo shapeshifter and a sunshine human. Each book is a stand-alone M/M spooky romance, but we hope you enroll in them all.

Brandon:

I'm pumped to be one of the first humans to attend a monster university, but a minor, negligible, insignificant issue arises almost immediately: My new roommate wants to drag me to his underground realm and take my soul.

He's a nøkk who could almost pass for human, except his webbed fingers and entirely black eyes give him away. In my attempt to befriend him, I give him three drops of my blood, a black animal, and a bottle of vodka (I hear it's a nøkk thing). Which apparently triggers some ancient bonding ritual. My bad.

I must admit I'm into him. Maybe those online tests that say I'm only *mostly* straight are right. But there are a few hiccups: I can't know his real name. He won't show me his true form. And he's both an omen and a cause of drowning ... which is troubling, since he's on the water polo team with me.

Still, something about him calls to me, even if it shouldn't.

The Nøkk:

This human is mine.

Stay away from him.

The Nøkk and the Jock *is a monster-human bi-awakening M/M romance starring Brandon Fernandez, a golden retriever of a human being, and the prickly, melancholy nøkk. It features puzzling emoji text conversations, a monster who can stop waterfalls in midair, and drunken scareoke (monster karaoke). HEA guaranteed.*

PLAYLIST

The Nøkk's playlist (courtesy of my 15-year-old, who created an "emo Norwegian boy" playlist in literally two minutes):
"Monster"—Skillet
"Wolf in Sheep's Clothing"—Set It Off
"Blood//Water"—grandson
"Thnks Fr Th Mmrs"—Fall Out Boy
"Thank You for the Venom"—My Chemical Romance
"Teenagers"—My Chemical Romance
"I Write Sins Not Tragedies"—Panic! At the Disco
"Hayloft"—Mother Mother
"Hayloft II"—Mother Mother
"N.M.E."—Set It Off
"Comatose"—Skillet
"Body"—Mother Mother
"Brain Stew"—Green Day
"Dance, Dance"—Fall Out Boy
"So Long"—James Marriott
https://music.apple.com/us/playlist/the-n%C3%B8kk-and-the-jock-part-one-steve/pl.u-yZyVDKmu1AL4L

Brandon's playlist:
"The Best"—AWOLNATION
"Whatever It Takes"—Imagine Dragons
"Burn the House Down"—AJR
"I Like Myself (Most of the Time)"—K. Flay
"Give a Little"—LeGrand

"My Way"—Frank Sinatra

"Toxic"—Britney Spears

"bad guy"—Billie Eilish

"Bohemian Rhapsody"—Queen

"Let It Go"—Idina Menzel

"I Feel Like I'm Drowning"—Two Feet

"Naked Kids"—Grouplove

"The Monster" (feat. Rihanna)—Eminem

"I See You"—Missio

"Darling" (feat. Missio)—Said The Sky

https://music.apple.com/us/playlist/the-n%C3%B8kk-and-the-jock-part-two-brandon/pl.u-zPyLAeLCq9VoV

Author's Note

If you're familiar with Scandinavian folklore, it will quickly become apparent to you that, while much of *The Nøkk and the Jock* has some basis in traditional stories, I took some pretty damn big liberties in portraying the magic system. I was told that I'm somewhat off the hook, since there aren't any nøkks around for me to ask to do a sensitivity read. (Although I did have a Norwegian friend read an early version. Thanks, Susann!) But then my brother reminded me that he's convinced our Scandinavian mother is directly descended from jotun, aka frost giants, and I could ask her. (Side note: When we confronted her with her mythological Norse ancestry, she didn't deny it, so it must be true.) Except she's not allowed to read my books ... even though apparently she does so anyway. I discovered this when I found her one-line five-star Amazon review of my first book. That's such frost giant behavior. Still, it doesn't mean she gets to read my words about sexy water polo boys getting it on in the shower. Thus, since I could not ask any nøkks or other mythical creatures (aka my mother) about their magic, please don't take my portrayal of them as canon. It's not.

Content warning: recreational drinking, reference to recreational drug use, explicit sex, swearing, abandonment/rejection by a parent, death (in the past, off page) of a loved one, drowning and threat of drowning, body shaming, fistfights, bullying.

Series Memo

Notes from the Organization of Monster Enhancement

Two decades ago, a spontaneous anomaly affected the world. Approximately thirty-three percent of the human population was permanently transformed into different beings of various classifications, soon labeled as "monsters." Some individuals shift into and out of their secondary form. Others were permanently changed and have no shifting abilities. An additional subset of previously deceased beings was resurrected; while most of these undead individuals are harmless automatons, a rare few have sentience.

Monsters walk among us and deserve our respect. Like all humans, they live, learn, work, eat, play, and, of course, love.

Bro how the heck
Do tournaments
I am confused
—Jasper McAdam

I

Brandon

I'm in the vodka aisle of Brainz Liquor with my water polo teammate Clay, plotting how to charm my roommate-to-be: a nøkk. Charm as in "make the nøkk my friend," not, like, "cast a spell" or "perform a ritual" or whatever. At least, that's my goal.

But I'm having trouble getting started.

Scratching the back of my neck, I squint at dozens of clear glass bottles on the janky shelves. "I wish the tradition called for beer," I say, throwing up my hands. "What if I just pick him up a six-pack of an IPA? Would that be a total mistake?"

I look around the cramped shop, with its squeaky wooden floors and antique bottles shoved way up high into the rafters. Is anyone else here buying vodka?

A cyclops and a fellow human loiter at the closest refrigerator case to Clay and me, arguing over whether they should get PBR or Natural Light. (The correct answer is neither.) On the other side of them, three thunderbird shifter girls are selecting a twenty-four-pack of Boowery beer. Local microbrew. Nice. Also, not helpful.

I'm overthinking because this is more than buying a present for a potential friend at a new school. I'm setting the tone for a whole new *era*. Creelin U is the first monster university in the country to welcome humans, and as one of those historic first students, I want to do my part to foster good human-monster relations. Hence, booze.

Except … I'm stuck. You'd think by my junior year of college I'd have the best brands of liquor down pat, but nope. I learned early on that the hard stuff and I don't mix well, so I know very little about it. Beer? Yes, especially in the offseason. Weed? Fine, on occasion. Tequila? I could call up my uncle who makes his own and ask. But vodka? Nope. This gap in my knowledge explains why I've been studying row after row of bottles for the past half hour. It also explains why, when I saw Clay strolling in for a bottle of spiked O negative or something, I roped him into assisting me.

Clay, however, is no help at all. He may be wing to my flat on our water polo team, and thus my new best friend, but I'm learning that he doesn't know much more than I do about buying alcohol.

"If vodka's the rule, then you give him vodka, Fernandez," Clay says sagely, like he's some guru monk in a movie. He's not. He's a vampire. Except he's got a California surfer-boy drawl, so he's more *Point Break* than *Lost Boys*. When I met him, I told him so. The next day, he took me to the theater in town to see a new release, demanding that I watch a movie from this century. He hates anything old. In return, I made him watch *Better Off Dead* on the laptop in my dorm room. No one disrespects my eighties movies. We've now had four movie marathons, but neither one of us can get the other to agree that their movies are better. I'm good with it. Next up is *Dead Poets Society*.

Arriving on campus early for water polo has rid me of most of my new-school jitters, since I have built-in friends on the team. We've developed the sense of belonging that comes from bonding about the common enemy of having to set our alarms for zero dark thirty during summer break. We get up at dawn, grumble about it, practice for a few hours, then go to brunch. The group is truly starting to come together to dominate in the pool.

But a few nerves remain. I'm worried about how our team is going to do once we're playing for real. I'm worried about keeping up my grades for my scholarship. And I'm *really* worried about whether my new roommate is going to like me. If he doesn't, this whole year will suck like last year … and the year before. I can be a lot—too much for some people—and I want to get started on the right foot.

You might think I could've avoided this issue by getting my own room in town, and you'd be right, but my scholarship covers the cost of the dorms, and plenty of Creelin juniors and seniors live on campus.

"Just because the design's badass, what, like, it's better?" I ask dubiously. I gesture at a label with an old-school flash tattoo design and then to another one that seems to be dripping in blood. "Does all vodka taste the same? I've heard that, but I dunno. What do I do?"

Today is move-in day for returning students; newbies— which includes all humans plus monster transfers like my roommate—arrive tomorrow. Except I'm already here for polo, and he's coming from Norway, and I guess there aren't a lot of flights or something.

I wonder what his name is. The school didn't tell me. All I know is that he's a nøkk, which is a monster I'd never heard of before, so of course I looked it up on Witchipedia.

Nøkk (also known as näck, nixie)

Shapeshifting water spirit originating from Scandinavian folklore, who takes the form of a handsome man to lure people, especially pregnant women and unbaptized children, to the underground world to take their souls. The dangerous and mysterious nøkk is often melancholy because he lacks a human soul and will never find salvation. Presenting the nøkk with a gift of vodka, a black animal, and three drops of blood is tradition, and in return, the nøkk will teach the giver a special form of music. The nøkk can stop waterfalls in midair, and the scream of the nøkk is an omen of…

I don't like the idea of my new roomie being melancholy. I want him to feel like he belongs, which is why I'm here shopping for this traditional gift for him.

Clay frowns, his black pompadour slicked back to show his pale, blueish skin. "Yeah, huh. Hmm. Pick one *you* like."

"That's the problem. I don't like vodka." I stare at Clay. "Do you?"

"No. I drink blood." He flashes me his fangs.

I burst out laughing. "Oh my god, I can't believe I asked you to help me."

He points at a bottle shaped like a black crystal skull that's sitting at eye level. "Buy this one. The bottle's *sweet*."

The price tag on the shelf makes me clear my throat. I pull out my phone and navigate to the app with my bank balance. Same tiny number to get me through the weekend. My scholarship should hit Monday, but I keep wishing it will magically fund earlier.

I turn to Clay. "It's also sixty bucks. Is it really that good? Doubt it." I run my blunt nails down my cheeks. "I dunno what

I'm doinggg."

"Witchipedia didn't specify a kind, did it?" Clay asks.

"Nope."

"Then I don't think the brand matters."

"What if he doesn't like me because I pick the wrong one?" I mutter.

Clay pats my bare bicep with his cold hand. It feels like being hit with a frozen chicken breast. "He will. Or he'll answer to me."

I rub my arm. "Pretty sure you can't vampire-aura someone into being my friend."

"I could try. Besides, everyone likes you. I don't know what you're so worried about."

"I just want to have a better start than I did at my old school. Not being able to hang out in my own dorm room sucked."

"Still. You're trying too hard."

"Whatever." I don't care if I'm trying too hard. This matters. Who my roommate is matters, and I want to make the best first impression I can.

I tilt my head and again study the choices. Finally, I spy a dusty bottle of charcoal-filtered vodka on the bottom shelf for $10.99. Perfect. I snatch it up. "This'll do. Let's go." Now I have to find this zombie everyone says doesn't card people. "Everyone" being our teammate Phil.

I don't see a zombie, but there's a brown-haired harpy with wire-rimmed glasses perched behind the cash register, texting on her phone. She looks familiar. Ah, she's the Creelin U student body association rep who gave me an early orientation tour. Bingo.

Walking up to her like I've done this a million times, I set the bottle on the counter and beam at her, but her head's down. She scans the barcode and tells me the price, and I hand her a crumpled twenty my grandma gave me for my birthday. Then she looks up and squeals, "OMG, Brandon!"

"Hey there." I bite the inside of my cheek. Crap, she remembers my name. What's hers? "I didn't know you worked here!"

Clay shuffles behind me, and I see his hand move over his mouth as he tries not to laugh. Dammit, he can read me well already.

"Yeah, it's a new job. Closest store to school. Better pay than work-study." She winks, and her wings unfurl. "Are you starting to find your way around?"

Putting an elbow on the counter and leaning in closer, I say, "I am. I've almost got the cafeteria figured out, and I know where all my classes are going to be. Thanks so much for your help."

"You're welcome," she says brightly. "It's ... *different* having humans on campus, but I think this year's gonna be great."

"Yep, it is." My eyes slip from hers to the Visa/MonsterCard logo on the counter. "First group of humans enrolled at Creelin. It's gonna be, uh, new." What else can we talk about? Help.

A pause. Then comes the dreaded question. "Totally sorry, Brandon, but can I see your ID?"

My stomach sinks.

No, I can talk my way through this. Cheeks burning, I dig in my pocket for my wallet and nonchalantly pass over my driver's license. I'm going to have words with Phil next time I see him.

The cashier holds my ID up and studies it. Her brows knit together. "Um, this says you're twenty."

Clay snorts quietly and murmurs, "Wait, you're not old enough? What the hell, Fernandez?"

I shoot him side-eye. "I'll be twenty-one in less than a month.

That's just *days*. Let's have a party. Karaoke. Know what? I'm inviting everyone who wants to come. You could join us." I give the cashier my most charming smile. "Can't you round up?"

The harpy presses her lips together in an apologetic pout. "I'll get in trouble." Her eyes shift to the back of the store, where a zombie, likely the owner, is sweeping.

"I thought he was cool." I jerk my head his way.

She shakes her head. "He's absent-minded, but he can be strict. Sorry. Karaoke sounds fun, though. Are you going to do it at Scareoke?"

Where's the local Scareoke franchise? I nod anyway.

"I'm not sure I can make it, since I'll probably have to work, but thanks for the invite." She taps the vodka bottle with her talon. "Can't you come back on your birthday?"

I lower my voice, press my hands together like I'm praying, and look at her intently. "Look, I'm not actually buying it for me. It's a present. I need vodka to befriend my new roommate. Please. He's a nøkk. Do you know any nøkks? I've never met one before. They're rare in the United States, and I want to make him feel welcome—"

"I still can't sell it to you if you're underage." She wrinkles her nose in a kindly way so her glasses push up her face. "I'm sorry."

Dammit, Phil.

Sighing, I pass the bottle to Clay. I hope he's older. He flicks his eyes to the ceiling, shakes his head slightly, and hands her his ID. He exchanges an amused-slash-annoyed look with the cashier, then addresses me. "Dude, why didn't you just ask me to begin with?"

I scowl. "Didn't think I needed to. Phil said they don't card here."

Clay puts a hand on his hip, turning to fully face me. "You trusted *Phil?*" He rolls his eyes, and the harpy starts to roll hers, too—Phil's pretty well-known, I think, since he's a seven-foot-tall Sasquatch—but then she reads Clay's identification.

"Um." She strokes her chin. "This also says you're twenty. And it looks really fake."

I burst out laughing. "Wait, you're not twenty-one, either?"

"Oops. Shit. I'm older than that." He sighs and pulls out his wallet again. "I hate my real ID."

I catch a glimpse of the identification she returns to him. "You have an *inverse* fake ID, Clay Cannon? Stuck forever before your twenty-first birthday, huh?"

With a pointed glare at me, Clay gives her his driver's license.

Her eyes widen. "Yeah, okay. You're plenty old enough. Thanks so much for shopping at Brainz! Hope to see you at the bonfire tomorrow night!" She bags up the bottle and hands it to Clay, along with *my* change, which he pockets. He waits to pass the vodka to me until we step outside into the warm but overcast afternoon.

Yes, even though he's a vampire, he can go out during the day. Eighties movies don't get everything right.

I pull out my phone and text Phil a string of emojis: whiskey glass, ID, red *x*, thumbs-down, knife.

He immediately sends me a middle finger emoji, and I snort, showing my phone to Clay.

"How come you never text in words?" he asks.

"Why would I use words when they"—I shake my phone at him—"give me so many emojis to use?"

"But what you send doesn't make sense sometimes."

I shrug. "You always figure it out." Then I sing, "Money,

please," as he and I start strolling back to campus.

Clay digs in his shorts and gives me the change. "I don't get a buyer's fee?"

"Nope."

Then he pats his pockets, his face looking pained. "Crap. I think I lost my room key."

I look back over my shoulder. "Did you leave it in the store?"

"No, I don't think so. You would've seen it."

"True. Then you can go check your room—did you leave the door unlocked?"

He nods. "My roommate was there."

"Well, if you don't find it, the housing office is still open. You can stop by there and see if they can give you a spare or something."

"Yeah, okay."

We walk a few moments, enjoying one of the last afternoons before classes start and we have less free time. Finally, I pipe up. "I wanted to buy the booze on my own—felt like more of a gift from me, you know?—but I'm glad you were there. Thanks for helping."

He nudges me with his shoulder. "You're welcome. Young'un."

"I should've known it wouldn't work, except I've bought beer before without getting carded. And everyone said the owner was cool."

"I get it. I don't normally get carded, either."

"That's because you turned twenty, what, nineteen or twenty years ago?"

He shrugs and mumbles, "Something like that."

Clay definitely doesn't act forty. Maybe vampires mature slower.

"What were you gonna buy?" I ask.

"Hmm? Me? Oh, I forgot. I was going to get a blood pop. It's okay, I can get one later."

It's a pleasant day, so we're both in tank tops. The sides of my shirt are sliced halfway down, and the breeze feels good. It ruffles my curly, overgrown hair, which is flopping in my eyes. I should've gotten it cut before I left home, but I was too busy.

"Continuing on," I say as we pass by a couple of girls, who wave at us. I've never seen them before. I wave back anyway. "How should I give him the three drops of blood?"

"You could let me bite you." A glint of hope sparkles in Clay's violet eyes. "And I can spit in a test tube."

I hold up a hand. "Ew. No. Gross. Pass." I purse my lips, and then the light bulb turns on. "I can get some microscope slides from the student store and poke my finger. That'd work, right?"

"Boring, but yeah. I guess." Clay's phone lets out a distinctive sound, but he ignores it. It's the WereScruff hookup app notification. I don't use it, because I'm straight—at least, if you ignore the online tests that say I'm not *100%* straight. You can't trust anything on the internet, and I round everything up. Like my age. But I have lots of LGBT friends like Clay who use the app and have heard that sound many times since I started college. "Let me know if you change your mind and want me to bite you."

I shove him. He laughs, and we cross the bridge over the Lin River. It rushes below us, dancing over rocks to a quiet pool downstream. My friends and I—along with a lot of other students—spend quite a bit of time on the banks of the Lin and Cree Rivers. Since the weather's been good, we've practically lived there the past few weeks when we weren't at practice, in the cafeteria, or watching movies.

"Where do you think I can find a black animal?" I ask. "Should I go to an animal shelter and adopt a cat? A black bear? What other kinds of animals are black? A panther?"

Clay snorts. "What the hell is he going to do with a black bear in the dorms? And where would you get one, anyway? Just catch the nøkk, like, a beetle."

I hum. "I wanna do this right, but I'm good with giving him something tiny and low-maintenance. Where do you think we can pick up a beetle?"

"Um. The forest." He does jazz hands as he waves at the groves of trees off the side of the road. The school's surrounded by a wooded area, which is currently bright green with late-summer leaves.

"Yeah, maybe." I bite my lip and do an up-nod at a mummy who's staring at me. Well, I think he's staring. With the bandages, sometimes it can be hard to tell.

Also, now that I think about it, it's felt like *everyone's* been looking at me since I got here, but especially today with the arrival of the returning monster students. What the hell?

"Is there something on my face?" I turn up my face to Clay for inspection like I'm a toddler needing someone to wipe off a milk mustache.

Clay raises an eyebrow that's the same blue-black as his hair. "It's fine."

"Okay, good. So why does it feel like I've been stared at all day?"

"You're human. Having you on campus is as new for us as it is for you. It's one thing to live in the same city, another to go to school together." As an afterthought, he muses, "Or maybe they want to eat you."

I smack his chest, which feels like hitting an Igloo cooler—from the inside. "Are you serious? I thought that was only in movies. Like, monsters don't actually eat people in real life, do they? None back home did." I don't think.

"Not that kind of eating." Clay smirks. "Have you seen yourself?"

"Yeah," I say. "I have a mirror. Wait, is the thing about vampires not being able to see themselves in the mirror true?"

Clay starts laughing. "Oh my god, dude, you're going to make me say it? You're hot, Brandon. All the monsters want to bang you."

"They do not!" I hiss, although the image of banging one of the thunderbird shifters we saw earlier comes into my mind. I've only ever been with human girls. What would it be like to get together with a *monster* girl?

He nods emphatically, pulling me out of my reverie. "They do. Humans, too."

"Whatever."

"And yes, I can see myself in a mirror. Sheesh, it's like you get all your info on vampires from the movies."

I smile. "I love movies."

Clay shoves me.

We pass through the gargoyle-guarded university gates, and I study them, watching for movement. Apparently some are statues and some are real, but humans can't tell the difference. At least, I can't. They all seem like stone.

"Huh." I bite my lip, thinking over all the looks I've been receiving. "I was wondering what was going on. I got in the wrong line in the cafeteria this morning—you know, the one with the bloody food for the werewolves? At any rate, everyone was star-

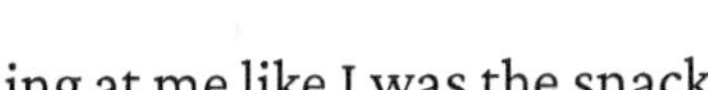

ing at me like I was the snack."

"To be fair, your blood does smell delicious," Clay says reasonably.

"Go away, vampire. You're not getting any of this." I jokingly point to my chest. "And how do I smell different from any other human?"

He laughs. "Okay, fine. You just smell like a good, normal human. But that's what's up. They all want in your pants. Guys, girls, nonbinary folx. Humans. Monsters. I think it's your face. And that hair."

"Whatever," I repeat, although I'm excited for what the school year will bring. Maybe I'll find the girl of my dreams. Or at least get laid.

And I'm already getting my biggest wish—to belong. Back home, I was too much for some people and not enough for others. At a new school on a very diverse team with all kinds of monsters as well as other humans, where everyone brings something unique to the group, I'm feeling accepted. Finally.

Clay stops short as a spider scurries past us on the ground. With lightning-fast speed, he scoops it up and keeps it cupped in his hand. "Here's your black animal."

"Thanks! Come with me to the student store?"

We smile and coo at the little spider as we head in to buy microscope slides ... and maybe get a container for the nøkk's new pet.

2

THE NØKK

Hoisting my backpack over my shoulder, I step off the airplane in front of the precious toddler cyclops who kicked my seat the entire trip from Oslo. I yawn. My back aches from hours of keeping my elbows close to my body to avoid touching the bogeyman seated next to me. I did not sleep. My eyes feel as dry as sand.

But I am finally here. JFK Airport. New York City.

For months, I had been feeling an intense longing that would not go away: a need to leave Norway and start over. Now, as I set foot on solid ground, my throat is thick, and I blink back tears.

I have arrived. It is time to start my new life away from my homeland. I am not wanted there.

Humans and monsters alike shuffle down a series of long corridors, headed for baggage claim. A recorded female voice comes over the loudspeakers every few seconds with a new announcement like "Welcome to the United States. Please have your passports available for inspection. As a reminder, phoenix shifters are required to delay self-immolation and rebirth until exiting the terminal. Rideshares are located on the lower level by gate A56. Acid spitting and fire breathing are strictly forbidden inside the terminal area."

I walk by a mirrored wall and catch a glimpse of myself amid all the other passengers. Dark eyes lined with black eyeliner. Straight green-black hair with long bangs. Pale skin. Skinny jeans, tight band T-shirt, studded belt, and Converse high-tops. My body form is unstable, though, my outline fuzzy around the edges.

Focus. Maintain your appearance. I look again, and now I appear more solid. Good.

After what seems like several kilometers of walking, we enter an enormous room full of hundreds of monsters and humans standing in lines that snake back and forth. Booths with glass walls, occupied by immigration officials, await us at the far end.

My heart palpitates, and I am hit with a sudden headache. My instinct tells me to turn around and get back on the airplane and go home. Flee. While I have traveled before, it has been with my cousin, never on my own.

But no. I can do this. I have a plan: Pass immigration. Get my bags. Go through customs. Take the train to Pennsylvania. Start anew, and hopefully better, college experience.

It is a good plan. I did not leave Norway only to immediately return.

A uniformed human with a strong New York accent says, "US citizens over to the right. Permanent residents to the right. Everyone else to the left. Move along, people. We haven't got all day."

Bleary-eyed, I get in line behind a family of centaurs from Italy—judging by their passports—and in front of a pair of humans from Peru. I fidget and yawn again. My body feels hollow, and my muscles are twitchy.

I am told that if a human travels in a natural manner, like walking or floating down a river, they do not move faster than their soul. As a result, those methods of travel feel harmonious and pleasant. But if a human travels by machine, their soul needs time to catch up, hence the sense of disorientation upon arrival at their destination. It can take just a short while for body and soul to rejoin if the human travels by car, which explains their need to periodically stop and stretch on long trips. After airplane travel, the soul needs longer to find its body. Humans call this feeling "jet lag," and it can take a day or more for the soul to return and the human to feel well again.

Since I do not have a soul, jet lag cannot be the reason for my physical discomfort right now—shortness of breath, tense stomach, overwhelming thirst. Maybe it is simply anxiety.

A speaker crackles. "Will the owner of a mythic broadsword please return to gate C3 to retrieve a lost item?"

The queue moves forward slowly, and eventually I make it to the counter with an immigration official—a human—sitting behind a clear partition with a little slot at the bottom. Biting my lip, I pull my passport out of my jeans pocket and accidentally drop it on the ground. Cursing my clumsiness, I pick it up, slip it through the opening, and hold my breath.

Before the official opens my passport, he points to a taped line on the floor in front of a camera and says in a bored voice, "Stand there."

With a rolling feeling in my gut, I follow his instructions. I assume the camera takes my photograph, although there is no outward sign that it did anything. As my headache comes on stronger, I return to the opening in the glass. The man is scowling at the computer.

"Is this your true form?" He taps on the monitor. "You're not showing up in the facial recognition database."

Scratching my ear, I move my weight from one foot to the other and sigh. "No. It is not my true form. Do I need to shift?"

The official makes an impatient noise and holds out an open hand, gesturing to the crowd behind me. "Shifters have two choices if they wanna enter America. Show your true form, or fill out the F3917 application."

"Can you give me the application?" *Please do not make me transform in public.*

He puts both hands on the counter and looks down at me. "Sure, but it will take seven to ten days to process, and you have to stay in the airport until it's done."

I blink at him. My stomach drops. My heartbeat speeds up. I paste on a smile and clasp my hands together. "Okay. I will comply."

It is not unusual for shifters to have to show their true form in circumstances like this—ones involving identification. I do not know why I expected anything different. I guess I had not thought it through. Or maybe it was wishful thinking. I am used to not having to prove my identity at home, and indeed, in some situations regulations require shifters to remain in human form.

Quickly, I move back to the line on the floor and shift into my true form. Everyone around me takes two steps back, but I cannot tell if they are simply surprised or if they are repelled. I always assume it is because they are repelled. After all, my human mother has told me how ugly I am. How horrified she was when she gave birth to a nøkk instead of a human. I glare at them.

The immigration official gives a little cough and then recov-

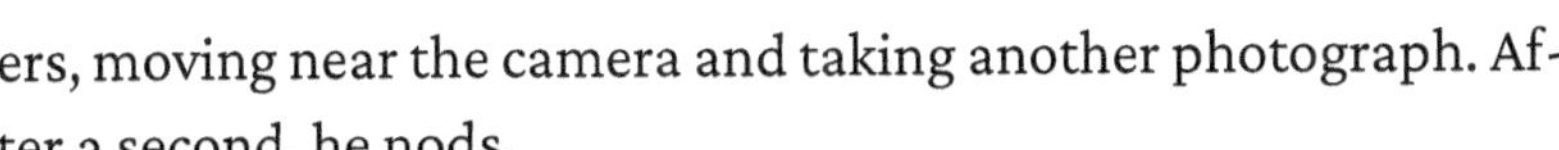

ers, moving near the camera and taking another photograph. After a second, he nods.

I shift back and return to the window, unable to meet anyone's eyes, my arms tucked tight to my sides. While monsters are integrated into society, and there is little overt prejudice, I am still an outsider.

But now the official is staring at my passport, scratching his chin, and muttering to himself. "Okay, that's a match, but … Hmm." He picks up a phone and dials. "Fran, could you please come over? I've got an irregularity with a Norwegian citizen's passport." He turns to me, seeming to want to keep going on other questions while we wait. I take that as a hopeful sign. "What is the purpose of your visit?"

"I am here for college. On a student visa."

"Where are you staying?"

"Pennsylvania." If I can make it into the country.

A uniformed banshee with a name tag that says "Supervisor" strides over and stands next to us. "What's the problem, Reggie?"

"This gentleman's passport"—Reggie indicates me—"has a blank where the name goes. I've never seen a passport without a name."

The banshee takes my passport and flips through it. She turns to me with a hand on her hip. Then recognition dawns in her eyes. "Ah. Norway. You're a nøkk?"

"Yes." She must be able to tell by my eyes and my fingers. And my photo, I suppose.

"That explains it." She addresses Reggie. "He's clear on that front. Protocol S2524."

Reggie's eyes get big, and he looks at me. "Ohh. Okay. No names. I get it." He turns to the supervisor. "Never seen a nøkk before or had to invoke that protocol."

"In twenty years it's only happened a few times," she says.

"Got it. Thanks, Fran."

"Yep." She gives me a nod. "Good luck, nøkk."

"Thank you."

Reggie stamps my passport. "Welcome to the United States."

"Yes. Thank you." I move past him as quickly as I can, breathing more freely the farther away I get from that encounter.

The next area is the baggage claim, and my belongings are waiting for me—a small mercy. I rent a cart and hoist my bags onto it, walk through the "Nothing to Declare" part of customs, and then I am in the chaos of international arrivals. People are everywhere—humans, monsters—hugging, kissing, exclaiming.

No one greets me, but I was not expecting anyone. I wrap my arms around my stomach to stave off the loneliness, and after a moment, it dissipates.

Keep going.

I pass by a store full of American flags and T-shirts. I do not need those, although I do need to get a US telephone number. Thankfully, there is a store at the airport that can take care of this for me. The salesperson asks me what name to put down on my account, and I tell him the first one I think of, which makes him chuckle, but I refuse to change it after I blurt it out.

It is not easy being a nøkk.

While I do not want to give my father my new number, he can still get in touch with me by email or traditional nøkk magic, so there is no sense in withholding it. I text him that I have landed.

I do not get a response. He is probably out looking for his next victim.

I step out of the store, blinking rapidly and searching for

guidance signs. There are so many people surrounding me that it is difficult to determine where to go.

But eventually, I see the sign for directions to the train station.

Excellent.

THE TRAIN is waiting at the platform when I get there. I drop my luggage off in the vestibule at the end of the train car and find my assigned seat, which is on the aisle. Already in the seat across from mine, facing me, is a human child who looks deceptively cute, next to his mother, I assume, who is by the window. They are seated so they will be traveling backward, I believe. Remembering the toddler on the airplane, I am wary of being kicked, but the child's mother seems to be distracting him. I put on my headphones and begin listening to a rock playlist on Spookify.

The human child unabashedly stares at me, and for a moment I worry I have shifted back into my true form. But no, when I glance down, I look like a human. Mostly. I stare back until he looks away. Then I pick at my black-painted fingernails.

The train takes off toward Pennsylvania, and I settle in for the ride. I am not feeling well. Constantly moving, being away from a water source—it is getting to me. My headache has lessened, though.

I will be fine. I am sure.

My mind wanders to what my roommate will be like. In Norway, I lived at home when I went to university. I have not shared a room before.

I do not look up when the train stops at the first station, but when it starts again, a passenger comes walking down the aisle carrying a large coffee. The passenger trips, and the cup arcs out of his hand. Before I think about it, I am out of my seat at monster speed and hovering over the child to shield him. The scalding liquid ends up spilling on my back. Better me than the human child. I am more able to heal myself.

The passenger yelps, "Sorry! I'll go get napkins."

When the child's mother realizes what happened, her eyes grow wide, and she takes her child into her lap. "You saved Chris!" she says, checking the child over. He seems to be unharmed. Then she turns to me. "Oh my goodness, are you okay?"

"I am fine," I say, my skin burning. I focus to make it regenerate. While I am not the best at partial shifts, I make the pain mostly go away.

She starts clucking at me. "No, you're covered in coffee. Do you want to borrow a jacket? Or do you need something else? I'm just so sorry."

"It is okay. I will simply put on a different shirt," I say, and stand to go down to the baggage area.

She reaches out a hand to take mine, ignoring my webbed fingers. "The stains may not come out. Let me give you money to replace it, at least?"

"I could not accept."

"Can I buy you a drink? What do you like to drink?"

A vodka sounds nice, although the drinking age is higher here than in Europe. Or a big glass of water. I am also a true Norwegian and love coffee. "I am fine."

I walk down to my bags. I take out a clean shirt and change in the vestibule, then return. The passenger with the coffee cup reappears with napkins and four drinks in a beverage holder, three

of which he passes to us, apologizing profusely. I accept the coffee, which is scalding hot, while Chris drinks what appears to be
cocoa cooled with extra milk. Having satisfied himself that the
damage is repaired, the passenger continues to his seat.

Sipping her own coffee, the mother smiles at me. "What is
your accent? Somewhere in Europe?"

"Yes, I am from Norway."

"Are you going to be in the United States long?"

"Yes. I will be here for the school year. I am attending Creelin
University."

"Oh! Creepin U! I mean, that's what people in town call it. I
live in Creelin." She starts scribbling on the back of a scrap of paper. "I'm Kellie, and this is Chris, and if you ever need anything
while you're in school, just give us a call, okay? My wife and I
would love to have you come by for dinner sometime. Especially
since you saved Chris from getting burned."

I take the paper as if it is an offering. "Yes, thank you. I will."
I have no intention of taking her up on it, but it is a kind gesture.
Also, it does not hurt to know local people, just in case.

She seems safe. I do not feel a pull to take her soul.

I have never felt that pull, but I am always wary and on the
lookout for it. I do not want to be like my father.

"Can I have your number?" she asks.

"Um. Yes." I pull out my phone and tell her the number.

She texts me a "Hey, it's Kellie" message. "Do you mind me
asking what you're studying at Creelin?"

"I am a music major," I say.

"How fascinating! Tell me all about it!"

And while Chris the child plays contentedly on her phone,
Kellie listens as I tell her all about the kind of music I like to play.

The kind I hope I will get to play when I arrive at Creelin—very modern music on the electric guitar. Not the traditional nøkk music. Although I am officially signed up to play the violin, I brought my guitar as well.

I think I may have made my first friend in the United States. I need to be careful about making any more, though. After knowing what happened to my mother, I could not bear to indulge my true nøkk nature. But hopefully I will not meet anyone who triggers that instinct.

We arrive at the Creelin train station.

"Would you like me to give you a ride to school?" Kellie asks, as she gathers up her belongings and her son.

"No, thank you. I am fine," I say.

"You're sure?"

I nod. "There are taxis."

"Be sure to text when you get settled in," she says. "Even if it takes a few days."

A lump forms in my throat. She is acting more motherly than my own mother. "I will keep in touch, yes."

I take a taxi cab to the university, get to the administration building, and find my room assignment. A chatty troll walks with me to the room.

Holding my breath, I open the door. There is no one inside, but it is nevertheless obvious that someone has already moved in.

I wonder who my new roommate will be. And what will it be like living with a human?

3

BRANDON

Clay and I head into Mummy Mocha, which is located on the first floor of the CU library. The gold-and-blue decor is all fake crypts and sarcophagi, but I dig it. I've been in here a few times since I arrived at school, and I can tell I'm going to be a regular.

"Dammit, we forgot to look for a container for Spidey. Do you think, if we ask, they'll have a jar of some kind here? Or maybe we just use an empty coffee cup," I say to Clay, as the spider crawls around his fingers.

"What do you need a jar for?" someone asks from behind us.

We turn and see a tall, dark, and handsome man. I've already heard of him—Sethem Adham, crush of all the monster boys on campus. The ones who are into guys, that is.

"I'm giving my new nøkk roommate this spider," I say. "But we need something to put him in. And hi, I'm Brandon, and this is Clay."

"Nice to meet you. I'm Seth." He grins. "I have just the thing. Give me five minutes."

I look at Clay and shrug. "Thanks, dude," I say to Seth's departing back.

The line moves fast, and when it's my turn, I order a sarcophacappuccino over ice.

"Do you want anything?" I ask Clay.

"Nah. I'll get blood later."

I pay for the coffee with some of my remaining cash—grateful that the cafeteria will supply me with food for the weekend—and while we're waiting for Seth, we sit at a table and I down my drink. The caffeine hits me, and I feel more energized. "Help me prick my finger," I say.

Clay scrunches his nose. "And I really can't drink your blood?"

"Nope. Gimme." I gesture at his hand, and he sighs and lets me poke one of his sharp nails into the pad of my index finger. Then I smear three drops of blood onto the microscope slide I just bought and cover it with a little square piece of glass.

"Too tempting, Bran," Clay says, looking at the blood longingly and licking his lips.

"Not for you, and not sorry," I say, setting the slide in the bag with the vodka and sucking my finger to stop the bleeding.

Seth returns holding a small jar, which he places in my hands. "Here you go."

It looks like something from ancient Egypt. I furrow my brows. "Where did you get this?"

"I'm a mummy shifter. I have access to lots of jars." He winks.

"Thank you. This is awesome." I hold up the small jar, which has a metal lid that isn't at all modern, and inspect it. "Can I punch a hole in this to let the spider breathe?"

"Do what you wish," Seth says, with a go-ahead gesture.

I pass it over to Clay, who uses one of his fangs to make a hole in the metal. Then we set the spider in the jar, and it seems to be content. At least, it's not shriveling up or anything.

"I appreciate the use of the jar," I say to Seth. "Let me get you a coffee."

"Dude, I work here," Seth replies through a chuckle. "I get plenty of coffee. No need."

"What about me?" Clay asks.

"Do you want coffee?" I ask.

"You know I don't."

"I'll let you pick the movie next time, even though it's not your turn."

He seems mollified.

"See you around?" I say to Seth.

"Sure thing!" But he's already smiling at some guy across the room.

CLAY SKEDADDLES to see if he left his key in his room, and I'm whistling as I take the stairs inside Karloff Hall two at a time, paper bag in hand. Although the gothic, gray stone buildings of Creelin U are imposing, inside it's a different world—sleek and modern, with fast internet. This place is the coolest. I've only been here a few weeks, but it's already starting to feel like home.

I open the door to my room and startle a dude who's sitting, shoulders slumped, on the twin bed opposite mine. My new roommate! Adrenaline surges through my body, and I suck in a deep breath.

He lifts his head, and our eyes lock. My heart starts beating so fast I'd be worried if I didn't know I was healthy. My skin is tingling. I'm unable to peel my eyes from him, and he seems to be reacting the same way.

My new roommate's eyes are super dark, with no whites—so dark that I can't tell the shape of his pupils. On top of that, he's wearing heavy black eyeliner. Those fathomless eyes flick over me rapidly as he takes me in—I'm still in my ripped tank top, shorts, and flip-flops. His face is extremely symmetrical. He licks his full lips and then drops his gaze to the floor. He's dressed all in black, and his clothes fit closely to him—not skintight, but definitely not loose. A dark gray hoodie sits beside him on the bare mattress. His body is long and lean, but his form seems fuzzy, like the outline of his body is staticky.

His straight, shoulder-length greenish-black hair falls over his eyes and contrasts with his extremely pale skin. But other than his eyes, he could pass for human. Except for his slightly webbed fingers and that static thing.

I want to erase the distance between us, and I don't know why. I just want to touch him.

"Hi! I'm Brandon Fernandez!" I say cheerfully, bounding over to him and holding out my hand to shake his.

Tilting his head up toward me, he takes my hand. His skin is cool, but not cold like Clay's. Energy pulses from his long, slim fingers to mine, and I shiver in pleasure. I'm very aware of my own heartbeat. I don't want to let his hand go.

His eyes again catch mine, though his dark hair obscures them. "You may call me Steve." Steve's voice is lilting, reminding me of running water. He has a Norwegian accent. I mean, it has to be Norwegian, though I have no basis for comparison. I don't think Steve is a Norwegian name, but what do I know?

Also, he's ... *fascinating*. I keep staring at him, those black eyes drawing me in. But I don't want to be rude, so I force myself to let go of his hand and look away. My fingers immediately throb with the need to touch him again.

A backpack and a few oversized duffel bags sit in the middle of the floor, along with two black cases—one large, one smaller—that must hold musical instruments. Each duffel bag has a small red flag with a blue-and-white cross stitched on it. That must be the flag of Norway. Then my gaze returns to him.

Steve's tongue darts out to lick his lips. He pushes his hair behind his ears. I'm breathless, and I don't know why.

"Nice to meet you. I brought you a present!" I blurt, shoving the paper bag at him. He takes it gingerly, like it's going to explode. I pull out one of the desk chairs, turn it around backward, and straddle it, hanging my arms over the back. I have goose bumps, even though I don't feel cold.

He opens the bag, and his eyebrows squish together. "What ... what is this?"

"Three drops of my blood, a black animal, and vodka." I tap the chair back and bounce my knee. "There's a spider in the jar. I couldn't find a cat on short notice."

Steve gives me a look like I have zombies crawling out of my ears. "Um. Okay. Thank you."

"Did I mess up?" I ask, rubbing my bottom lip. My chest tightens. "I was trying to welcome you to the United States. I Boo-gled it. Witchipedia said to give a nøkk those three things."

Steve narrows his eyes. "Did the website inform you that I now have to teach you an enchanting form of music?"

Does he not want to do that? Did I accidentally invoke some magic I was unaware of? My throat constricts, but I wave a hand. "I just wanted to give you a present. I don't care about you teaching me anything."

"That is the reason for the tradition," he insists. "People give the nøkk these gifts to avoid being drowned and to learn music. Now I have to educate you." He opens his mouth like he's going to say more, but stops. I'm distracted by his bright white, even teeth. Finally, he says, "I insist."

Warmth radiates through my chest. I smile and clap once. "Well, if you insist, Clay and I were talking about going to do karaoke for my birthday. It's coming up. You can go with us! Do it then."

"Oh my gods," Steve mutters. "Teach you the music of the nøkk at a karaoke bar? No. That is not done."

"You don't have to teach me nøkk music. Just sing something, and it'll count. Can you sing 'Let it Go'?"

Steve throws his shoulders back. "I most certainly cannot. Nøkks sing about loneliness and longing for salvation because we are not children of god. We shed tears for our lot in life."

Is he serious? I think he is. "I'm sorry to hear that. 'Let it Go' makes me cry. Sure, it's a girl-power song, but don't we all have shit that we want to get past? So, what about it?"

His lips press together in a slight grimace, and he shakes his head. I hold my breath. Then, finally, he says, "Yes, I can come to your celebration."

Steve with no last name kind of looks like a movie star. I'm not sure which one. He just has that vibe about him. Handsome. He's handsome, I think.

Something flutters in my stomach. "Yuss! I'll let you know when we have firm plans. Thanks, Steve-o!"

"No," he says. "It is only Steve. Not Steve-o. You can call me Steve."

It's funny the way he says I can *call him* Steve. Maybe this way of talking is just a nøkk thing. "Oooh-kay," I say slowly, chewing on my lip. My shoulders drop.

Seeing my face, which must look hurt, he says, "It is best if you call me Steve."

"It's not your actual name?"

"It is not."

I *knew* it. "Are you under witness protection?"

He wrinkles his nose. "No. Nøkks do not readily share our real names. Only someone fully bound to a nøkk may know their name."

Bound? I raise my eyebrows. Now I'm really curious. "Are we ever going to be bound so you can tell me it?"

"No."

I want to ask him why not. But I can respect nøkk culture. I rub my face and then gesture at the bag. "Do you at least drink vodka?"

"Yes. The nøkk drink vodka and coffee."

"Only vodka and coffee?"

"And water, I suppose."

"Fascinating," I say, questions bubbling up inside me. I want to know all about him. "I'm sorry; you're not a test subject or something. I'm just interested in you, that's all. I'm headed to the cafeteria in a little bit. What are your favorite things to eat? Maybe I can bring you a snack."

"No, that is not necessary. I do not eat very much. But when I do, it is fish, mostly, or fruits and vegetables."

"That sounds healthy. I'm mostly on a health kick, too," I say, patting my stomach. "I'm in training for water polo." I point to the bed he's sitting on. "You want this side of the room? It's not too late to switch if you want the other side. I don't have that much stuff."

"No, we do not need to change. This side is acceptable. Thank you." He pushes his dark hair behind his ears, which are small and cute. "I have a question for you," he says, and I nod a few times. He tilts his head. "Are you always like this?"

My stomach sinks. Am I already too much for him?

R.I.P.

4

THE NØKK

The moment this human, Brandon Fernandez, bursts into my new dorm room, he ignites a palpable desire within me to drag him to the underground world and force him to give me his soul.

My fingers suffer with the need to touch him. I am lightheaded. Something shifts near my heart, my breath seizes in my lungs, and I fight the yearning to take him. Could this desire overpower me?

It had better not. I have seen the pain my wretched nøkk father caused my poor human mother.

Brandon is so beautiful that he is hard to look at. His curly, dark brown hair tumbles around his chiseled, perfectly proportioned face. His brown eyes dance with mirth and mischief. Dimples flash in his cheeks. *Dimples!* His ripped shirt exposes the dark tan, hairless skin covering his broad torso. Silvery stretch marks move as his stomach goes in and out. A brown nipple peeks out at me. This Adonis *must* be mine.

At least, that is my first reaction.

My next is to flee ... to save him. No one who seems so pure should be around a soulless monster like me. My desire to rescue him grows even more acute when, after a moment's hesitation, he opens his smiling mouth and continues cheerfully chattering away.

"Yes, I'm like this. So, tell me everything about you! What's it like being a nøkk? Where are you from in Norway? How was your flight? When did you get to the US?" Brandon asks, his eyes alight. His fingers grip the back of the chair as he straddles it, and sexy veins snake up his forearms. I want to lick them.

With each new rapid-fire question, I lose the previous one, so I can only answer the last. "I arrived in New York this morning."

"You must be exhausted. You'll have jet lag." He leans toward me, bringing with him the mingled scents of sunshine, salt water, and piña colada sunscreen. I shudder in pleasure. Those three things may be my downfall. His skin looks velvety soft. "I went to Tokyo once for water polo—my varsity high school team made it to the international championships. And oh, man, the jet lag got to me. Although I don't think the time difference between Norway and Pennsylvania is the same as Arizona to Tokyo. Do you need to take a nap?"

If he had not told me he was a water polo player, I would have figured out that he did something in the water from his swimmer's build—narrow hips, broad shoulders—but also from the sun-lightened ends of his wild, dark hair. I glance away and look out the window. What would he feel like next to me? His warm body against mine? That is a very dangerous thing for me to be contemplating.

What was his question?

"I have periods where I recharge and periods when I am active. I do not always need to sleep. When I am here—in the human realm—I tend to follow human rhythms. So, yes, I think I am tired."

Is he going to pepper me with questions forever?

"Aww. Well, maybe you can get to sleep early. Say, the Witchipedia article I read said nøkks are shapeshifters. Are you?"

Apparently so. "Yes." I sigh.

"So why did you choose this shape?" He appraises me, and I bloom under his gaze. "If you could be anything, why did you decide to look like this, specifically?" I stare at him, but he does not shrink from my gaze. "Sorry, is that a rude question?"

"No, it is not rude." I shrug and try to think of a way to tell him why without revealing too much. I shapeshift because I despise my true form. It is hideous and repellent. I finally add, "I do not know. This is an easy form for me to be in." Relatively easy.

"I have so many questions," he continues. "The article said you—nøkks—take the shape of a handsome man to lure women to water. So is that why you picked this form?"

"*People*, not just women," I correct, my cheeks hot. He thinks I am handsome?

Brandon raises an eyebrow. "People, then. Why do you lure them in?"

I do not. I never have. But now I understand why the nøkk take souls.

Because I lust for you, Brandon. Because I fantasize about what I would do to you. Because you triggered something within me that no other human ever has.

Those are not the right answers, and I cannot say those things to him anyway. "Why do any of us do anything?" I huff. "It is what I am supposed to do. My nature. Are you always this full of questions?"

"Yeah. Kinda." He kicks the carpet with his heel. "Sorry."

Now I feel bad. "It is okay." Maybe I can change the subject by giving him some unthreatening information about myself. "I am at home in the water. I chose Creelin because of its proximity to the Cree and Lin Rivers—in addition to its music program, of course."

He gives me the brightest smile I've ever seen. I want to capture it. Make it the centerpiece of my existence. Do anything to make him smile again and again. "Excellent. I love the rivers. My teammates and I hang out at them all the time. You should join us!" Dimples again.

I want to learn everything I can about this human, but I must not allow myself to. The more I know, the more I will want to take his soul. I feel that thirst as a soreness in my chest. I nod instead, trying to calm my accelerating breaths.

"Can I keep asking you questions?" he asks. Resigned, I nod again, and Brandon scratches his belly. "Is it true that nøkks are an omen of death?"

"No. We are an omen of drowning, not death."

Brandon scrunches up his face to think about that, and it is bloody adorable. I need to have him. I can take him.

I must resist.

He bites his lip, and I want to be the one doing that. "But isn't that the same thing?" he asks.

"Not always."

"Hmm. Witchipedia was wrong." He taps the back of the chair and pushes himself up, then gestures at the brown bag he gave me, which I set on the bed. His waist is just below my eye level, and I cannot help but look at his shorts, which have a mouthwatering bulge. I want it. I want *him.* "Do you want to keep the spider or let it go?"

"I am not sure how to care for a spider. If you are in agreement with me doing so, then I will let it go."

"And you said you didn't want to sing the song from *Frozen.*" Brandon winks.

Despite my discomfort with being in a new place and Brandon's overwhelmingly beautiful presence, I laugh.

"Do you ever shapeshift into a horse?" He steps closer to me, and I hold my breath, because he is too alluring. My cock thickens in my tight jeans.

"Sorry?" I say, clenching my fists and releasing them.

"In *Frozen II*, the nøkk was a horse. Or kind of water and a horse?"

"That is a brook horse. They are ... a cousin. Something different. Or sometimes they can be a nøkk in disguise. But I have never taken its form."

"Oh, okay." He runs a hand through his hair. "I'm kinda hungry. Do you wanna come to the cafeteria with me?"

I do. I want to know more about this strange, gorgeous man. I sit on my hands. "No."

"Need time to unpack, huh? I'll leave you to it. Want me to bring you back something?"

Keeping him safe takes precedence—he needs to stay away from me. I shall figure out food later. "No."

"Cool, man. I think I should wear a real shirt to the cafeteria, though. Not this ripped-up thing. Air conditioning."

Brandon whips off his shirt. His belly button is distractingly cute, surrounded by the pretty silver stretch marks on his abdomen. He strides past me to the dresser, and I do my best to avoid memorizing the planes of his very beautiful back. It is proving difficult to know where to place my eyes—other than staring at my feet—because this room is very small. Finally, Brandon pulls out a white T-shirt and shrugs it on.

I touch my face and rub my temples, trying to distract myself from him.

"What's your cell phone number?" he asks.

I drop my hands. "Sorry?"

"In case of emergency or whatever, we should be able to get in touch with each other." He pauses. "You do use cell phones, right? I know you're a water spirit, so does it get all wet when you go in the water?"

Gods. Brandon all wet. My cock is really going to get hard. "I do not go in the water with my mobile, and I only use one when I am in the human world. When I am in, um, where I am from, I do not need one to communicate."

Please go. I want you too much, and I cannot have you. You need to leave, Brandon.

"Oh, interesting. By the way, how come you speak English so well?"

"I went to monster school in Bergen. We are taught English from an early age."

Brandon wiggles his cell phone. "Number, please." He opens up a contact expectantly.

This man wants to have access to me beyond this room. I. Am. Fucked.

"I do not have my US number memorized yet," I say, pulling out my phone. I should not encourage more contact between us, but "No, because I want you too much" and "You have triggered my nøkk instincts to possess you" are not things to say out loud.

"So I just put you in here as Steve? That's it?"

"You can list my last name as Jobs."

He stares at me. "You're kidding."

"When I was in the store getting the number, they asked my name, and that is what I told them."

Brandon starts giggling, and it is infectious. Something floats up out of my chest into the heavens. "Okay, so I'm rooming with 'Steve Jobs' from Norway. Only not really," he says. He types, then looks up. "Hit me."

I tell him my number, and he enters it in his phone, then texts me a string of emojis—thumbs-up, laughing face, sunglasses face, alien face, clapping hands, and merman. I am not sure what to think. But I am preoccupied with every single one of them. What do they mean? What do they say about Brandon? Will they bring me closer to him?

I cannot get closer to him, I scold myself.

"Text me if you change your mind and want me to bring you something back from the cafeteria. And call me Bran if you like. That's what my friends call me. Or Fernandez—I'll answer to that, too. My friends think I'm weird, because I only text emojis, but I'm sure you'll figure it out. Adios!" He waves and is gone, the door clicking quietly behind him.

I blink at it.

When he was here, it was all I could do to control myself, keep myself from taking him, but I can breathe easier now.

This is going to be a very long year. I can tell my fixation on him is only beginning.

I am curious about his gift, so I open the paper bag. As I expected, there is a large clear bottle of some kind of vodka, which I set on my bookshelf. It looks forlorn, since there are no other decorations on my side of the room. It is not the traditional liquor, brennevin, which I imagine might be hard to find in the US. But he gave it to me, and I will treasure it.

Next, I pull out a small jar with a hole punched in the top as if someone used a claw to puncture it. The spider is small, but alive. I open the window and let it climb out to the nearest tree branch. I kind of want it to come back, but it is better for the spider to live outside.

The jar is pretty, and I set it on the windowsill. I wonder where it is from.

Would Brandon's soul fit inside it? It would not stay long, given the hole in the top, I suppose.

Do not think of such things.

I reach in to make sure the bag is empty and feel a painful slice across the pad of my finger. I pull back my hand. A bead of blood is forming where I have been cut on a sharp edge of some kind. I suck my finger, then pull out a clear, rectangular glass microscope slide with a square cover over a smudge of blood.

Brandon Fernandez *gave me his blood*. He said that earlier, but I had not processed what he meant, given how overwhelmed I was by *him*.

Oh gods, no. Panic races through my veins, and I realize what is happening too late. Before I can stop it, the blood from my cut migrates under the square cover and mingles with his.

A surge of power rips through me, zinging across my skin and making the hairs on the back of my neck stand on end. I suck in a breath. Does he realize what he has done?

He has initiated the bonding.

Not only has he triggered the nøkk instinct to take his soul within me, he has taken the first step toward voluntary mating.

I must save him. I need to find another roommate. I cannot make Brandon suffer without a soul, nor can we be bonded, especially without his informed consent.

I grab my room key and bolt out, bashing my hip on the doorknob in my haste. Quite a few people are carrying boxes and bags into the dorms, while others appear to be headed in groups to the cafeteria for a late lunch or early dinner. As I race across campus, a number of students—mostly shifters, I think—are throwing Frisbees or sitting on the lawns in the quad, playing on their phones and talking. They all seem to be monsters, which makes sense, because I was told most of the humans are arriving tomorrow. At least, no one else calls to me the way Brandon does.

In the administration building, I go to the housing office. I reach the window right before a vampire, who slides behind me. I pace, waiting to be noticed.

A zombie wearing a twin set and a scarf over her shoulders looks up at me from behind the counter. "May-may I help you?" Her voice is a moaning rasp punctuated by grunts, but pleasant enough. I am impressed that a zombie can speak so well. But CU is run by ghosts and zombies, so maybe some are more articulate than others.

"I need to switch rooms." My voice wavers. "My roommate and I are not going to be able to live together in harmony."

She clucks her tongue, her words slurring. "I'm so-sorry to hear that. You can pu-put in a transfer request, which we'll evaluate in about two-two weeks."

"Two weeks?" My nerves go haywire, and my chest hurts. I try to control my panic. That may be too late. I wring my hands.

The zombie nods. "Could be-be three." She grunts. "Enrollment sort-sorted out first, and then we move-move people."

For a moment, I am unable to speak. Finally, I say, "Okay, well." Better late than never. I will just have to avoid him as much as possible until I can leave. "Please put me on the list."

"Yessss." She hands me a clipboard to fill out. My hands jerk, and I drop the pen and have to pick it up.

I can do this.

Then I pause, my hand suspended, as I stare at the question marked "Name." My mind blanks, and I sigh. It has been a long day, and I do not have the energy for this. *Calm down.* I clear my throat. "I am not sure how to fill this out. I do not remember what I put on the transfer forms for my name."

She tilts her head and grunts. "You're the nøkk?"

"Yes."

The vampire behind me stiffens. I wonder why. Does he not like nøkks? I am not sure if there are any others in the United States right now.

The administrator slurs, "We know-know your name issues. Put-put down 'the nøkk,' and we'll take care-care of you. Do-do you have a pseudonym?"

"Steve," I say.

The zombie smiles at me. At least, I think it's a smile. It is more of a grimace, but it seems kindly. Maybe. "I'll note it. Do-do you request we call you-you that?"

"Please."

With minimal extra assistance, I finish filling out the form and hand it back to her. "Two-two weeks at the earliest," she re-iterates. "It may be long-longer. For now, I suggest you-you settle in as best you can."

Exhaustion suffuses my body, but I force myself not to yawn. My phone pings, and it is Brandon. He has sent me another string of emojis: thumbs-up, waving hand, stick of butter, pretzel, slice of pizza.

What by the monster gods does that mean?

But he texted me. It makes my heart beat faster, which I am sure some of the monsters around can sense.

The zombie administrator hands me a copy of the form. "Here-here you go," she says.

"Thank you. Please let me know about the room change as soon as possible," I say. "It is absolutely urgent."

"Yes-yes. Next?"

As I turn to go, the vampire in line behind me looks at me as if he is sizing me up. I ignore him.

I walk back to the dorm and consider whether I should unpack my bags. I could go stay in a hotel for the next couple of weeks. But that might insult Brandon. I can instead use the time to come up with an excuse to leave that will not make him feel bad.

When I step into the room, I look around. Now that I have met him, the space is charged with his presence. His blood on the slide. His scent. Hints of his personality, with a water polo game schedule and a poster for a movie called *The Princess Bride* on the wall.

If I have to remain, I may as well move in for the time being, so I go about setting my clothes in the dresser, my laptop on the desk, and my guitar and violin in the closet. I should eat something, but the time difference and travel are catching up to me, and I feel lethargic. I drink a glass of water from the en suite bathroom sink before pulling a pillow, sheet, and duvet out of one of my bags and making up my bed. Then I undress and crawl in, even though it is not late at all.

I would be more comfortable if I shifted into my true form, but I cannot chance Brandon seeing it—both because it would frighten him and because he would never speak to me again if he knew what I really look like. Of course, for his sake, it would be better if we did not talk to each other … but I will admit I like hearing his voice. My cock likes it, too, but I do not jerk off. I would not want him to walk in on me. My cock hard, I sink into sleep the moment my head hits the pillow, the travel and distance overpowering me.

In my dreams, the deep fjords of Norway are framed by tall mountains. I am swimming with the silver fishes in the cool darkness. Then I am naked with a warm, gorgeous Brandon, whose soft skin I explore. Rub up on. Lick. Kiss.

I wake very early the next morning, before the sun rises, and my sheets are soaked with my spend, as if I were a teenager. My handsome roommate is asleep in his bed two meters away from me, his curls spread across his pillow. I did not hear him come in. I suppose I needed to sleep more than I originally thought.

While I want to study him, I feel horrible. The dehydration water spirits feel when we are away from a water source is like a hangover. Pounding headache, nausea, dry mouth, and disorientation—I have all of that right now.

A shower may alleviate some of the symptoms, and I need to wash my sheets.

I bring my clothes and toiletries into the bathroom and step under the spray of the shower. The water revives me somewhat. I stay there as long as I can, then dress and return to our bedroom.

Brandon is gone.

Part of me is relieved. Part of me wants to hunt him down and force him to be mine.

I haul my sheets to the laundry room and then sit on my bed until boredom and cabin fever overwhelm me and I am compelled to go outside. I take off to explore the campus and find where my classes are, so I will be ready when they start on Monday. Then I return, put my sheets in the dryer, and slip out again.

When I go down to the river, though, I find that there are many students, including merfolk and selkies, along its banks. I am not used to being with other people when I recharge. I decide I will come back later. I turn and walk away.

I sneak into the dormitory in case Brandon has returned, but he is still not there. Once my laundry is dry and I can remake my bed, I will walk into town. I intend to stay away from the dorm room that houses the one thing that I cannot have.

5

BRANDON

"I don't know how to tell you this, so I'm just going to say it," Clay says quietly, as we make our way across campus to the indoor pool for water polo practice. It's earlier than I'd like to be up on a Saturday morning. Zombies are mowing the grass and taking out trash, helping the ghosts get the school ready for the day. "I'm pretty sure your nøkk is looking to change roommates."

I flinch, although it's slow, since I'm still waking up. I huddle deeper into my oversize hoodie. "How do you know that?"

When I returned from the cafeteria yesterday, Steve was already asleep, only a bit of his dark hair showing at the top of his bedding, so I went to Clay's room to watch movies. We watched a recent release—his choice, I kept my word—and *Dead Poets Society*. Then, this morning, Steve got up early to shower, and I realized I was late for practice. I quickly stripped down, shoved on my Speedo, put my pajama pants back on along with the hoodie, and headed out before he was done. Leaving without saying goodbye felt wrong, but I had to hurry to meet Clay.

"I saw him at the housing office last night," he says. "They got me a replacement key."

"You actually had lost your key already, Cannon?" Before he can answer, I continue. "Never mind. He doesn't want to stay with me?" The idea makes my heart sink, and I stumble in my flip-flops. I'd thought I was having better luck here than in Arizona, but maybe not. And I don't understand this pull I feel toward Steve.

Last night, I really needed to jack off, but with him there, I didn't do anything. I'll have to take a long shower after practice.

Clay shakes his head sadly. "Sorry, dude."

"I'll talk with him when I see him next," I say. "Maybe there's some misunderstanding. I thought I made him laugh yesterday."

I thought there was some connection between us. Like he could be a friend.

"Maybe so." Clay doesn't sound convinced.

We get to the locker room and stow our clothes, keys, and phones in our lockers before taking our towels to the pool and dumping them on the bleachers. Then we jump into the salt water, joining everyone already there swimming conditioning laps. The moment I get in the pool, I relax. There's just something about being surrounded by water that makes me feel better. Energized.

But as I start swimming, I'm thinking about what Clay said. My roommate doesn't want to live with me. He's already trying to get away.

Because he can't stand me.

Except ... he was nice to me. So what's the deal?

My body goes rigid, and I jab angrily at the water, my form all wonky. That's the thing about being underwater: It's just you and your thoughts. Nowhere to hide from them. Only a black line on the bottom of the pool to follow. It's like when there's no music on in a car. Too much emptiness.

I need to get my head straight. I owe it to the team to give it my best at each practice, so I do my best to shove Steve's dark eyes and mysterious nature to the side, instead focusing on getting faster and stronger.

When I come up for air and stop at the end of the lane, Coach is crouching down to talk with Clay and me.

"You were late, Fernandez," Coach says. "You too, Cannon. That means ten extra laps at the end of practice."

"Yes, Coach," we both mutter.

Then we start drills. I'm grateful for the distraction.

There are a number of other humans on the team: Ashton, Bailey, Diego, Ren, and Carlos. Only Ashton is from Pennsylvania. The rest are like me, recruited from around the country specifically to come to Creelin for polo. Then there are the monsters. Besides Clay, there's Phil, the Sasquatch with incorrect information, Nick, who's a Loch Ness Monster shifter, some mermen and dragon shifters, and a gnome. Fifteen of us total.

The program here has traditionally been good. Opening it up to humans means all eyes will be on us, so the school worked hard to attract the best available players. Some people think humans are at a disadvantage playing against monsters, but I think that's narrow-minded. I'm enthusiastic about the upcoming season. We got this.

I'd better be optimistic. We have a lot to prove. If we don't show that humans and monsters can compete together at this level, it will set back human-monster relationships.

So, no pressure. In fact, Creelin's whole experiment is putting the school under a microscope. At least, that's what the harpy said when she gave me the tour.

The team does drills, and then we run plays and practice taking shots on goal until the two-hour session is over. Everyone else goes inside to change, and Clay and I do our extra laps after agreeing to meet the team for breakfast when we finish.

By the time we head back to the dorms, the sun has risen all the way. My body's feeling strong, and my brain's clear. That's better. In my room, though, there's no sign of my roommate. His bed is stripped.

I'd lived here by myself for a few weeks, and I'd gotten used to having the space—an empty bed, a bookshelf waiting for books, a desk with nothing on it. Being alone meant I had freedom to stroke one out in peace.

Now, there's a pillow and a crumpled duvet on his bed—I'm not sure where his fitted sheet is, but maybe it was gross from travel—combat boots on the floor, and the bottle of vodka on the shelf. I spy the jar from the spider sitting on the windowsill. Where did he put the slide with my blood?

I text Steve a glass, drop of blood, shocked face, wave, and pool.

He leaves me on read.

I frown at my phone. Then I catch the time. Shoot, gotta go. I race into the shower to wash off the salt water from the pool—I prefer my own toiletries but don't like dragging them down to practice every time—and book it down to the cafeteria to have breakfast with the team.

Steve isn't in the cafeteria. Not that I look.

After I choose scare-rambled eggs, bacon, toast, and orange juice, I sit down across from Phil and shake my fork at him. "Dude, Brainz Liquor totally checks IDs."

Phil cocks his head and sips his coffee. "No way."

"Way."

"They didn't check mine," he says defensively.

I roll my eyes. "That's probably because"—I gesture at him—"they thought you were older than you are."

Phil's twenty, but with his Sasquatch hair and height, he could pass for whatever age. He waxes his whole body for polo, but his hair grows back so fast, I don't see why he bothers. We've had to help him every week, but ripping off the hair is just an exercise in pain, as far as I can tell. I wish he'd let himself be, as is.

"Sorry, man," Phil says, and his regret looks genuine. At least from what I can see of his face.

"It's okay," I mutter.

"Did it work, though? Could you get the vodka?" Phil bites into his bacon.

"Clay got it for me. He's older than he looks."

Clay elbows me in the ribs—like being stabbed with an icicle, I swear—and I stick my tongue out at him. "Don't make fun of nontraditional students," Clay says.

"I wouldn't dream of it," I say, smiling at him.

"At least you could buy it in the end," Phil says. "Did your roommate like it?"

My face falls. "Yes? I don't know. I thought so. Maybe? He seems distant. And I haven't been able to talk with him much. I just want to have a good year. I want him to, you know, like me. Be a friend."

"Keep trying," Clay murmurs. "But if it's not meant to be, don't force it."

I blink at him. I told him what happened to me before. He knows how much it matters to me to have a good experience at school.

But he may be right. I can't force someone to like me.

"So," Phil says. "Who's going to the bonfire?"

Everyone raises their hands.

"Get your roommate to go!" Nick says. He's got a Scottish accent, though he says he's been in the US since he was "a wee one." He's our backup goalie.

"That's a good idea," I say. "I'll ask him. Although I'm worried he'll say no. He's said no to almost everything I've suggested so far."

"I'll come with and reinforce the invitation," Clay says. "Besides, I want to formally meet a nøkk."

"Fine," I huff, and take a bite of my toast. I text Steve a flame emoji, followed by a celebration horn, a mug of beer, music notes, and a thumbs-up.

He leaves me on read.

"Is anyone going to the orientation by Dean Yaga today?" I ask.

They all shake their heads. "It's just for humans," Clay tells me.

"Ah. I'm not sure I need it, since I've been here a little while."

"You might as well go," Clay says.

Before we head to the dorms, I pull Clay into Mummy Mocha so I can buy Steve a coffee and a fruit cup. I have the impression that Steve doesn't take great care of himself. And he seemed so ... lonely.

When Clay and I step into my dorm room, Steve's sitting at his desk doing something on his laptop. Like before, he startles when I walk in, but this time he seems to brace himself, holding on to the seat of the chair.

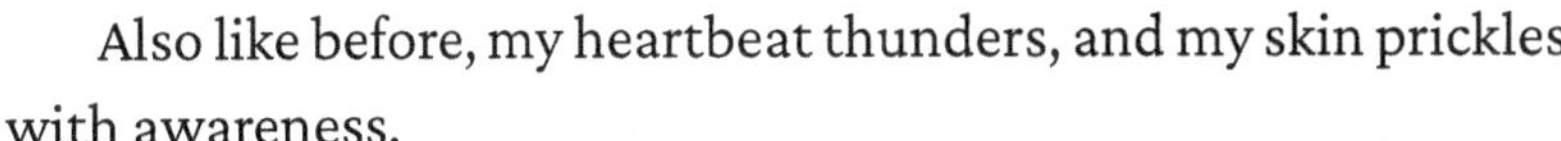

Also like before, my heartbeat thunders, and my skin prickles with awareness.

Clay steps forward and holds out his hand. "Hi, I'm Clay Cannon. You're the nøkk?"

Steve rises and shakes his hand, then returns to his seat. "Yes. You may call me Steve. It is nice to meet you, Clay."

Clay winks and gives Steve his charming smile, looking him up and down in his usual flirty way. A flash of protectiveness goes through me. I don't want Clay being his player self with my new roommate. I elbow Clay—which is like poking a glacier—and he looks at me, frowning.

"He's not interested," I mutter, although I don't know that for sure. I clear my throat and turn to Steve, setting down the coffee and food by him on the desk. "Brought you breakfast."

Steve's eyebrows rise, and he blinks a few times. "Thank you." He sniffs the coffee, then takes a sip and looks more content.

"Hey, you made your bed! Something spill on the sheets?"

"Um, yes. Or ... they needed to be cleaned."

"Cool. Wanna go to a bonfire party at the river tonight?" I ask, smiling. I don't know why Steve makes me smile. He just does. There's something about him that I want to ... protect. Guard. Take care of. He seems so lonely, and I want him to be happy. "I hear it's tradition, and the dean looks the other way."

"No, I do not care to go," Steve says. His Norwegian accent is so cute. Even when he's glum, his voice still comes out all musical, the syllables moving up and down in inflection like a cosine wave.

"Do you have something else going on?" I ask.

"No."

"You just want to be alone?"

He hesitates. And that's when I know I've got him. I'd leave him alone—reluctantly—if I thought he actually wanted to be alone. But he doesn't.

"Come on," I coax. "You don't have to stay if you don't like it. But I think you want to come."

He shrugs. "I guess. I do not know ..."

"Don't know what?"

"How to be with a large group of people. I can be ... awkward."

"Me, too," I say cheerfully, and put my hands on his narrow shoulders. Steve shivers, and I feel something pulse between us. Weird. Pleasant, though. I let him go after giving him a squeeze. "Come be awkward with me and Clay."

"Speak for yourself, Fernandez," Clay says, crossing his arms.

"Come on, old man. You can show us how it's done."

Clay rolls his eyes. Steve is watching us like we're playing tennis. "Old man?" he asks.

"I was twenty when the Halloween Wave hit," Clay explains. "And it took me a while to get back to school. I needed to get used to being a vampire, first. Then I got a job, but I didn't like it, so I decided I needed better education. It's not like I won't have time. Unless someone shoves a stake into my heart, I'm pretty much immortal. Now I want to learn as much as possible."

"That's remarkably wise," I say.

"Don't act so shocked," Clay says. "Just because I sound like I don't have that much going on doesn't mean I don't want that to change."

I take a minute to puzzle out all those negatives before saying, "Sorry. I wasn't trying to insult you. You're brilliant. I'd just been wondering."

"It's a touchy subject. All these young kids at school, and here I am feeling old. But I don't look it."

"You don't really act it, either, if I'm honest."

Clay glares. "Do me a favor. Don't be honest."

"Ha ha. Okay. Fine," I say. "Steve and I will lie to you."

Steve furrows his greenish-black brows. "I do not lie."

"I'm kidding." I grin. "Well, kidding about you and me lying. Not kidding about wanting you to come to the bonfire." A pang hits my heart, and I give him my biggest puppy dog eyes. "So, now that we've settled Clay's old-age, or maybe age-old, issues, will you come with us tonight?"

Steve nods, and I feel like I won something major. *Yuss.*

After chatting a bit more, Clay and I take off—him to his room and me to the human orientation. I can't wait to get through that and hang with Steve tonight. I want to get to know him better.

6

THE NØKK

At the bonfire, I learn that I am not the only one who wants Brandon Fernandez. We pass by werewolves, vampires, incubi, gorgons, and humans, all of whom turn to stare at my roommate.

Yes, he is that beautiful. And he does not seem to be aware of it, which makes him even more attractive. As I follow Brandon and his friend through the clusters of students at the bonfire by the river, I want to growl at every single being who gets close to my human.

I want to destroy them for even looking at him, because my instincts tell me that he is mine.

Even though my brain reminds me I cannot have him. I do not want to hurt Brandon through my proximity—or tempt whatever he has triggered inside me—but I also said I would attend this event.

Has Clay told Brandon my plans to change rooms?

I do not know how to behave now—I feel helpless and stuck. And embarrassed, if Bran does know.

In short, things are awkward.

Worse, though, I am … jealous, even though I know I have no right to be.

The longing for Brandon is even greater than my desire to return to my source—to join the others who are swimming and splashing in the river. They appear to be having fun, and I am most myself when I am in the water. It is rejuvenating, reinvigorating, refreshing—and helps me get to my full powers. But all I am doing is watching everyone react to Bran.

My father has told me my entire life that I would want to drag humans to the underground world. I always thought that was him trying to explain what he did to my mother.

Now, though, I am starting to understand my father—unfortunately—because I am feeling the same urges, I think, that he did. They manifest in a desperate lust that I can barely contain.

All I think about is Brandon. All I want is him.

I need to get my head on straight.

I do not think this hunger is only a result of the gifts Brandon gave me—or our blood commingling—because it began when he first walked into the dorm room. I think it is a reaction to something intrinsic to *him*. His energy calls to me, and my entire being wants to answer.

But I cannot—must not—take his soul. He has a shining light, and I must not deprive him or the world of it.

We pass the crackling bonfire and head toward an area where drinks are being served. Brandon looks over his shoulder at me and smiles, and it makes the electrical circuits in my body go wiggly. *Dimples.* "Want something?" he calls.

You. I shake my head.

He gazes at me, as if checking to see whether he should hand me a drink anyway. I am anxious and dehydrated, yes. But I will not accept any more gifts from Brandon. Even though I want to.

I spent much of this afternoon in the shower, trying to tap into the power that water gives me. And I might have been thinking about Brandon as I gave my cock attention. He needs to never find out about that.

Clay takes a bag of blood off a table, and Bran pours himself a beer from the keg. Just then, a harpy girl comes up to them and throws her arms around Bran. Her wing almost hits me in the face, and his drink sloshes to the ground. "Bran!" she cries.

"Hey," he says, wiping his hand on his shorts. "Good to see you again."

Again?

She nods at Clay, and then they all look at me.

Bran smiles warmly and gestures between the harpy and me. "Um, this is my roommate, Steve. Steve, this is ..." Bran trails off. He does not know her name. I am irrationally happy that he does not know her name.

"Savannah," the harpy says, either unfazed by or oblivious to Bran's blunder. "Nice to meet you!"

"Yes," I say, remembering my manners, even though something about her makes my temperature rise. "It is nice to meet you, too." I say the common phrase, but I wish I could say what I mean, which is: "Go away and leave my human alone."

"So when are we going to Scareoke?" Savannah asks Bran.

Wait, they are going on a date? I thought he wanted me to do karaoke for him—in payment for his gift.

"Let's go on my birthday—three weeks from tonight," Brandon chirps. "You'll be there, right?"

At first, I think he is still talking to the harpy, but then I realize he is addressing me. Something warms inside me. "Yes, I will go."

He looks pleased. But the harpy will not leave him alone. Finally, after she talks for a bit longer, she kisses him on the cheek and flies away. I want to scrape her touch off his skin.

Clay smirks and leans in close to Bran. "She wants you, dude. I told you."

Bran rolls his eyes.

"Excuse me. What did you tell Brandon?" I ask, unable to keep quiet.

"That everyone wants to get in his pants."

The vampire is correct, confirming what I had noticed earlier. Since Brandon is a beautiful ray of sunshine, he draws the attention of everyone around him. Especially monsters. Many monsters are forced by birth to be creatures of the dark, and darkness longs to know the light.

Like those creatures, nøkks are the melancholy part of nature, the sadness that is ever-present. We lurk in still water, the shadows of trees, and the decay of the forest.

Light is all I have ever wanted.

So I have a decision to make. I can proceed to complete my bond to Brandon, which he does not know about and has not consented to.

I can take his soul, an outcome I am resisting with my entire being.

Or I can have as little contact with him as possible, to save him from either of those two potentially disastrous situations.

Obviously, I choose the final option.

When Bran gets in a conversation with a Sasquatch about the water polo team, I slip away without saying goodbye, intending to return to the dorm room. Before I go far, though, I collide with a human.

"Excuse me," I say.

"Sorry, I didn't mean to run into you." He smiles. "Hey, I'm Kentley."

I remember my manners. I do not want to scare this human. "It is nice to meet you, Kentley. You may call me Steve."

"It's so great to meet you, too! I'm a little out of my comfort zone, all these monsters." He looks me up and down. "Wait, what are ... You're not human, are you?"

I shake my head. "No. I am a nøkk. And a music student."

"Oh monster gods, I'm sorry for being speciesist."

"I understand how this could be challenging for you if you have not interacted much with monsters before."

"For what it's worth, I'm a music student, too! I play piano. Maybe we'll have some classes together. What's your schedule like?"

We compare notes. I will have class with him a few days every week. "I will see you then," I say, somewhat cheered that I may have met someone I can talk to—who is human—and who I do not want to ruin. I excuse myself.

When I get back to my room, I pick the slide of Brandon's blood up from my bookshelf and set it back down again.

NOT EVEN half an hour later, the door flies open. "Dude, where'd you go?" Bran demands, his presence seeming to take over all available space in the room.

A thrill courses through my body like the strings vibrating on an instrument. *He is here.*

He should not be here. I do not want him here.

But, in reality, I do. I have never felt more conflicted.

"You looked as if you were busy," I say, glancing up from my electric guitar. I had not plugged it into the amp, to allow me to practice my fingering while minimizing the noise it would make.

"It's a party. You could meet people."

I stare at his beautiful self—the wild hair, lickable skin, and soft, friendly eyes.

Bran relents, his shoulders sagging. "Hey, sorry. I don't mean to butt in. I thought knowing people might make the first few days easier." He kicks at the carpet. "Is something wrong with me? Clay told me you wanted to change rooms."

Of course he did.

I set my guitar down on the bed beside me and scrub my face. "I do not think it is best for you to room with a nøkk. We can ... It can ... It may not be safe."

"Safe? You're not going to hurt me. I thought you were registered with the Organization of Monster Enhancement."

"I am."

"Then it's fine."

No. It is not fine. You do not know how much I want to kiss you. How much I want to complete the bond.

Or take your soul.

I huff. "I just thought it would be better," I finally mutter, not wanting him to know my thoughts, because those are surely too much.

Bran's face falls, and I want to kick myself for making him sad. I want him to never look this way again. "I wish you'd reconsider," he says quietly.

"Why?" I ask. "You do not know me."

"My last two roommate situations were … not good. One of them hated me—he thought I was annoying—and the other one had sex so much I never got to be in my own room. I was hoping this year would be different, and you seem like a cool guy. Will you at least give us a chance as roommates? Please?"

I stare at him. I should not give us a chance as anything. That is a bad idea. What choice do I have, though, with not being able to move for two weeks at least? Moreover, he will want to move soon enough, to get away from me.

And I cannot deny Brandon. Finally, against my better judgment, I nod.

"Thanks, man," Bran says, and he squeezes my shoulder with his warm hand. I want to lean into him like a flower toward the sun.

I nod. "Go back to the party. I want to go to sleep."

"Okay," he says. "If you're sure you're okay."

"I am fine."

After a moment, Bran nods and leaves.

The moment the door closes behind him, I shift into my true form, just for a breather. I am not a very good shifter—I cannot hold my human form forever. It is much more natural for me to be in my true form, and I need a few moments without pressure.

I resolve to stay away from Brandon as much as possible, even if we remain roommates.

And I do so. On Sunday, he tells me he is going to hang out on the banks of the Lin River with some friends and asks if I want to come join them.

I shake my head and instead take a long walk in the woods, away from the school and people. Away from all of the students spending time with friends on the riverbanks. I want to be by myself. I bring sheet music and scribble down the notes for a song.

Midday, Brandon texts me a series of emojis that I do not understand, so I do not respond, although I analyze every single one of them.

I manage to stay away for most of the day, but when I get back in the evening, Bran is sitting on his bed with an open laptop.

"Hey!" he says, smiling wide, patting the space next to him. It makes my heart long for things I cannot have. "Wanna watch a movie? It's the original *Blade Runner*."

"No."

"Are you excited for classes to start?"

I raise an eyebrow. "I am not excited, no. But I am looking forward to it."

That is the truth. Once classes start, I will have more places to be besides this dorm room: practice rooms for music, empty classrooms. Although I believe the library is open already.

"Come sit!" Bran gestures at the desk chair. "Talk with me. What have you been doing?"

"I went for a walk."

"Oh yeah? How was it? The forest is gorgeous. I'm not used to it being all green like it is here. Back home, it's a desert. Literally."

"It is kind of like my home," I admit. "Although the mountains are taller there."

"Oh? Tell me more about Norway!"

I look at him. "Are you sure?"

"Yeah, totally! I've never been to Europe. I'd love to go there. I'd love to go everywhere. Traveling is great."

"It is a very beautiful country," I finally say. "There are mountains, as I mentioned, and lakes and fjords, and towns of various sizes. Oslo is a big city. I live in an area that is not as populated."

"Bergen, right?"

He remembered. A smile breaks through my normal somber expression, and I feel like I might be glowing. "Yes. That is where I started university. It is the closest city to where I am from."

"I wanna see pictures," Bran says, and he starts typing on his laptop. After a moment, he says, "Whoa, is this it?" He turns the computer so I can see the screen.

"Yes, that is my home."

"So cool," he whispers, and even more *want* blossoms inside me. "I wanna see it sometime."

"Maybe you can," I say, before I can help myself. But the smile on Bran's face takes my breath away.

Dimples.

We click on some more photos, and I identify different places I know.

A whole series of photos showing bingo cards appears, and I cough. "What are those about?" Bran asks.

"We like bingo in Norway. Nøkks especially."

"Oh. Huh. Cool."

"Why do you text only emojis?" I ask, wanting—needing—to know.

He grins. "If you think about it, we don't need words to communicate. We can communicate through other means, like art, music, and emojis."

"Music?"

"Absolutely. Don't you think it's easier to say something in a song, sometimes? Like, you can show someone the lyrics—or even just the melody—and it conveys a mood or emotion better than spoken words."

I stare at Brandon. *He understands.* "Yes, I agree."

"Or it even happens with movies and books. There's something that the creator had to say, and it takes that long to get it all out. What they want to communicate can't be compressed into a little sound bite, you know?"

"I do know."

"So, I like to use emojis. If I send a monster or a mermaid, I'm usually thinking about the students here. If it's food, it's likely because I'm hungry. If it's a face, then it's probably what I'm feeling. Or I'm asking you what you're feeling. With all of them, I'm limited to the options on the keyboard, so sometimes it comes across a little weird."

Being around Bran makes me warm inside and out. "And you want people to figure it out?"

"That's the idea. Although if you're Phil, you just send me the middle finger emoji and call it good."

I give him a small smile. "I do understand what you are saying about words not working."

We sit for a beat, gazing at each other. *Brandon, how I wish I could give you something, even if I have nothing good to give you.*

I study his parted lips. I can feel his breath pass over my cheek. I want to touch him, to move closer—

"So, what's your first class tomorrow?" Brandon asks, and whatever trance we were in breaks.

"Sociology. Then performance seminar." I need to volunteer something. He has already shared so much with me. "I am told I will need to play the violin for placement in the orchestra." I sent in an audition video to get into the school, but I will still need to be placed.

"Oh, that's so cool! Do you want me to listen to you practice?"

Part of me wants to play for him. To show him who I truly am—because I can usually express myself through music.

If I do not accidentally enchant someone, of course.

That is the risk whenever a nøkk plays music. And I do not want to ever enchant Brandon. In the unlikely event that he were to ... be interested in me, I would want him to feel that way on his own. Not because I kidnapped him and stole his soul. Not because we completed the bonding he started by commingling our blood. Not because I forced him with my monster powers. But because he actually liked me.

He is too tempting, and I need to say no. I shake my head. "That is not necessary. I am an adequate musician."

"Then good luck! I'm sure you'll do amazing," Bran says, giving me the biggest smile anyone has ever sent my way.

THE FOLLOWING morning, I do not "do amazing."

Sighing, I take the violin off my shoulder, set down the bow, and wait for the classroom furniture to stop dancing. I glance around at the sleeping faculty members and try not to think about how massively I am already failing in my new university.

This is not the way to make a good first impression.

The orchestra director had sent us an email telling us to bring our instruments for performance seminar. I delivered both my violin and guitar cases and my amp—along with electrical adapters for US plugs—earlier in the day so I would not have to carry them plus my school rucksack all over campus.

When it was time, I cleared my throat. "I am Steve. I am a nøkk. I do not know if I will send everyone to sleep, but I am signed up to play the fiddle." Over my protest.

But as my father is overseeing my schooling, what he says goes—although he has not called or texted since I left Norway. That does not really surprise me. I am not sure how many souls he has taken, but it is more than the number of years I have been alive. He is surely busy prospecting for another human to enchant.

"I suppose we should've thought of that before we enrolled you, but it seems we didn't," Professor Lopez, the orchestra director, said gently. "Forgive us; we haven't had a nøkk before. Why don't you go ahead and play? If you need to stop, then do so."

I lifted the violin to my shoulder, intending to play something light. But as soon as I started, the entire room nodded off and the desks and chairs started dancing. I had to grab the music stand before it flew to the ceiling.

I guess my performance is over.

After a few minutes, Professor Lopez blinks awake.

"Sorry, professor," I whisper. "That was an accident. When I get nervous, I slip back into our traditional music, and I had not accounted for how powerful it is, especially in an enclosed space."

And I am not presently strong enough to hold back its power. I need to go down to the river, but between finding my classes and avoiding my roommate, I have not done so and have been relying on the shower. Not being recharged has made me sluggish, and it is no wonder I accidentally played an old song.

Professor Lopez blinks and adjusts his tie under his sweater vest. "I guess you were correct." A few other strings faculty members yawn awake, glancing around as if wondering how they got to where they are.

"I am truly sorry."

Professor Lopez gives me a tight smile. "That's quite all right. We'll have to work with you to figure out how you can perform. Generally speaking, playing in a soundproof room where no one else can hear it isn't the point of music. Is there anything you can do so it isn't so … enchanting?"

"I believe that when I play a traditional nøkk instrument, the effects are worse. I know I am enrolled to play the violin, but I also brought my electric guitar. May I see if that causes less of an issue?" A hopeful flutter arises in my chest. I may be able to tell my father that I am unable to study the violin and am forced to play the guitar.

That would be a dream come true.

"I'm not familiar with the traditional nøkk instruments. What are they?" Professor Lopez asks.

"Fiddle, flute, and harp."

"Well, yes, let's try to avoid those until we come up with a solution." Most of the others are now awake, and the professor looks around. "Why don't you give the guitar a try."

I plug my amp into the wall and my guitar into the amp and strum an experimental chord.

All eyes are on me.

So I go for it, playing a song I heard on the radio yesterday. While I long to get lost in the music, I'm acutely aware that I need to not enchant everyone.

Even so, I enjoy myself for a few minutes, making the kind of music I love.

When I glance around, everyone is awake, which is an improvement.

Professor Lopez smiles. "That was terrific. While you are wel-

come to practice the violin in the soundproof rooms, what if we focus on the electric guitar for your coursework while you are at Creelin U?"

"Yes, professor," I say, smiling.

I am pleased. Studying the guitar is exactly what I wanted.

WHEN I AM done with my class, I lock up my instruments in the music building and head to the dorm. Having looked up the water polo schedule, though, I make sure to leave before I think Brandon will be coming back. Instead of going to the cafeteria, I stop by the housing office again. The zombie lady is wearing a dress with a big floppy bow at the neck and a pencil skirt, and she looks at me with concern. At least, I think it is concern.

She shakes her head the moment I get to the front of the line and moans, "No-no, Mr. Jobs. We-we are not-not ready for transfers yet."

"Thank you," I say quietly, "but that is not why I am here. I need to withdraw my request."

The zombie looks surprised. "You-you're sure? You were-were adamant before."

No, I am not sure. I wish there were a nøkk here to ask. Because I do not think I am imagining the bond between Brandon and me. I felt that surge of power. Legends say mingling blood is the initial step.

But I told Bran I would not change rooms. "Please take me off the transfer list."

The zombie nods. "It-it is done."

I check my phone and realize it is time to go to my next class, so I walk as fast as I can across campus.

Brandon texts me a series of emojis that I think means he is going to the river: ocean wave, fish, beach umbrella, swim shorts, and pixelated monster. If he is at the river, I should stay away. I will take another shower. That water will give me enough strength for now.

By the time the school day is done, I am exhausted, hungry, and dehydrated. I also have not seen my roommate at all, which was my goal, so I should be pleased.

After bathing again, I crawl into bed.

When Brandon walks in after dinner, he takes one look at me and kneels down beside me on the floor.

"Hey," he says. "Are you okay?"

"I am fine," I say.

I can sense that he wants to chat, but I turn my back to him and do my best to fall asleep. I do not want to be tempted to take things I cannot have. I do not know how I am to survive sharing a room with my biggest temptation.

7

BRANDON

Tuesday morning, I get up early for practice, and Steve is sleeping in his bed. Something eases in my chest. He's here, and he's safe. He doesn't look well-rested, though. His eyes look more sunken than I remember, like he might be sick.

I want to leave him something to help him feel better, but I don't know what he needs. Something about Steve pulls me to him, though. I'm not sure whether it's how he seems to quietly observe everything, his cute little mannerisms—like how he doesn't use contractions—or how he dresses like he's an emo guy from the early 2000s.

I just want to get to know him. Is that too much to ask?

I quickly throw on my bathing suit, hoodie, and lounge pants and book it to the pool complex, where Coach beats our asses. But I suppose that's the right thing for him to do if we're going to win a championship this year, which is always my goal. This team's motivated to prove that monsters and humans can succeed together, so we're all putting in extra effort.

I spend the entire practice wondering how my roommate's

doing, and the moment we're done, I head back to the dorm, still in my Speedo with my towel wrapped around my waist.

My haste pays off, because I catch Steve in our room.

Happiness bubbles up inside me when I see his cute face, that dark hair, those webbed fingers. There's just something about him that I can't seem to get enough of.

"Hi!" I chirp, rubbing his shoulder so he wakes up, water falling in my face from my wet hair. "How have you been doing? Are you ready for the second day of school? Do you know where today's classes are?"

Steve blinks at me, his dark eyes looking almost like they have a film over them. The outline of his body seems more staticky than it was when I first met him. His eyes take in my bare torso—covered in stretch marks from when I weighed double what I do now—and he swallows hard. I take a step back and give him space to sit up. He does so, but he keeps his duvet around him.

He's wearing a dark gray T-shirt that's many sizes too big for him, and I can see the waistband of his gray plaid pajama pants. He yawns and says, "I am fine."

Alarm bells ring in my head. Something is wrong, and I want to save him ... but I don't know what to do, since I don't know what I'd be saving him from. Himself?

I stare at him. "Are you sure? I haven't seen you around. It must be a big adjustment—"

"I am fine, Brandon." His hands grip his mattress like he's afraid he'll float away. Is something wrong? Do I smell bad? I don't smell like chlorine, because there isn't any in our pool. Does he not like my stretch marks? They're part of me—part of my history.

I put my hands on my hips. "Want me to grab you some coffee like yesterday?"

He shakes his head, pressing his lips together.

I sit down on my bed, across from him. I want to ask if I did something wrong, but I can take a hint. He doesn't want to talk to me. In fact, it seems like he can barely look at me.

That hurts.

I run my hand over my face and grab my clothes so I can shower. I smile as brightly as I can. "If you need something, just let me know."

"Thank you," he says quietly.

When I'm done with my shower, though, Steve hasn't moved. How many times can I ask him if he's okay?

One more. "I can bring you back some breakfast."

"I am fine," he repeats.

Maybe he's just not a morning person. I check my phone. "Sorry, I gotta get some food before class. Catch you later?"

He nods.

I race down to the first floor of the library and into Mummy Mocha, where I buy myself breakfast and Steve a coffee and a fruit cup from the same redheaded kid who served me before, who I learn is named Tanner. Steve's in the shower when I drop off the drink and food. I can't hang around to see if he's looking better, since I have to run to get to class on time.

BUSINESS CLASS in a monster university features rows of students with laptops, some playing on their phones. There's a whiteboard at the front of the room and a screen that projects the professor's computer screen. In other words, it's a normal classroom.

Except the person next to me has oozing skin. There's a group of incubi in the front row that most people steer clear of because they don't want to have someone feed off their sexual energy, even inadvertently. And there's Seth, from Mummy Mocha, chatting with two other guys.

Like everywhere I go at Creelin, I feel as if everyone's eyes are on me. I never got this much attention back home. I scan myself to see if I wore something weird, but no, my shorts zipper is up, and my shirt doesn't have any stains on it.

The professor—who I think is a ghost—passes out a syllabus and starts talking about what we're going to cover this term, and it feels like every other class I've attended my whole life. With each new class I attend, I relax a little more.

I go back to the dorm room after Integrated Business Management, but Steve isn't there. I text him a bed, waving hand, book, laptop, and merman.

He leaves me on read.

I hang out as long as I can before Intro to Monsterkind—a mandatory class for humans—but I don't see him, and I end up having to run all over campus the rest of the day.

Then he sends me a waving hand emoji. *He responded!*

I peek at the text every chance I get, my heart feeling lighter.

I'M ABOUT to go to dinner, and my phone rings just as Steve walks in. I look at the name displayed on the screen and answer the call with a smile.

"Baby girl!" I coo. The corners of Steve's mouth turn down.

He goes over to his desk and opens his laptop.

"Hi, Bran!" Hearing my younger sister's voice brings a lump to my throat.

"I miss you. How are you?" My voice warms.

"I'm okay." A pause. "I wish you weren't so far away. Are you going to be able to visit at all this year?"

"I'll come home for winter break. Can you wait that long to see me?"

Viviana sighs the kind of weighted, exasperated sigh that only a teenager can muster. "I guess."

I wave at Steve, mouthing "Dinner?"

He shakes his head.

I shut the door behind me and return to my call, walking down the hallway. "You can do it. Are the kids at school treating you okay?"

Another sigh. "I guess."

A flare of protectiveness surges through me. "Do I need to fly back and have a friendly discussion with any of them?"

"No. Romeo moved away."

"That's a relief." He was a jerk. "So you think school is going to be good this year?"

"Yes. I just miss you."

"I miss you, too, baby girl. How's Mom and Dad? And Ofelia and Ruben?" Our older sister and brother.

"Mom and Dad are here. Wanna talk to them?"

"I do, but I want to talk to you first."

"Okay. Ofelia and Ruben are at work."

We chat for a while, and she gets me caught up on all the high school and family gossip. Then I talk with my parents for a few minutes before joining the team at dinner. I eat fast so I can try to

get back to my room and chat with Steve. When I return, though, he's not there. I stay up as late as I can, but he doesn't come in until I'm almost asleep.

THE FOLLOWING morning, we have a break from polo practice, but I'm still up before Steve. I go and get coffee and breakfast and return before he leaves the room.

Steve's been looking paler and paler, to the point where his skin has a gray tinge. Of course, given that he's a shifter, I'm not sure of his natural color. But it's clear he's not doing well. He's got dark circles under his eyes, and his hair has gone really lank.

"Do you need to call your parents?" I ask, passing him the coffee, which he accepts and sips. His face relaxes a bit at the taste, which makes me happy, but I'm still worried about him. "Are you missing them?"

He snorts. "No. I am not missing my family."

The way he says it is so final. I suppose not every family is as close as mine is.

"Is there something I can do?" I ask. "Have you been eating enough? Do you need me to bring you something?"

"I am fine."

He doesn't look fine. He looks like he's about to collapse. I don't know what to do. "Should I take you to the health center? Do you need to see a nurse?"

"No. I am fine," he grits out.

A helpless sort of anger flashes through me. I stand up and put my hands on my head. "If you say you're fine one more time, we may have to have words. C'mon, man. You know something's wrong. What is it?"

Steve clams up. I suppose demanding that he talk to me wasn't the right move, but I don't know what is.

"I gotta get to class," I mutter. "But you can tell me what the problem is. I promise I won't judge you. I just want to help. I like you."

He looks at his feet.

Finally, when it's clear he isn't going to give me anything to work with, I sling my backpack over my shoulder and take off.

But I vow to start a one-man mission to cheer Steve up.

"I'M WORRIED about my roommate," I tell Clay, when he catches up to me for lunch after my monster history class. I text Steve a purple monster, sunglasses, waving hand, lobster, and steak.

He leaves me on read.

"Oh? Why?" Clay has a bag of blood on his cafeteria tray, and he comes over to join me in the human food line. I knew I'd miss the southwestern dishes I'm used to—my mom's green chili stew being my favorite. But at least there are the familiar monster-ella sticks and French frights. The vending machines sell Ghosta-cola. Today, though, I just grab a turkey sandwich, an apple, and chips. Clay and I go to the nearest clerk, who is a zombie. I hand him my ID, and he swipes it to pay for the food.

"Steve seems ... moody. Morose. Melancholy," I mutter to Clay.

"Maybe he's missing home. We all get a little homesick." He digs in his pocket for his ID and sighs. I roll my eyes and let the zombie scan my card again.

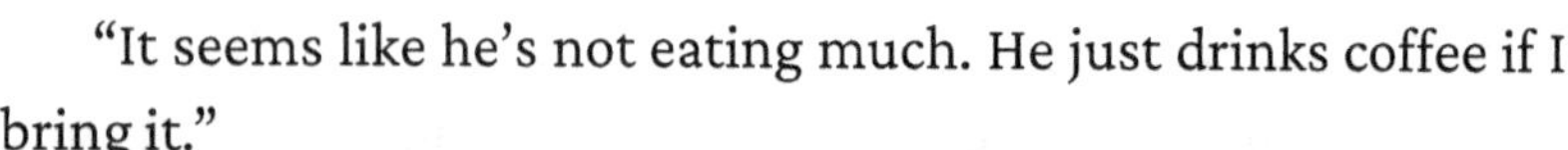

"It seems like he's not eating much. He just drinks coffee if I bring it."

"Hmm," Clay says. I spot Phil, Bailey, Ashton, and Nick at a table, and we head over.

"Can we join you?" I ask.

They nod and make way. My phone pings with a text, and as soon as I put my tray down, I look and see a message from Steve. It's the heart with a bandage on it. That makes something inside me ache.

"What's up?" Phil asks, noticing my expression.

"My roommate's bummed out."

"You're living with the nøkk?" Nick asks.

I take a bite of my sandwich. "Yeah."

"He could be despondent because he hasn't immersed himself in fresh water," Nick says. "I can tell when I go too long without the right kind of water, and usually the fix is just to jump in a lake."

Phil nods. "Nick is correct. Nøkks are nature spirits. They can get depressed when they aren't in a natural environment. I know a couple of nymphs, and they have the same issue. Has he gone to the river yet?"

"I have no idea," I say.

"Maybe that's the problem. If he's away from his home water source and busy with classes, he's probably off schedule and needs to recharge to restore his health and get his full powers. Or at least to improve his mood. Get your nøkk in the water," Phil advises. "See if that cheers him up."

"Will do," I say. "I never knew any of this stuff, and it's interesting. Maybe I should major in monster kinesiology instead of business."

"Maybe," Nick says. "That sounds cool."

"What's up with everyone else?" I bite into my apple.

"I've got a date tomorrow," Clay says.

I look at him in surprise. "You do? Who with?"

"This guy from my Victorian literature class. Wanna come?"

I scoff. "I'm not coming on your date."

"I don't know that it's really a date," Clay admits. "I told him that a bunch of us were hanging out, and I asked if he wanted to join us."

"That sounds about right. You were too nervous to ask him out for real?" Phil says.

Clay shrugs. "I like the guy."

I grin. Even after just a few weeks, I can tell that Clay can be a player, but he can also get shy if he really likes the person.

I can't wait to find Steve and see if I can make him feel better, so when the rest of them start discussing favorite snack foods, and Clay goes off on a tangent about the taste differences between synthetic and real blood, I beg off.

When I step into our room, I'm pleasantly surprised to catch my roommate sitting on his bed ... but he looks terrible. His dark hair hangs in hanks over his face, and his eyes have even more of a film over them. His cheeks are sunken, and his entire body seems like he's barely hanging on.

I wince. This is absolutely unacceptable. I march up to him with a big, determined smile. "How are you doing?"

He shrugs, and something about that shrug is so lost that I can't stand it.

"That's it," I say. Bending over, I slip my arms under his legs and back and hoist him up like a bride. While he's not light, he's not heavy, either. I can carry him to the river, no problem. I work out.

"What are you doing?" Steve yelps. I like his weight in my arms. I like how he smells—like clean water. I like how cool his skin is and how soft his hair is against my neck. My pulse zips along faster.

He's too weak to even hold on to me properly. It makes my heart hurt.

It also makes me want to scold him, and I do. "I'm taking you to the river. Since you obviously haven't gone on your own. You know that proper self-care is important? You can't just go about barely eating or drinking, and, if you're a nøkk, not getting in the amount of dunking you need."

"What are you, my doctor?" Steve mutters.

"No," I say gently. "Just a friend."

I mean that. I want to be his friend. I like him. There's something about him that makes me want to be near him all the time.

I carry him down the stairs and outside. We get some looks. But it's an indication of how bad Steve feels that he doesn't protest any more or try to get me to put him down.

Turns out it's a long damn way to the river when you're carrying someone else, and I'm sweating by the time I can see the water, but he needs this. Some of the returning guys on the water polo team have shown me the areas that are less crowded, and I head for one.

Finally, panting, I arrive at a quiet part of the riverbank. I shuck off my shoes, throw my wallet, phone, and keys on the ground, and wade into the water with Steve still in my arms.

He yelps again when the water first hits him, and then it's like he's gotten an infusion of pure joy.

Yes! A deep relief comes over me, and I suddenly want to cry.

Everything inside me goes light and giddy, and I'm sure that's nothing compared to what Steve's feeling.

His whole body relaxes, and he closes his eyes. His face fills out—it had been so gaunt, almost skeletal, now that I think about it. But now his skin isn't gray. It's still pale, but that's the look I think he chose.

Steve splashes, then does this merman-like dive. Before I know it, he pops up way upstream. Fastest swimming I've ever seen.

He's clearly not human, not governed by the laws of physics. He cuts through the water like he *is* water.

He surfaces, then dips down again.

My despondent roommate's suddenly joyful, and it makes me laugh. He whisks by, and I splash him. It's ineffective, since he's already wet, but it's fun. Then I take off swimming. My clothes weigh me down, but I'm only wearing a tank and shorts, so it's not too bad.

I chase after Steve in the river, laughing, and he pretends to let me catch him. We both know that's not possible, since he's so fast, but it's still fun.

"So, what have we learned?" I shout.

"That you are a very slow swimmer?" Steve replies.

"Rude. No, we've learned that we don't let you go more than a day without being in the water. I think you should go every day. It's nuts. I go swimming more than you do." I blink as an idea occurs to me. "OMG, that's it!"

"I'm sorry?"

"You should join water polo! You'd get course credit for athletics, and you could help your mental and physical well-being. Win-win. It's a saltwater pool, so no chlorine. That might make it close enough to river or ocean water to meet your needs. Plus you'd get to spend more time with me," I tease.

"That's true," he says quietly. Like that's actually something he'd want. I know I can be annoying and pushy, but it's nice to think that he's not utterly repulsed by me. "I am not into sport," Steve says.

"But you're a good swimmer."

"This is also true. I do not know how to play water polo, though."

"They can teach you. At least try out. I think you're a shoo-in. You'll pick up the rules fast, and we need help if we're going to beat Shuford this year. The game is fun—it's like a combination of basketball, a swim meet, and hockey, only you can't really move, and the water actively works against you."

"I will not have that problem, I do not think," he says. He swims so that he is right next to me, water dripping down his now-radiant face. "Brandon, thank you for taking care of me. I am sorry I did not … I did not pay enough attention to what I needed, so it got bad. You saved me."

I wave a hand. "Anyone would do the same thing."

"No, most people would not walk the kilometer or more you did to bring me to the river. Most people would not keep after me to do better. I am most grateful to you."

His lips part as if he is going to say something else, and his solid, dark eyes hold mine. He's not blinking, and neither am I. I want to move closer to him, to touch him. It feels like he's casting some sort of spell on me, and I think I like it. I fixate on his lips. I'm hyperaware of every part of my body, and … to be frank … my dick is chubbing up, even in the cool water, which is a little con-fusing. But Steve's beautiful—

There is a rustling in the leaves on the riverbank, and we both turn our heads.

Clay is standing at the water's edge, his blue-black hair shining in the sun. "Watch out for the kraken," he calls.

"What?" I shriek, and lurch for the bank, the spell broken.

Clay and Steve start laughing. Steve's laugh is like a singing brook. Clay sounds evil—an evil surfer from California.

"There's no kraken, is there?" I mutter.

"They exist, but they aren't in a river in Pennsylvania." Clay pauses. "Well, I don't know about that, actually. A few are enrolled as students."

"Come on in, you jerk," I say, splashing him.

It's a hot day. Not one to stay away from water, either, Clay rips off his shirt and shorts, then hops off a rock into a deep area wearing only his boxer briefs. We splash each other, and I've never seen Steve so animated. He needs this. I'm going to have to remember to give it to him.

"Are you going to join polo?" I ask him, when we're all waterlogged.

"Yes, okay, I will try out," he says. "You talked me into it."

"That's great," Clay says. "Coach'll be all over that. We need all the good swimmers we can get."

"Their need is apparent, if they have accepted Brandon," Steve says with a smile.

I splash him.

Steve's laughing and chatting, and it seems the most natural thing in the world. Now that I've seen him this way, I hope he can be this free more often.

8

THE NØKK

I was wrong, and Brandon was right: I needed to take better care of myself. In my defense, I have never lived this far away from a water source, so I have never had to think about going out to one or making a point to get in the water. I just … was in the water. Even when I went to school, I still came back home to the lake. I thought I could get away with dousing myself in the shower—especially since I wanted to avoid Brandon and his friends, who were often at the river. But that was not enough.

Thankfully, Brandon is not gloating.

He is, however, even more irresistible than he was before, which is a major problem. He hauls himself out of the river and sits on the bank, his shorts soaked. The golden light of late afternoon highlights the beautiful planes of his torso under his thin, wet tank top. Water runs down his forehead. He is unbelievably attractive, and I remind myself—again—that I must not steal his soul. The fact that he saved me does not mean I should spend more time with him.

The idea of not spending time with him is getting harder and harder to fathom.

I lazily paddle around, letting the water rejuvenate me. Clay wades out, chats with Bran for a while, and says goodbye. Soon it is just me and Brandon, the sun's warm rays hitting us, Brandon sitting quietly and watching me.

"So should I come with you to practice tomorrow?" I ask, not ready to leave the river, although I am not feeling so sulky since I am in the water.

"Yeah, definitely." He nods. "Do you have a bathing suit?"

"I do not." In my true form, I do not need one. And, in the past, I have rarely swum in human form.

"Then let's go buy you a Speedo, Steve-o. Or you could borrow one of mine," Brandon says.

That makes my cock want to stand up. "No, I can buy one."

"Do you know where to go?"

"No, but Boo-gle is a thing," I say, a teasing tone in my voice for the first time since I arrived in Pennsylvania. The water really is a cure-all.

"I can come with you," Bran offers. "I'll take you to the Creelin sporting goods store."

"Why are you so annoying?" I huff playfully.

His face drops, which makes my stomach sink. "I'm sorry. I know I overstep sometimes."

"No, Brandon." I catch his eyes. "You are charming."

His cheeks flush. "Are you feeling better now?"

"Yes," I say.

"Are you ready to get dried off and go shopping?"

"What, now?"

"If you want to come to practice tomorrow, you'll need swimwear. I'll take you to town."

ONCE WE ARE back at the dorm, Brandon says we need to shower before going out, which means I get to sit on my bed and listen to the water run and try not to think of him all soapy and naked. The way I have thought of him every day since I met him. When we are both cleaned up and dressed, we go out to where his car is parked.

"Why did you transfer to Creelin?" he asks as he navigates his older SUV toward the downtown area, Spookify playing on the sound system.

I bristle. "The opportunity came up."

Bran glances at me, and his expression tells me he knows I am lying. Or that there's more to the story.

"If you have to know," I say, "I did not ... Things did not go well for me at my first university."

He furrows his brow. "I'm sorry to hear that."

"There are a lot of nøkks in Norway, but even among them, I am different. I do not want the same things that they do. I know it is my true nature to take souls, but I do not want to do that." *Normally.* "My father wants me to play the traditional music of the nøkk. I want to play the electric guitar. I felt left out, and I thought perhaps in a different place I could be more myself." I pick at the chipped black polish on my fingernails.

"Aww, Steve." He frowns. "I'm sorry that happened to you. No one's treating you badly here, right?" His voice takes on a more menacing tone than I thought he was capable of.

"No. The people I have met here are nice. I know I stick out, but at this school, everyone sticks out a little bit."

Brandon nods, and we drive to the store.

I WALK UP to the first bathing suit I see, one that's black and blue, pull it off the hanger, and move to go to the front to pay.

Bran stops me with an arm across my chest. I try not to lean into it. "Dude, no. Sorry. You can't just buy it. You have to try it on. You want it to be super tight. You don't even want to be able to get a finger in the waistband, because then the opposing team can grab hold of it and pull it down."

That thought is not pleasant. Well, it would only be pleasant if Brandon were the one pulling it down.

"Okay," I say.

"Get a size or two smaller than you think you are. Want some help?"

"No," I say, smirking. "I can figure out how to put on an obnoxiously small bathing suit without your help."

Brandon holds up his hands. "Okay." He slaps my ass when I turn away, and I want to lean into that, too—even a rough touch is still contact. "Go get 'em."

I glance over my shoulder at him as I enter the tiny changing room, my butt stinging slightly. He is not ... interested in me, is he?

No. That is not possible. I believe Brandon is straight—based on his interactions with the harpy and whoever his "baby girl" is.

While I could shapeshift into a larger size to make the bathing suit fit properly, the size I am now is the same as my true form and therefore the easiest for me to maintain.

I shed my clothes, then shimmy the Speedo on. It is very tight. Ridiculously so. But I can see how that would be a good thing in competitive sport.

I gaze at myself in the mirror. In this form, I have a lean torso, not overly muscled. I wanted to be ideally proportioned. In this tiny garment, my cock looks big.

"You okay in there?" Brandon's voice interrupts my thoughts, and my cock gets a little plumper.

If he is going to interrupt me, then he is going to get the full effect. I slide the curtain open with a whoosh and step out. I show him that I cannot stick a finger in the waistband very well. My cock is surely outlined by the fabric.

Brandon eyes me from the top of my head to my webbed feet. He bites his lip, and his nostrils flare. "Yeah, that works. You look good, Steve."

His words make my heart rate increase. "Thank you. I will buy this one," I say, and slip back inside. I put on my clothes and emerge holding the scrap of fabric.

"Can I ask you another question?" Brandon asks, as we head toward the cash registers.

"Yes."

"Why don't you tell people your real name?"

I decide the reason doesn't need to be a secret. "If someone uses it who isn't another nøkk, my family, or bound to me, it will kill me."

Brandon gasps. "No way."

"Yes, it is true."

"I guess most monsters have some sort of weakness or Achilles' heel, huh?"

I smile at him. "I believe so. But the ways of the nøkk can be unusual. We have a flair for the dramatic. Just ask my uncle, who shapeshifts into an old boat so he can sink, taking people down with him."

We pass a group of surly monsters who are loudly looking at the bathing suits. They give off vibes I do not like.

"Are they on the team?" I whisper.

"Not on Creelin's team. They must be from Shuford," Brandon murmurs. "Our rival. That's what I'm guessing, anyway. Phil told me Shuford's team has at least one werewolf and a hydra, plus some mermen." He inclines his head, and I take a look.

"Yes," I confirm. "That is a werewolf and a hydra."

"There's no point trying to whisper," someone sneers behind my back. "Werewolves have superior hearing."

"We didn't mean to insult you," Brandon starts.

"You're too weak and harmless to worry about. What are a couple of pretty boys like you doing in the Speedo section? You're Creelin Cockatoos?"

Brandon puts his hands on his hips. "Yeah. So?"

I turn and see the werewolf, who scoffs. "Just nice to see that there won't be any competition this year. Can't believe they have humans on their team. It's like they want to lose."

A sudden anger comes over me, and I want to protect Brandon with everything I am. I will not let any monsters hurt him. Ever.

Including me.

"Be quiet," I say, my voice low, and they all turn to look at me.

"Who are you?" the werewolf asks. "You weren't on the team last year."

I do not answer. Instead, I say, "You will go now."

The werewolf makes an incredulous noise. "Don't tell me what to do. Prick."

"*You will go now*," I repeat, with emphasis. While humans are more easily affected by my powers, nøkks have some sway over monsters as well. The merman, especially, looks at me oddly.

"What are you?" he asks, finally.

"I am a nøkk," I say menacingly.

"Come on, guys," the hydra says. "We'll beat them in the pool. We don't have to do anything now."

I don't know if it is due to my enchantment or not, but they turn and leave. I glance at Brandon, who does not look scared. More like curious.

"What?" I ask.

"That was so cool of you." I flush at his praise. "I'd heard that Shuford were a bunch of dicks, but I didn't realize they were that bad. I think we'll definitely be needing you on the team."

"I just want more time in the water."

"Win-win, like I said. Come on, let's buy your suit and get out of here."

I nod and follow him to the cash register.

THE FOLLOWING morning, Brandon wakes me up with coffee. "Time for practice," he mutters, and ruffles my hair. He is leaning over me, and I want to reach up and pull him into bed with me.

Then he moves to his side of the room, drops his pajama pants, and slides on a Speedo. I stifle a groan. I only get a brief view of his taut, round ass, but having him changing in front of me is starting to be a problem, because he is so mouthwateringly beautiful.

I slip on my new Speedo—with difficulty, because it is very tight—and a hoodie and sweatpants and go with him to the pool, where he introduces me to his teammates.

The coach, a walrus shifter, takes one look at me and grins. "You're the nøkk Fernandez mentioned? Jobs?"

I nod.

"I'm Coach Rosmarus. Let's see what you can do." He gestures to the pool.

I jump in and immediately feel energized. I cut through the salt water, going to the other end and back in a flash. Then I do it again.

When I come to a stop at the coach's feet, he whistles and nods. "You definitely have the water skills for this game."

"You're faster than a cat up a staircase," Phil, the Sasquatch, says.

"When have you seen a cat go up a staircase?" the Loch Ness Monster shifter with the Scottish accent—Nick, his name was Nick—asks him.

"My mom loves cats."

"Regardless, he is fast," Nick says.

Coach grins widely. "While this is unprecedented, I think we can find a place for you, at least provisionally. Welcome to the Creelin water polo team, Steve. You're a Cockatoo now."

We practice with a yellow ball, and while I am not as adept with it as the other players are, my speed and natural instincts in the water make up for it.

Bran grins at me, and I wish I could belong to him.

But I cannot.

"You're coming with us to Scareoke when we go, right?" he asks at the end of practice, when we are headed to the lockers.

"Um," I say.

"Come on! It's gonna be my birthday. You can finally sing 'Let it Go' for me."

I agree, because I am obliged to teach him music in exchange for his offering, and this seems to be how he is interpreting that. Even though it is a terrible idea. I nod.

But I will still do my best to stay away the rest of the time, because he is much, much too tempting. Even if I want to see him, it is best for him if we do not interact more than necessary.

9

BRANDON

"Fernandez!" Coach calls, blowing his whistle. We just finished our Saturday practice, and everyone else has already headed to the locker room.

I jog over, still wet from the pool. "Yes, Coach?"

"Can you take this?" He holds out a net bag filled with gear. "Put it in the storage room. And see if Steve needs a hand. He's putting away the scoreboard equipment, but I'm not sure he knows where it goes."

Steve's back to giving me the cold shoulder, and it's making me feel cruddy. The past few days, I've only seen him here at practice or when he's asleep. What did I do wrong?

Other than forcibly buy him a Speedo. Give him some weird gifts. Throw him in a river.

Okay, that's me getting in his business quite a bit. Maybe I'm trying too hard and need to just let it go.

Ha. My favorite song.

I can't have another bad roommate situation, though. I need to confront him about it. I have to know what's going on.

I leave wet footprints behind me as I pad over to the storage closet. "Hey, Coach asked me to bring in the—" As I step inside, I trip over a bucket that had been propping the door open, and it skids to the side with a loud clang. The door slams shut, leaving us in complete darkness. "Balls," I finish weakly. I reach out for the door handle, feeling around, find it, and push. Nothing. I pull. Nothing. "Um. Is the door ...?"

"Stuck?" Steve's low, musical voice comes from maybe five feet away. Close enough to hear easily, but not so close that it makes me jump. "It seems so. It was difficult to open when I came in, which I believe is why the bucket was there."

"Crapola."

Steve huffs. "Do you have your mobile?"

I pat my hand down my bare torso and hips to my Speedo. Like I've hidden a phone next to my balls or something. "No," I say after a moment. I'm not sure why it takes me so long. "It's in my hoodie."

"I do not have mine, either." He sounds annoyed.

"I'm sorry. I didn't mean to lock us in. I don't mean to do any of the stupid shit I do. It's just a mistake."

He huffs.

"What?" I protest. "I swear, it was an accident. Someone will find us soon. I'll pound on the door."

"I believe that you did not mean to trap us."

"You don't sound like you believe me."

"I do."

"Why are you avoiding me again?" I blurt. "I thought we were getting to be friends, what with you joining the team and all. Now you barely stay in our room. Sometimes I can get you to talk to me, and other times it feels like you don't want to be near me.

It seems like you don't like me."

My pulse is pounding, and my mouth has gone as dry as the Arizona desert.

"I like you," Steve says quietly.

"Doesn't feel like it." I realize I'm pouting, and I try to stop. It's not very mature to pout, and I need to stop. Still, something inside me wants everyone—but especially this guy—to like me. "What did I do wrong?"

He sighs. "You did not do anything wrong."

Our surroundings are silent as a tomb. "I told you why it was so important to me to have a good roommate situation. I'm trying my best to be easy to get along with."

"I apologize," Steve says. "I did not want to hurt you. That is why I requested the room change: so I would not hurt you."

"You're not going to hurt me."

"I am not sure about that," Steve admits. "When I get around you, it is hard to control my nøkk ... urges."

"What kind of urges?"

Something about the way he's talking makes goose bumps rise on my skin. And my cock twitch.

He pauses. "I want to take your soul."

I laugh, and then I realize he's being serious. "Wait, really?"

"Yes. That is what my instincts are telling me to do."

"How, exactly, would you take my soul? I suppose I should be scared, but I'm more curious than anything else."

"I drag you to the underground world, and there is a ritual." He pauses. "I believe it involves paperwork."

"That doesn't sound so bad," I joke.

"Can you hear yourself?" Steve sounds incredulous, and he repeats, emphasizing every word, "*I want to take your soul.*"

"Are you going to?"

"No," he mutters. I hear the scrape of his bare foot, like he's kicking the ground.

"Then that's your answer."

"But it is very bad. My nøkk father took the soul of my human mother. He takes many souls, perhaps in an attempt to force the humans to fall in love with him. It never works. Or maybe he takes them simply because he wants to and he can, I suppose. She has never forgiven him or me. She is now soulless, trapped in the underground world, unable to ..."

He trails off. I wait for him to say more, but he doesn't, so finally I say, "I'm sorry to hear that. But you're not your father. And it sounds like you don't want to be like him."

"I do not."

"Then you'll be your own person. And you're not going to take my soul."

"I know I should not," Steve admits. "I am trying not to."

"Do you think you will be able to avoid it?"

A moment later, he says, "Yes."

"Then can we try to work our roommate arrangement out? Have you hang out with me more?" I'm not entirely sure why this matters so much to me, but it does.

"Yes, okay," he whispers.

"Thank you." Relief courses through me.

"Do you realize that you trusted me with your blood before you even knew me at all?" Steve says abruptly.

I'm not sure why he's bringing that up now. "The Witchipedia article said to."

"Did the article say that it is the initial step in the bonding process?"

"What kind of bonding?" He'd mentioned bonding in the context of knowing his real name, and I am so damn curious as to what it means.

Steve pauses. "I do not know how to explain it. There are three steps for a nøkk to ... find companionship, I guess is the word. Or a mate. The first step is to exchange blood. The next is to exchange a kiss."

A mate. Something more than friends or roommates. Someone to kiss. Or do more with. A *boyfriend.*

I shiver, and my cock thickens.

What is going on? My body apparently likes the idea of being Steve's *mate.*

Would I want to kiss Steve? I haven't really thought about kissing a boy before. Except for when I was taking those online tests, that is. They all said I wasn't straight. Even when I took them a second time.

Huh. Maybe there was something to those.

Here in the darkness, I can't see Steve, but I've memorized him. I know the way his dark hair shines in the sun. I like his voice. I like how he seems so reserved, but in reality, I think he's just a little lost and unsure.

So, maybe, yeah. I like him.

And maybe what I've been feeling is ... Oh, damn. Horny as hell.

I adjust myself in my bathing suit.

Clay's going to have a field day with me.

I clear my throat, my voice husky. "What's the last step?"

"Giving them your heart. Then you may know a nøkk's real name."

My pulse pounds. I shrug. "That doesn't sound so bad, either."

Would I want to be a nøkk's mate? At least, *this* nøkk's mate?

I think I might. The way I'm getting hard in this wet bathing suit tells me that. I feel bad when Steve's not around. I want to know everything about him.

Steve lets out an exasperated sigh. "I would be taking away your free will."

"Why? As long as I know what I'm getting into and making my own choices, how is that different from any other relationship?"

Steve waits a long moment before he answers. "Because you would be locked in, without the ability to change your mind. And even if you do not consent, I still *could* take that choice away through force. I have been battling my fierce desire to make you mine every day since I met you."

Oh, damn. I shudder, but it's the anticipatory kind, not the scared kind.

Shit.

Steve wanting me ... That's kind of awesome.

I'm *interested* in Steve. Regardless of whether I know his real name or what he looks like in his natural form. It's almost like he's an online friend: I know him by his username and personality. That's been enough for me to form close friendships in the past—especially with people who love eighties movies as much as I do.

The bonus is that Steve's here in person.

I like him. Yeah, that's the bottom line. I like Steve not-Steve the Norwegian nøkk.

But is he truly interested in me? Other than this intrinsic-nature thing? Other than me inadvertently trapping him with my blood? Other than these "urges"?

I'm not sure, and right now I don't want to ask.

I can have a secret crush on him for a little bit while I sort this out.

I realize that he's confessed his desire for me, and I haven't responded. I say, my voice husky, "I trust you. Just because you *could* do something doesn't mean you *will*. And it's no reason to stay away from me. Based on the evidence so far, you're perfectly fine."

"But I have been trying to stay away from—"

There's a creaking noise, and the door opens. Coach stands in the doorway, silhouetted in the light beyond. Both Steve and I are blinded. I pick up the bag of balls again and hold it over my crotch, willing my cock to deflate.

"Thanks," I say. "The door got stuck."

Coach grunts. "You're welcome. Next time keep the bucket in place." He looks at Steve and me with some suspicion, but I'm starting to get cold, so I drop the bag and edge past him, Steve close behind me.

I turn to Steve as we enter the locker room. "Have lunch with me after we get changed."

After a moment's hesitation, he says, "Yes, okay."

As we walk to the cafeteria, there is a tension, a prickling, an energy between us that I cannot get enough of. And I am not sure what to do with it.

Steve admitted that something in his nature calls me to him. And I admitted—to myself—that I'm okay with that.

But where do we go from here? He's doing everything in his power to resist ... me.

Once we get our food, Steve and I sit awkwardly and stare

at each other. It was easier to talk in the dark. Confessions came when we weren't looking at each other.

So instead of confronting him about his feelings, I ask him about music, and we discover that we like the same bands. We have an easy conversation after all. If we aren't going to end up bonded, maybe he can be my friend, anyway.

AFTER LUNCH, Viviana calls, and I excuse myself. Steve heads off to the dorm, and I sit down in the quad to chat on the phone. "How's school going, baby girl? Anyone catching your interest? Some special guy?"

"Um. Well. Maybe. There might be an enby kid I like."

"That's cool." I never figured my sister wasn't straight, but there's no reason why heteronormativity needs to rule the day.

I freeze. Am I a product of heteronormative thinking? Like, have I assumed I'm straight just because I grew up with that as the default? Is that why it's taken me so long to sort out what I'm feeling about Steve?

The thoughts I've been having in the shower should've been a clue, because he's who I've been picturing when I stroke one out. Not that I want to share that with my kid sister.

But Steve mentioning my being his mate—and his desire for me—wasn't the first time I'd been attracted to him.

"You're quiet," Viviana says.

"Sorry, sis. I'm just thinking that I might be into a guy. Pretty sure I am, actually."

"Really?"

"Well ... I can't stop thinking about him. I always want to

make sure he's okay. When he talks, I hang on every word."

"That's cool. Is he cute?"

"Yes. I mean, yeah, but he's a shapeshifter, and so far I've only seen him in human form. Human-ish. Anyhow, I like him for him, not for how he looks." I bite my lip. "And I might like him *that way*."

"Have you considered kissing him?"

I tilt my head. "Kinda?"

With Steve, kissing is weightier than just "Let's kiss." Apparently, with the nøkk, it would mean more.

I think I'd be good with that. It might be reckless, but I have to follow my heart. And my heart's telling me that Steve's my person.

"Then do it." She giggles. "I'll tell you if I kiss my crush."

I blink, older-brother instincts activated. "You're eighteen. Way too young."

"Whatever."

"Okay, fine. Just be careful."

"I promise." Her voice gets sly. "Promise me you'll kiss your roommate if you want to and he wants to."

I nod, though she can't see it. "I promise."

THAT EVENING, I'm sitting with Clay in his room watching *The Goonies* on his laptop. When Andy kisses Mikey by mistake, I blurt, "I want to kiss Steve."

Clay spits out some of the blood he'd been drinking, and it spatters his shirt. He glares at me. "What did you just say?" He wipes his face with the back of his hand, then shakes his head in disgust and stands up.

"I'm having these … feelings about him."

He strips off his bloody T-shirt and grabs a fresh one. He walks into the bathroom, washes his hands and face, slides the new shirt over his head, and returns all cleaned up.

"Explain," he says. His Cheshire cat grin makes his fangs more prominent.

"It's hard to describe. I mean, I haven't really felt much for guys before. Until him. Steve's … interesting to me. I know he's a shapeshifter and that he can take on any form he wants. Because of that, I almost don't care what he looks like. It's funny—he's beautiful, even though he's so damned emo—"

"He's very cute," Clay says. "But if he weren't beautiful, would you still be into him?"

"Yeah, definitely. Steve intrigues me. Or maybe I should call him not-Steve, since it's not his real name. I don't like calling him the nøkk, because it makes him sound like the representative of a whole species rather than an actual person. He may be the only one in the US, but he can still have a name."

Clay stares at me with an eyebrow raised.

"I just … *like* him. I like how he views the world. I like the expression on his face when I make him laugh." I look at my hands, and they're trembling. "So am I bisexual? Or pansexual? Because I still am attracted to women, at least in theory. But … also … Steve."

I expect Clay to shove me or make fun of me or something. He doesn't. Instead, he pats me on the back. "Do *you* think you're bi or pan?"

"I'm not sure. I've never felt the way I do around him with anyone else."

"Then maybe you are. Do you need to put a label on it?"

I think about that a moment. I'm a human. I'm a junior. I'm a water polo player, a teammate, and a student. I'm a son. A friend. A brother. I've got all kinds of labels.

Do I need one more?

"I'm not sure. I'll try it on for size and see if it fits."

"Or see if it's too tight. Like our Speedos."

I roll my eyes. "You know why Speedos have to be tight—to protect our modesty."

"Our water polo team has no modesty whatsoever."

I grin, thinking of Steve trying on a bathing suit. "Likely so." Then I let out a breath. Okay, then. "Pansexual. I'm going to see if that's me. In fact, I think that's what I'm going to put on a form if I'm asked about it." I pause. "Can I be pan if I've never done anything? Like, do you have to actually have sex to be a certain sexuality?"

Clay studies me. "I'm gonna let you ask any questions you want, even the obvious ones, because you're just a baby bi/pan—but you know the answer. No, you do not need to have sex to identify as a certain sexuality. It has to do with who you're attracted to, rather than anything else."

I nod a few times. "It's just ... I feel like I should be weirding out about it more."

Clay shrugs. "Meh. To me, sexuality is no big deal. Everyone has one, and it's slightly different for each person, so why don't we just let people be?" He tilts his head. "Gods, that sounds insensitive to those of us who were, or still are, persecuted for our orientation. Sorry, I don't mean that it doesn't matter. I just mean that it's okay if you like who you like, Fernandez."

I'm getting *very* sure that I'm attracted to Steve. I'm more interested in him than I ever have been in any other being on earth, and it's not because I'm intrigued that he's a nøkk, even if I have to admit seeing him swim is pretty much a religious experience. It's not because of how he looks, either. I can tell it puts some strain on him to stay in that form, because sometimes there's a blip and his outline fuzzes out for a second. When that happens, I catch a glimpse of his true form, and it's adorable—all green-gray and cute.

It's funny: While I'm attracted to his body—and it makes my dick hard, if I'm honest—his body isn't the most important thing. I like that, even though he's kind of melancholy, he has this joyous way of talking. I like how he listens to me—he makes me feel special. I like who I am when I'm around him, which is why it made me so sad when he avoided me.

"College is the time for experimentation, anyway," Clay reminds me. "So go for it. I'm not sure I get what you see in him, though."

"Why not?"

Clay shrugs. "He seems so morose."

"He isn't morose. He just gets despondent when he's away from water. He's fighting against his nature, too. He doesn't want to be a monster—or, at least, he doesn't want to do the things a nøkk traditionally does."

"It's tough when you don't like being in your own skin." Clay sighs. "I didn't want to become a vampire, but I had to accept it." He grins. "Once I realized I didn't need to be the Bela Lugosi stereotype and could just be myself, it worked out much better. I couldn't do anything about what had happened to me, but I could be who I really am."

"Maybe we all need to be ourselves."

"And being yourself means you're not entirely straight, huh? I guess that doesn't surprise me."

"Why? Are you interested, Cannon?" I tease.

Clay looks at me longer than I'd have expected. Finally, he shakes his head. "No. It's not because you're not hot or I don't like you. I do. But I don't think we have that chemistry, you know? I might prefer bookish guys."

"I think I prefer one very melancholic one." I stretch my legs out. "Now tell me who you're into that's so studious."

OVER THE NEXT few days, I become fascinated with gay sex. I keep looking things up: How to do it. What the tricks are. It seems both not complicated at all and incredibly complicated. I don't want to hurt someone—Steve—or be hurt. And I don't know if I want to be the one giving or receiving. Honestly, both sound interesting.

I spend a lot of time in the shower imagining what it'd be like to have Steve mounting me, pressing into me. Fucking me.

I want that. I've never thought about it before, but now that it's maybe an option, this whole world has opened up to me. One where things aren't as rigid as I thought they were. One where I'm not rounding up but am exploring the interesting smaller percentages.

When I admit to Clay that I'm looking shit up on the internet, he laughs his ass off. "Dude, it's not something you need to research that hard."

"It kind of is. Because I don't think ... I think it could be messy and hurt if I didn't do it right."

"Sex is mostly messy and sometimes hurts. But not too much, as long as you communicate with your partner." He smiles. "You'll figure it out. Don't stress so much about it."

His words don't help. I still stress. Or, at least, I think about the logistics *an awful lot*. And I wonder if what I'm feeling is close to the desire Steve apparently feels for me.

HAVING A ROOMMATE makes it tough to find alone time to jerk off, and that's even more of a problem when it's the roommate who's making me horny. Since Steve not-Steve moved in, I've mostly done it in the shower. Which is fine, but it doesn't lend itself to any kind of ... visual aids.

Anyway, he's not here right now. I think he's in class, so I can chance a little porn on my phone.

Gay porn.

I put my phone on incognito mode, and it's easy to find monster-human movies. There's so much to choose from. I find one with a water spirit who looks a bit like Steve and a human who looks a bit like—okay, a lot like—me, and turn it on, prop the phone against a pillow, then stick my hand in my pants and lie back on my bed.

It feels really good to stroke myself. I haven't had a good solo session in ages.

I fondle my balls, one at a time, then grip my cock and rub it so it thickens.

"Fuck," I whisper. Okay. This feels good.

I shove my shorts and boxer briefs down past my ass so my cock springs free and watch as the guys kiss on my screen.

Why is something as simple as kissing getting to me? Well, it's hot. The water spirit seems like he wants to devour the human—and the human is devouring him right back. They don't remove all their clothes to begin with, instead reaching inside each other's pants to stroke each other. Reaching behind to tease each other's hole.

This is ... educational.

Would I like that feeling? I'd need lube, which I don't have. I do have suntan lotion, though, and I grab some and use it for lubricant. So I'll smell like the beach while I beat off. There are worse things.

As the guys on-screen get more and more into it, they shed their clothes, and then the water spirit drops to his knees and takes the human's cock into his mouth.

I gulp. I want that. I stroke harder.

The guy being sucked is having the time of his life, but it seems like the guy doing the sucking is loving it, too. Especially when he reaches down and begins to play with his own dick.

Then they switch positions, so the human is now sucking the water spirit's dick. While some monsters have different anatomy than humans, the water spirit doesn't seem to be that different, other than his dick being really long.

How far are they going to go? Are they going to have anal?

The water spirit pushes the human down and starts licking his asshole, and I can't see what he's doing that well. Or imagine what it feels like. But the way the human is moaning makes me think I'd want to try this.

I want to try everything.

I'm not going to last much longer. I'm not going to find out how far they get, because I'm about to fling myself off the cliff of orgasm, right damn now, and it's gonna feel epic because I've needed to come for so long and I'm into this stuff that's so new—

The door from the hallway opens.

Shit.

My roommate steps in, catching me with my dick in my hand. Seeing Steve makes me start pulsing, and I shudder in pleasure as he stares at me with those dark, kohl-lined eyes.

10

The Nøkk

Oh my sweet monster gods.

Brandon looks debauched. His curls are sweaty, his shirt is rucked up to his brown nipples, his pants are down to his thighs, and his lovely cock is in his hand.

And he is coming.

While my instinct is to say "Sorry" and immediately leave, I am frozen in place as if he has cast a spell on me.

I simply cannot move. I can only stare. I do not know what my expression is, but Brandon's face has gone red. "Wait, Sorry, hang on," he says. He quickly pulls his pants up.

Finally, my body gets the message that I should not be gazing at him so intently, and I half turn back toward the door, which thankfully shut behind me.

Bran clears his throat. "Oh my god, I'm …"

"It is okay," I say. I swallow hard, my cock thickening. "Actually, it is very … You can … I am. I am not offended." I am turned on and trying to hide my own arousal from my roommate. I tug the hem of my hoodie down lower.

Brandon, now mostly clothed, scoots off his bed, grabs some fresh clothes from a drawer, and slips into our bathroom. I hear the water running, and I assume he is washing his hands and body where he came all over them.

But his phone is still playing.

And it is playing monster-human porn. I do not believe I am imagining things when I think that the pair looks like us.

Is there any chance that Brandon is interested in me as something other than a friend?

That is impossible. He has a girlfriend back home.

Brandon returns and hastily shuts his phone off. Then he runs his hands through his hair. "Ugh. I didn't think you'd be back. I didn't mean for you …"

"It is okay, Bran."

"Everyone does it at some point?"

"I suppose that is true, yes." I feel my cheeks heat. "In any case, I did not mind seeing you like that. It was … sexy," I admit.

Bran scrubs his face. "Okay. Hmm. I guess." He chuckles. "Except for my mom when I was about fourteen, no one's ever walked in on me like that." He gestures between us. "Living together, it's hard to get privacy." He tilts his head. "Oh my god, do you need me to leave sometimes, too? So that you can get off?"

My roommate has now shown me what it looks like when he comes. That will be material for my time alone.

I must have a faraway look on my face, because Brandon smirks. "I'll take that as a yes."

"Um. Yes, I suppose. We do not need to plan that. It is okay. I will be fine."

"Okay. But if you need some private time, just let me know."

"Thank you," I say, for lack of any other words, and I feel my body temperature rise about as high as it gets. "I need to go …" I gesture at the door. I want to get out of this room as fast as I can, so I drop my rucksack and leave for a walk in the forest.

I want to talk with someone. Unfortunately, I do not know very many people. I could text my father, but he would not understand. My mother …

Then I remember Kellie, who is one of the only numbers in my phone.

It is suddenly hard to swallow. Kellie could not know that her simple words would affect me so strongly. But my mother never paid attention to what I was doing or how I was developing. All she did and does is complain about what my father did to her. While she has a right to complain, it leaves no room for her to think about her only son.

I list off my classes, and she tells me that she knows one of my professors, who is friends with her wife.

I wait a moment trying to decide how to respond, and during that time, a text comes in from Brandon. As usual, it is a bunch of emojis that I do not understand.

I never know how to respond to his texts. But I look forward to them. I spend a lot of time trying to figure out what is going on inside his head. Every set of tiny digital hieroglyphics he sends makes me feel closer to him.

I send him a waving hand. That gets me more emojis in return: water droplets, waving hand, eggplant, peach, blushing face. My lips part.

He is not flirting, is he?

I return to my other conversation.

> My roommate is very nice. He is also very handsome. I have to stay away from him as much as possible, because otherwise, I fear I would get too close to him.

Steve

> Too close? Oh, honey. Do you not feel like it's safe to have friends?

Kellie

A tear wells in my eye. Nøkks are loners, because we are hideous creatures without souls, and if we are with people, we will destroy them. But maybe I can take the first step in trying to be a friend. Or more.

> It is not safe, often, for me to have friends. I fear they will reject me if they somehow see my true form. Or that I will give in to my monster instincts and harm them.

Steve

> Ugh. I hate it when we judge people based on looks. There is so much diversity in humans and monsters alike. I think we should celebrate that. I think those differences make us more beautiful. And your monster instincts are natural, too. If you suppress them, you're suppressing yourself.

Kellie

The thing is, I am not sure whether my true self is worth knowing, either.

I keep texting her until I get to where the Lin waterfall flows, and then I thank her again and say goodbye.

I look around. I am alone. I risk changing into my true form and diving into the water.

Peace. Joy. Tranquility. This is who I am. I revel in the freedom for seconds or minutes; time is irrelevant when I am one with nature and my surroundings.

Until I hear leaves rustling, and I quickly shift back into my human form. I worry that I am going to get caught in my true form and not ever be able to change back, but I suppose that is an irrational fear. It has never happened, not to any shifter I have ever heard of. Changing form without wanting to? Yes, that happens—but I have never experienced that, either. I hope I never do.

THE NEXT WEEKEND, we have a polo scrimmage against Shuford College. I recognize the werewolf and the hydra from the sporting goods store, and there are others on the team who are meaner.

I'm fast in the water, but even I get kicked and held down. The point of water polo appears to be to do the most damage that the player can get away with without either referee seeing. Since this is just a practice, our coaches are refereeing. And while ours is whistling for penalties big and small, the Shuford coach is only calling the most egregious fouls.

We are all going to be bruised at the end of this scrimmage.

"We really need to beat them," Nick says, treading water.

"How did our team do last year?" I ask.

"We lost. They don't let us forget it, either."

"This year will be different, then." I set my shoulders and take off. I am determined to score on their hydra goalie.

But while I can cut through the water better than anyone on our team, the hydra seems to be everywhere at once and pulls off save after save. While some water polo games can be very high scoring, in this one, we have barely scored at all.

The werewolf is cackling. Something in it activates a force in me. I need to defeat them. Brandon passes to me, and I dart around a merman, fake out the hydra, and put the ball in the net before they know it. Then again. And again.

We beat them, but barely. The Shuford team leaves, muttering curses at us. Did we just motivate them to play dirtier next time?

Things get worse when my father calls. I stare at my phone and rub my face before answering. Needing to be alone when I talk with him, I head toward the woods surrounding the school, walking on a well-worn path among the shady trees.

"Hei, Pappa," I say, trying to keep a sigh out of my voice. I do not want to talk with him, but I also do not want him to know that.

He asks me in Old Norse—the language of the nøkk—how my classes are going and if I am learning the fiddle.

It is best to tell him the truth. "I have not been able to play the violin. When I do, I put everyone to sleep," I say. "It is not practical for them to have me study that instrument, because no one can stay awake to teach me anything."

"Then they are not respecting the nøkk," he says, sounding irritated. But he always sounds irritated.

A rustling in the trees makes me look around. I spot a dryad dashing through the forest as fast as I can swim. I do love being at a school that welcomes nature spirits like me.

I scrub my face with my free hand. "I am not sure what to say to you."

After a brief silence, he asks, "When are you going to gather your first soul? It is disappointing that you have not done so yet. When are you going to be a real nøkk?"

"I am a real nøkk, Pappa. Just because I do not want to rob a human of their soul does not mean that I am less."

He lets out a derisive snort.

My heartbeat speeds up. I want to ask him how Mamma is, but there is no benefit in doing so. He does not care about her, and she does not care about either of us. It is probably best if she and I pretend the other does not exist.

The line is quiet for a moment. Finally, I ask, "Can I help you with something?" Pappa does not deserve my politeness, but I will give him respect anyway.

"I just want to ensure you are a credit to the nøkk culture."

If I do not bite my lip, I will scream—and I do not want to cause anyone to drown. Why do I have to be like him to be a nøkk? Can I not be myself?

I just say, "Yes, Pappa." And I hang up.

DURING THE FIRST few days of school, people dressed up in good clothes with fresh haircuts—except Brandon—and they carried unblemished notebooks to class or had their laptops open with new documents at the ready. Now that we are squarely into the school year, people are starting to relax more. With humans on campus still a relatively new phenomenon, a lot of the shifters are remaining in their humanoid forms. But there are exceptions.

On Friday, I walk into my cryptid biology class, and one of the swamp lizard shifters is in her true form. I have never seen one in that form, and when I see her I gasp, my heart freezing for a moment, then pounding.

Because she is so brave. She somewhat resembles me in my

true form. In addition, she is wearing pajamas and looks like she just rolled out of bed.

The other thing that impresses me is that no one seems to care.

Is that what it is like being yourself? I am so used to everyone (okay, my mother) focusing on how people (okay, I) look, I forgot that some people do not. Maybe more than some.

I stare at the lizard shifter throughout the lesson, wondering what it would be like if I went out in public in my true form.

After class, I catch up with her and tap her on the shoulder. She turns with a smile.

I shuffle my feet. "Do you mind if I ask you some questions?"

"About what?"

"I am ..." I pause and try again. "This is not my true form. I am not a type of monster that humans traditionally find sexy. I appreciate you coming to class today this way. Do you ever get any comments on not being all ..." I wave my hands, not sure there is a way to say what I mean that is not insulting. To tell her that I am both judging and not judging her by her looks.

But she does not seem to take offense. Her laugh is strong and fierce. Her green teeth and black eyes make it clear she is more like me than like a human. "I don't care what anyone thinks or says. This is who I am. They can deal with it. If they don't like the way I look, that's on them. Not on me."

I am unclear on how to respond. She may be right, but I have never thought about it that way. I have always thought that I needed to mold myself to fit in. To be like everyone else.

But maybe ... I do not.

I *don't.*

Maybe the point of college—or part of it—is to figure out

who I am.

"Thank you," I say. "You have been very helpful."

"I hope you do show off your true form. We can handle it," she says, and she waves goodbye.

Would I ever be brave enough to show my true form to Brandon?

I am supposed to be meeting him for lunch. He has talked me into going to the cafeteria more often. I get in line for food and select some fish and vegetables. As I move past the cashier, though, Bran waves at me from the table where he's sitting. He is accompanied by Clay and that harpy who is always fawning all over him.

I look down at my tray.

I am not hungry anymore.

I set my tray in the return and leave.

BRAN BURSTS into the dorm room like he always does. I should be used to it by now, but it still startles me.

"Hey! How come you bailed on me in the cafeteria?" he asks. "I thought you saw me."

"I did," I say, "but then I decided I was not hungry."

"Were you *really* not hungry?" He hands me some fruit: an apple, a banana, and an orange. "Because I know you don't have to eat as much as I do, but you have to eat *something*. And keep up your strength for polo."

I am touched by his gift. Brandon is always bringing me gifts. "Thank you."

"You're still coming to my birthday party, right?"

"Yes, I will come," I say.

"Cool," he says. Then he checks his phone. "I have an afternoon class. Catch you later?"

"Yes, I will—*I'll*—see you later."

Brandon tilts his head. "You just used a contraction."

I shrug. "I am—*I'm*—trying to loosen up."

He touches my shoulder. "That's nice. But, you know, you can just be yourself." Then he leaves, and I miss him before the door closes.

If it is his birthday, I should give him a present. It is the least that I can do, given how much he has done for me. But what kind of present? Bran does not seem to need much, although I do not believe he is rich.

Perhaps I should give him something only I can.

I smile and pull out a piece of paper.

II

BRANDON

"Woo-hoo!" Clay calls. He whistles loudly between his fingers, showing off his fangs as we walk past the gargoyles at the entrance to Creelin U. I still can't tell which ones are real and which are statues. "It's not every day your boy turns twenty-one."

"Like you've ever done it," Phil says, hiccuping from our pre-gaming in my room. "Aren't you, like, stuck at twenty forever?"

"Shut it," I growl. "It's my birf-day. Let him be."

It's Saturday night, and I haven't seen Steve since water polo practice this morning. He said he'd come out and celebrate with us, but so far, he's a no-show. I drop him a pin with the address for Scareoke. I'm sure I'll have a fun night either way, but I don't want him to be all alone. He deserves to have friends.

I text him a robot, music notes, a martini glass, birthday cake, and microphone.

He doesn't read it immediately.

The karaoke place is a long walk from campus, but none of us wants to drive, least of all me. It's a warm night, although the weather's going to turn soon and get all spooky and fall-like. Halloween-y.

Weenie. I giggle. Must be the vodka Clay bought me. He gave me that kind in the black skull bottle—the sixty-dollar one. Sheesh. But he never seems to lack for funds ... at least, when he hasn't forgotten his wallet.

After walking halfway across town, we enter Scareoke. The entire water polo team—except Steve—is here, and that's good.

I really hope he can make it, though.

My phone pings with a pin from Steve, and my heart races. He's coming. *Yuss*.

Clay points us to a reserved area with a great view of the stage, Phil claps me on the back and shoves me in that direction, and suddenly everyone is buying me shots and drinks like Dangerous Mouse and Sleepy Hollow. I have no idea what's in them, and I know enough not to drink them too fast, but it's challenging when people are giving them to me right and left. Word's gotten out that the human's got a birthday, I guess.

We're sitting in two large booths, with extra chairs added, loudly deciding what songs to sing, when Ren asks, "How's it going with your roommate? He's great in the water, but he's quiet."

I don't want to talk about Steve behind his back, so I just shrug. "He's fine." I glance around the table. "You guys are spiffed up tonight. I'm used to everyone in Speedos or pajama pants and hoodies."

They all look down at their jeans and real shirts. "Anything for you, Bran," Clay says.

I draw everyone in for a cheers by putting my shot in the middle of the table. They all hold up their glasses, and we down a drink called Ghost Dusters—even Clay, who doesn't usually bother with alcohol because he says he doesn't get drunk.

"Who's going to sing first?" I ask eagerly. I love karaoke.

Raising his hand, Phil says, "Me!"

I shoo him to the front. He lumbers up, his tall, hairy frame dominating the stage, and the MC hands him a mike. While I'd thought Phil liked rap, for some reason, he starts singing "My Way," Frank Sinatra–style. I know the tune, because my grandma used to listen to it. He's surprisingly good, belting out the high notes with ease.

Phil finishes the song with a flourish, and everyone bursts into raucous applause.

"Huh. Sasquatch has some pipes," I say admiringly.

"Best idea ever," Nick says, toasting me with his drink.

"I dunno," I say. "Phil seems to have thrown down the gauntlet."

"And I'll pick it up," Clay says, sauntering to the stage.

When the notes of the song he chose start, we all howl with laughter at the vampire singing "Toxic" by Britney Spears, the blueish undertones of his skin glowing under the lights.

I get a fit of giggles when he does one of her dances, his black-blue eyebrows expressive. While his voice is just so-so, the dance is perfect, and he brings down the house.

Clay waves at me to come up and join him for the next song, and now I'm really feeling the alcohol. He helps hold me up as we sing "Bad Guy" by Billie Eilish. It's horrible and off-key.

I love it.

I'm about to ask the MC to put on "Bohemian Rhapsody" by Queen, but the words die on my lips as Steve strolls in.

My heart starts beating erratically, and something zings along my spine. He waves to us and looks at me with those dark, fathomless eyes. The room quiets somewhat, watching me watch him.

I like him. I want him.

"Steve! Hola! Come on up!" I say into the microphone, and Steve obliges. I thought he might refuse, but he is a music major, so maybe he's okay with performing.

He stands next to me and shifts his weight from foot to foot. We're the same height, and kind of the same build. Now that he's here, my evening is complete.

"Are you going to sing something?" I ask into the microphone. "This is my roommate, everyone."

"Yes, good. You asked for 'Let It Go.' I will sing that for you," Steve says into the microphone, and everyone hoots and hollers. "And happy birthday." Even Steve can't suppress a smile. He whispers something to the MC, who nods.

I hop down back to our seats, and Clay follows me. At the table, I sip a glass of water, because I don't need to be puking my guts up on my birthday. I still am not one for hard liquor.

Under the lights, Steve resembles a rock god, with that shoulder-length black-green hair that's now—since he's properly hydrated—shiny, eyeliner, and tight black jeans with a studded belt. Combat boots and a band T-shirt complete his outfit, and his pale, slim fingers hold the microphone in a sensual caress. The edges of his body are still staticky, like he's not holding his shift.

The iconic music starts, and Steve opens his mouth to sing, starting in low tones.

The room quiets.

Goose bumps erupt all up and down my body. Steve's eyes close, and suddenly the world is nothing but him and the music, all of us under his spell.

His voice is like a singing brook. Like a waterfall. It's natural and enticing, sweet and sensuous and also kind of dangerous.

Steve hits every note. He's better at this than any Disney princess.

The music he creates makes my skin tingle and the hairs on the back of my neck stand up. His voice sends pleasant flutters through my belly. I'm rapt, wanting to look nowhere else.

As Steve starts the first chorus, he opens his eyes and looks at me.

Clay whispers in my ear, "Watch out. Nøkks can have an allure."

He certainly does have an allure. I don't understand it, but I want him to never stop singing. This emo boy.

This guy I have a crush on. This guy I might want to be bonded to.

When he reaches the climax of the song, Steve throws his arms out, and he brings the house down as he hits the high notes, ending with a final flourish.

The room is quiet for a moment. Then the whole audience bursts into applause, as if it was a real concert.

In some ways it *was* a real concert. Steve has a voice like none of the rest of us do—even Phil. Steve smiles shyly and bows. The crowd roars some more.

He walks off the stage and over to us, and I make room for him next to me. He murmurs in my ear, his cool lips brushing my skin. "Happy birthday. Do you want me to teach you a song as well? Or are we even?"

"We're even. I loved hearing you. Do you want a drink?"

He shrugs. "Sure, fine." He gets a glass of vodka from a waiter

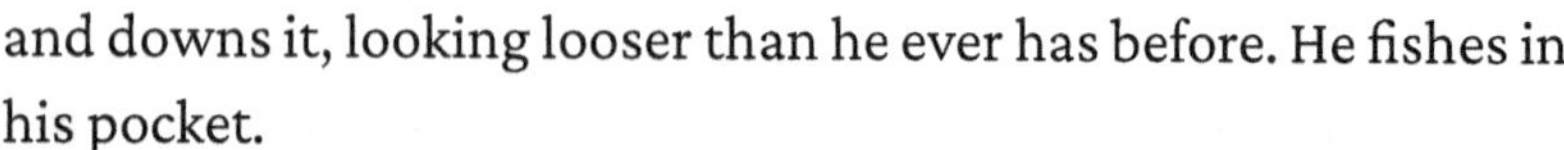

and downs it, looking looser than he ever has before. He fishes in his pocket.

"Don't worry about the drinks," I say. "We've got it."

"No," he says. "Well, I mean, yes, I am—*I'm*—happy to pay for mine, and I would like to treat you, but I also wanted to give you this." He shoves something into my hand.

It's a folded piece of paper. I open it up. It's sheet music, with notes written by hand. "What's this?"

Steve's cheeks flush slightly. "It's a song I wrote for you for your birthday."

My jaw drops open. "You wrote me a song?"

He nods. "I ... I will have to sing it for you in our dorm, because I will need my guitar. It is—*it's*—not on any karaoke playlist, of course."

I throw my arms around him and give him a hug that he returns after a moment, his grip surprisingly strong, given how slim he is. But I suppose he has monster strength. I love how he feels next to me.

I *definitely* have a crush on him.

"That's the coolest present ever, Steve. Thank you so much."

Steve smiles at me, and it does something to my insides. His smiles tonight might be the first I've ever seen from him when he wasn't in the water, and I treasure each one.

"You are welcome," he whispers.

Savannah the harpy walks in, along with two other girls, and when they spot us, they make a beeline to our table.

"Sit down," I say, scooting so we can accommodate them in the booth. I'm between Clay and Steve, both of their cool bodies pressed up against mine. Steve's feels more familiar. Perhaps because I live with him, I'm used to the way he smells. Not bad at

all. Like water or water plants or something. I dunno. I'm pretty drunk.

"You definitely are," Steve says.

I wonder if I said something out loud.

"Yes," everyone at the table says.

"Oh no."

Clay shoves at my bicep. "It's your birthday. You should get laid."

On my other side, Steve stiffens. "I can, uh, leave our room for some time if you want to use it."

For some reason, Steve's offer irritates me. I brush both of them off. "No. I'm happy where I am."

Another song starts up, and we all begin to sing along with the person up front.

STEVE'S HOLDING me up as we go down the street. I think it's a street.

I'm drunk.

"I know that," Steve says. He sounds amused.

"I guess you do. You're very smart."

"Perhaps. But you are smart, too, Brandon."

We walk a while longer, and I ask, "Where did Clay go?"

"He is making out with his date."

"He had a date?"

"I guess he met up with someone."

"I wonder if it's that guy he likes," I say, leaning farther into Steve and trying to be subtle about inhaling his hair, which smells like the freshest water.

"Does Clay date a lot of people?"

"I think so, but maybe he's just looking for the right one and it's taking him a little time to find them."

He falls silent. I want to tell him that I've been questioning my sexuality. That I may be trying to find the right one. That I'm interested in *him*.

I have enough presence of mind to know I shouldn't drunkenly confess all that to him.

Instead, I lean on him as we walk down the street and over the bridge, pass the gargoyles, and somehow make it home. The last thing I remember is Steve taking off my shoes and tucking me into bed.

I want to kiss him, but I fall asleep instead.

Sunday morning I wake up with a splitting headache, and Steve goes to the cafeteria and brings back food, including a coffee and a werebear claw for me and a coffee and an apple for himself. Again, I'm tempted to kiss him, especially when he later gives me an electrolyte drink.

"Someone once told me it was very important to stay hydrated," he says.

"Hmm. That person was smart," I mumble. "Why don't you feel bad, too?"

"Nøkks thrive on vodka. Besides, I drank less than you did."

"Lucky." I pout, and Steve smiles at me, which makes me focus, again, on his full, pouty lips.

I suppose with the whole nøkk bonding thing, though, we should be careful about kissing. Make sure we both want to do it before starting anything. He says he likes me, but I don't want him to be saddled with me if that isn't what should happen. I yawn.

"Do you want to sleep some more?" Steve asks.

"Yeah, I think so."

"Then I will go to the river. When I return, I will bring you lunch."

I smile weakly at him and snuggle deeper into my bed. "Thanks, man."

BY THE AFTERNOON, I'm feeling immensely better. Between pain relievers, electrolyte drinks, and sleep, life is back to normal. I do a few loads of laundry, take a long, hot shower, and eat the sub sandwich Steve brought me. When I'm done, I say, "Let's watch a movie!"

Steve looks at me like I've suggested that there's no such thing as nøkks. "A film?"

"Yeah! I don't have any homework left. Do you?"

He shakes his head.

"Then let's watch something. Come hang with me."

"Yes. Okay. Right," he says. With some words, he doesn't seem to have an accent, because his English is so good, but then the lyrical way he says other things makes it clear where he's from. I adore that about him.

"We can watch on my laptop." I point to my neatly made bed. "Just come over here, bring your pillow, and we'll make it like a couch."

Steve stands for a moment, suspended, like he's debating whether it's safe. I pat the spot next to me.

He swallows, nods, and snatches his pillow, then puts it at the foot of my bed.

Steve settles in with his back to the wall, and I join him, closer to the head of my bed, with my back also against the wall. His feet are tucked up next to his ass, hands holding his knees. I'm sprawled out, my legs wide.

And I'm trying not to hyperventilate because he's so close to me. I want him even closer.

I turn my laptop on, navigate to a streaming service, and start scrolling. "Do you have a preference?"

He looks fascinated at all the choices.

"What? Nøkks don't watch Ghouloo or MonsterFlix?" I tease.

"We do. But my father is old-fashioned, so most of the time I was out in nature."

"Makes sense." I hover the cursor over *The Princess Bride*. "What about this? It's one of my all-time favorites. But we don't have to watch it if you want to watch something else."

"I ... I do not know. We can watch what you want to," he says hurriedly.

I touch my shoulder to his. "Thanks."

The movie starts, and Steve at first pretends he's not into it.

"Do you want me to put subtitles on?" I ask. "I bet there's Norwegian."

"My English is good."

I grin at him. "I know it is. But that doesn't mean you don't want a little help."

Steve opens his mouth and closes it again. "I ... So far I'm understanding it. Mostly."

I pause the movie and click the subtitles to Norwegian. Then it keeps going. The way he exhales and settles in next to me, I know I made the right choice.

"Why do you like movies from the 1980s?" Steve asks.

"No one ever asks me that," I say, a lump rising in my throat. I pause the movie again. "My grandpa—my abuelo—he loved them. He babysat me a lot when I was little, because my parents both worked, and he would always watch them with me. So they remind me of him. They also often have this cheerful innocence and optimism. I dunno. I like thinking about him when I watch them." I swallow. "He died two years ago."

Steve looks like he wants to give me a hug. "I am sorry, Brandon. You must have loved him."

"Yeah, I did. I still have my abuela, and my mom's parents. But I miss his big, booming laugh and the way he played double solitaire with me."

"I wish I could give him back to you."

"That's a nice thought."

"But we can honor him. Thank you, Abuelo, for introducing Brandon to these movies as he is now introducing them to me." I restart the movie, and Steve goes back to watching the screen, but it's hard for me to see for a moment, because my eyes are too watery.

As the movie goes on, I notice that Steve's not giving off any body warmth. All he's wearing is a thin black T-shirt and jeans. "Are you cold? I could get you a blanket."

"I am not cold."

"But ..."

"Brandon," he says. I like the way my name sounds coming out of his mouth. "I have a lower body temperature than humans. I do not need a blanket."

"You sure? Even if you don't need one, it might be nice."

He nods.

I get up anyway and grab the hoodie I washed today. I hand it to Steve, and he looks at it dubiously. I raise an eyebrow.

When he sighs and slips the hoodie over his head, I feel better. He needs to be comfortable. I'm like a furnace next to him.

My hoodie is huge on Steve. I'm muscular, plus I like oversized hoodies, and he's a little smaller than me. The hoodie is black, with the logo of my favorite social media streamer. He picks at the embroidery and seems content. Then I think I see him sniff the fabric.

I know the hoodie is clean, but that makes me wonder ...

"Do I smell bad to you?" I blurt.

Steve shoots me a startled look. "No. Of course not."

"Okay. I was just worried. Nøkks might like different smells than humans, after all."

The edges of his ears turn pink. "You smell good, if you must know. You smell like sunscreen and the beach. I like the way you smell very much."

That makes me smile. Then I remember what he caught me using sunscreen for the other day, and my face heats.

So I focus on the Dread Pirate Roberts.

As the movie goes on, my eyes start to get tired. The next thing I know, it's dark, and my head is on Steve's bony but comfortable shoulder.

I yawn. "Hey. Sorry for literally falling asleep on you. I must still be worn out from partying last night."

"It's okay. The movie was good."

"Aren't you tired?"

Steve shrugs. "I do not need to sleep as much as humans do. It's more an indulgence than a necessity."

"Hmm. Well, sleep with me for a little bit."

"I beg your pardon?"

I think about what I just said. "I meant that literally, too. It's late. I'm tired. Lie down." I snap the laptop closed and haul him down with my arms around his middle. I grab the pillow on the way, and then we're lying together on my narrow mattress. He huffs but makes no attempt to move away, so I consider it a win.

I used to have this black cat who wouldn't want to be touched, but she also wouldn't want to be far from me. She liked being just out of reach, never quite able to be cuddled.

Steve reminds me of her. Only I've caught him, at least for now—and he seems willing.

With Steve in front of me, both of us on our sides, I have a sense of everything being right. I fall back asleep fast.

I DRIFT TO consciousness in the middle of the night with my dick hard against a soft ass. I thrust my hips and groan. That feels good.

Then I startle fully awake. I'm not with a girl. It's Steve in my bed.

Shit. I don't want to be a perv. I like him very much, and he likes me, too. But that doesn't mean I can just rub myself against him without his permission.

I pull back, not wanting to scare him. He might be awake, since he said he didn't sleep much. But he doesn't move, and before I can do anything else, sleep takes me over again, and I contentedly doze off.

12

THE NØKK

Lying next to Brandon in his bed, with his scent all around me, is an exercise in self-control.

He draws me to him not just because he radiates heat, but also through his sunny personality. I am not tired, but I have no desire to get up—not when he is so close to me.

I sink into recharge mode and drift for a while. I would like to relax fully and shift into my true form, but that would be too risky. He might wake and see me.

So I simply enjoy having him behind me. His breathing is heavy, so I know he is asleep, but he does not snore. I think I would find it cute if he did, anyway.

In the middle of the night, though, he starts rubbing a very large erection against my ass, and it is all I can do not to press back into him. I want it. I want to kiss him and touch him and take him inside my body.

But he is asleep, unaware of what he is doing, and it may mean nothing.

I wish it meant everything. Because no matter how chipper

and sweet Brandon is in the daylight, he is also one of the sexiest beings I have ever seen. He is as irresistible—and seemingly inevitable—as the changing of the seasons. I know he is going to do me in. I just know it.

And yet I cannot seem to move away. I could get up and go over to my bed, my side of the room. I could leave the dorm and go for a walk. I could go swim in a river.

But I want to stay here, in Brandon's arms.

All night long.

When he wakes Monday morning, though, I have made sure to already be up. I do not want to make this awkward. I have changed into my Speedo and gotten dressed.

Brandon has indentations from his pillow on the side of his face, and I want to kiss them.

I clear my throat. "Water polo practice starts soon."

"Shit," Bran says. "Thanks." He hurriedly gets out of bed and strips off his sleepwear. I do my best to avert my eyes, but he is so beautiful.

I wonder about the stretch marks on his torso. But I do not say anything. They are none of my business, and besides, I think they are gorgeous.

Together, we head for the pool.

I HAVE MY guitar in my lap late one morning when Brandon opens the dorm room door. I look up, startled.

"Hello," I say. "I am surprised to see you now. I thought you had class."

"Canceled. Professor was sick." Brandon pulls out his desk

chair and turns it around, as usual, straddling it and hanging his arms over the back. "What are you playing?"

"I am just practicing."

"Cool. Can I listen?"

After thinking about it for a moment, I nod. I reach over and plug the guitar into the amp. I usually do not practice out loud, but this way I'm not only going over fingering.

Taking a deep breath, I start to play a pop song he recognizes, and he smiles. I make my way through the song, and at the end, he claps.

"So good. I can't believe how amazing you are. No, actually, I can." Bran's eyes sparkle. "Can you play me my birthday song?"

"Okay," I say. He goes to open his drawer to hand me the sheet music, but I stop him. "I do not need the music."

"Oh. Right."

Taking another deep breath, I begin to play Brandon's song, which I intended to reflect him. The happiness he radiates. I wrote it in a major key, which is not something I usually do. It is far cheerier than anything else I have ever written, the notes happy and never getting too low. On the contrary, it soars. At one point, the fingering gets very tricky, but that is the fun part for me. The challenge makes me happy. Almost as happy as being in the water.

I am fully focused on the music, concentrating on playing each note perfectly, but when I am done, I look at Brandon.

His eyes are unfocused, and his face is peaceful. Did I accidentally enchant him?

I wait for his judgment.

Bran blinks. "Wow," he whispers. "That was beautiful. I love it. I got lost in it, you know? Like, I was picturing being out in nature—hiking or something. Along a brook. With everything all sunshiny and warm."

I smile. "That was what I intended. It is what I think of when I think of you."

Then I worry I have said too much. That I am showing him too much of what I am like inside ... but Bran does not seem to mind.

"It's the most special birthday present I've ever received," he says, reaching over and touching my hand. "Feels like you really see me, you know?"

"I see you," I agree.

We gaze at each other for a few moments, and then it begins to feel awkward. I do not know what else to say. It is easier for me to express myself through music than through language—especially English. The way Brandon expresses himself through emojis.

"Will you play it for me again? Another time, I mean, not right now," he adds hastily. "I'd just like to hear it again. In fact, I'd love it if you'd let me record it and put it on my phone. Or maybe you could teach it to me?"

"I will do that for you, yes. And you can record it."

He pats my thigh. "Thanks, man. I appreciate it."

His phone buzzes, and he smiles at it. The screen reads, "Baby girl." I stiffen. "You can ... talk with whoever you need to."

Brandon stands and pushes his chair back. "Thanks. I gotta take this. See you later?"

I nod.

"Hey, baby," he says, answering the call and leaving the room. Before he closes the door, he gives me a little wave and a smile. The kind that makes my heart ache even more.

I begin composing another song, but this time it is in a minor key. That's more like it.

Except ... the music is not getting out my feelings the way it usually does. Maybe I need to talk with someone.

I glance down at my phone. I have a class starting soon. But I know what to do.

AFTER CLASS, I give Kellie a call. "Hello. This is Steve."

"Steve! Hi! I was wondering how school was going for you."

"It's okay. An adjustment."

"Are you making friends?"

It is funny how this woman from a train—who is not all that much older than me, I do not think—is more of a mom to me than my own mother. "It is hard for me to make friends, but yes, I think I have met a few people who could become friends."

"I'm so glad! It *can* be hard." She pauses. "Say, if you want to chat in person, you could come over for dinner tonight."

"While I do not need to eat much, it would be nice to talk with you."

"That's fine. It's just an excuse to visit with you, anyway," Kellie says warmly. She gives me directions.

When I'm done for the day, I walk to her home, which is not far from campus, and she lets me into the small but welcoming house. She gives me a big hug, and Chris waves at me from behind her. "Hi! It's so good to see you, Steve!"

I shuffle my feet and try to smile. "Hi. Thank you for inviting me."

"Of course! I knew you were a good one when you saved

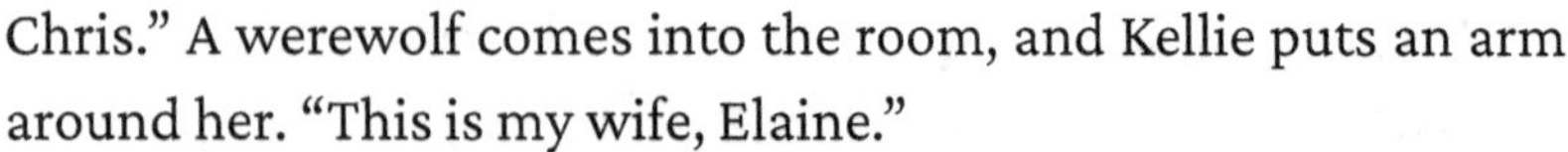

Chris." A werewolf comes into the room, and Kellie puts an arm around her. "This is my wife, Elaine."

"Nice to meet you," I say, shaking Elaine's hand.

"Same," she says. "I hear you're at Creelin."

"Yes. I am a transfer student from Norway."

"Well, welcome to the US. I hope you'll enjoy your time here," Elaine says.

Kellie says, "Dinner will be ready soon. We thought you might like fish, but don't feel obligated to eat if you're not hungry."

"Fish sounds nice," I say.

"Then join us."

They give me a tour of their cheerful home. It is full of framed, childish art, which I suppose was made by Chris, as well as books, comfortable places to sit, and a piano. I have always longed for a living situation this welcoming. I could have it with Brandon, I think. If he were mine.

Kellie fusses over me, which I am not used to, but the fish she serves is delicious, and I end up eating more than I normally would. "Everything is very good," I say. "Thank you."

We stay at the dinner table after we've finished eating, and I watch the sweet way Kellie and Elaine interact with each other. They tell me about their jobs and how long they've been here. Elaine works in the IT department at Creelin.

"How are things going at school, now that you've officially begun?" Kellie asks.

"It is good," I say. "I am focusing on the electric guitar instead of the violin, which is what I was supposed to be playing. But the guitar is what I prefer. I am finally being permitted to do what I want. It was not that way in Norway."

Elaine nods. "Creelin is an excellent environment to develop people into being their true selves. I'm impressed that they're letting humans attend this year. It feels very modern, which is a good thing."

"Yes, it is good to have humans and monsters studying together."

"What about friends?" Kellie asks. "It sounded like you wanted to say more when we were talking on the phone earlier."

"Um," I say, looking from one of them to the other. Because I do want to talk about Brandon. I have no one else to talk to. I would trust Brandon's input, but since it's about him, that's not going to work. And I'm not discussing this with my family or any other nøkk.

Kellie tilts her head, seeming to read my expression. "You don't have to."

"No, there is something I would like to talk about, but it is rather personal. Do you mind if I ask you a question?" I say.

"Not at all."

"There is a human I have a crush on at school. And I was wondering how it was to be in a human-monster relationship."

Elaine looks at Kellie, love shining from her eyes. "We have a great relationship. She's the best person I've ever met. And the prettiest. I think the world of her. We've faced some challenges along the way, but I guess we've mostly figured it out. There are times when I have to shift, but she accommodates me—gives me time to howl at the moon and roam free in the forest. But that's the main difference between us."

"I'd do anything for you," Kellie says, smiling at her wife. "But, Steve, what's up with you and this guy?"

"I am drawn to him, and he says he is attracted to me. But he keeps getting phone calls from a woman, and I think he might be in a relationship with her. I am not sure."

"You could ask him."

"True. But even if he is not in a relationship, every single person at school wants him."

Elaine chuckles. "I'm sure that's not true. But, okay, so he's popular. That doesn't mean you don't have a chance ... if he's right for you, that is."

"Maybe. But I have concerns. He activates something deep inside me—a nøkk urge to drag him to the underground world and take his soul."

Elaine and Kellie stare at me. I am worried I've offended them, but then Elaine breathes, "I know I shouldn't think this, and I'm only saying it because your concern makes it clear you're able to resist that urge—otherwise you would've taken him already—but it's kind of hot."

I do a double take. "Hot?"

"Sexy. You really want this guy, don't you?"

"I do."

"Then sort out his dating life, and if he's free, ask him on a date."

"There's another problem, though. Nøkk have a bonding ritual. I've never done it, naturally, but it involves exchanging blood, kisses, and hearts. And by accident, his blood has already mingled with mine."

"That is a complication. You—and he—need to be sure you want this bonding to progress before you move forward."

"I know." I pause. "But I kind of do want it to progress. Just not without his consent."

"It sounds like you know what to do, then," Kellie says, and I nod.

I am determined to talk with Brandon, but when I return from dinner, he's not in the room, and I fall asleep before he gets back. We do not have practice the next day, and I do not wake up until later than usual. I have been sleeping more here than I ever have. Maybe my body needs it when I am farther from home.

Brandon is gone again, but he left me a note to meet him at Mummy Mocha. The note warms me inside, and I hurry to get dressed.

When I walk into the coffee shop, though, I see Brandon sitting at a table with the harpy girl. Her wings are spread so that she's touching his shoulder, and their heads are together, looking over some papers.

I want to rip her away from him. I do not have any right to keep Brandon from talking to other people—or dating them— but that does not mean I have to like it.

I think about the sensation of Brandon's warm body against mine in bed, or even while we watched the movie—comforting, soothing. Those were good feelings, ones I treasure and would like to repeat. But desiring him also opens me up to moments like this, the acid in my veins when I watch this girl touch him. I want that to stop, but it may be out of my control.

I turn and walk away. I should go to class anyway.

BRANDON SLIPS into our room later that afternoon, when I am sitting on my bed playing with my phone. "Hey! I thought you were going to meet me earlier for coffee!"

"It seemed as if you had a study session," I say, trying not to sound hurt or sarcastic. I am determined to talk forthrightly with him about my feelings. To ask him what he wants.

But it is difficult.

He tilts his head. "Did you come by?"

I do not answer him.

Bran steps a little closer to me. "You're always welcome to interrupt me."

"I did not want to do that," I mumble.

"I'm inviting you to. It would've gotten me out of studying some monster history. I need to learn more about the Halloween Wave, but I can only study so much at once, and now I have the rest of the afternoon off."

"Oh," I say. "I am done for the day, too."

"How's your day been?" Brandon asks.

"Class was tough but good," I say. "The professors are challenging us to compose our own work to perform, and I am enjoying it very much."

"I bet you're great at that. I'd love to hear more of what you write."

"You might get enchanted."

He grins at me. "I already am."

I blink. Is he ... flirting with me? No, he couldn't be. Right?

"And you didn't even have to play any music to do it." Brandon's eyes alight on the bottle of vodka on the shelf. "Have you had any of that?" He points to it.

"Not yet, no."

"I'm not sure if it's any good. I had to go with what I could afford. And I don't generally drink vodka, so I couldn't really judge for myself."

"I am sure it is fine. And in any case, it was the gesture, the sentiment behind the gift that was important. Should we try it?"

He smiles impishly. "We don't have practice in the morning. I'm not that into hard liquor, but ..." He shrugs. "If I can't make bad decisions in college, when can I?"

"Yes, okay," I say. "We can drink the vodka." I nod a few times. While vodka does not affect the nøkk in the same way it does humans, maybe it will make it easier for me to start a conversation with Brandon that we need to have.

"You're so damn cute," Brandon says. "Hang on, let me go buy some soda." Taking his wallet, he slips out of the room, I presume to go the vending machine. He returns with a couple of cans of Ghosta-cola and pops one open. "Do you want soda or just straight?"

"I will drink the vodka straight," I say.

Brandon pours vodka into two paper cups from the water cooler, then tops one of them with soda and hands the other to me. He taps my cup with his.

"Skål," I say.

"Cheers, dude. To college day drinking."

He sips, then downs a bigger gulp, making a face. I want to kiss him.

The vodka warms me up. I think vodka was made for nøkk. Instead of being cool inside, I feel like fire is burning in my blood-stream. I smile at Brandon.

He blinks at me. "Whoa."

"What does whoa mean?"

"You're smiling."

"And that warrants an exclamation?" I ask.

"No, but you're usually all 'Life is tough, and I'm very emo.'" Brandon says it in a way that is not mocking, but he is teasing me nonetheless.

"Hmm. I am sorry."

"Don't be. I like you, and I like your smile."

"I like you, too," I admit.

"I see you," Brandon says. "I know you're trying to blend in—I think that's why you keep to your human form—but to me you always stick out." He hastens to add, "Not in a bad way. Just … I always notice you."

"I always notice you, too."

He scoffs, then swallows another sip. "There's a million guys like me. Ashton, Bailey, Diego. They all look like me."

"No, they do not," I say, then think about it. The guys he mentioned all have messy brown hair, tan skin, swimmer builds, and cute faces. They might have different ancestry, but when you get them together, they do look similar.

Except Brandon … Bran is different. He is more beautiful, yes, but my awareness of him is more fundamental than that. Maybe it is because he gave me his blood. I could pinpoint him immediately from anywhere.

"Is the vodka as bad as you expected?" I ask.

Brandon scrunches up his nose and lips. It is even more adorable than his usual expressions. "Wellll, yeah, kinda." He studies me. "You like it, though. Don't you?"

I am feeling as if this is how I am supposed to be. "Yes. It makes me … more myself."

"Cool." Brandon pours us each another drink, and we settle in next to each other on the floor, our backs to my bed.

"I enjoy this," I admit.

"Drinking with me?"

"Hanging out with you. It makes me feel … normal."

"You are normal."

"Hardly. I am the only nøkk in the United States, as far as I know."

"That doesn't mean you're not normal. And anyway, Witchipedia had a bunch of other words for nøkk, so maybe the ones who are here just call themselves something else."

"Maybe." I sip my drink. It is amazing how much better I feel with a little vodka in me.

Brandon giggles. "I think the alcohol is working."

"How does it feel for you?"

"Like the world is going swirly. Tipsy-turvy."

"Topsy-turvy?"

"That's what I meant." He drinks some more. "Oh, man. Vodka. Okay."

I like being with Brandon. I like it when he is loose and relaxed. He mostly is that way. But it is even better when he is giggly.

"The whole world is topsy-turvy," Brandon repeats. "I'm not who I thought I was."

"What do you mean?"

"I'm not straight, I don't think. The world is different now."

That confirms my hope, although Brandon's sexuality may be irrelevant to me, given his "baby girl" and Savannah. "Oh?"

"Well, I dunno. I've never been with a guy. And I haven't been attracted to guys before. But there is a guy I'm interested in now."

My heart sinks. I do not want to hear Brandon's confessions about his attraction to some guy. But I suppose I have brought this on myself by being friendly.

I sit upright, wanting to get away but trying not to be obvious about it. But Brandon tugs me back to him, and I get a whiff of his sunscreen scent. He smells like every warm beach ever. I am used to the mossy, dark lakes and frozen streams of Norway, but I have visited the shores of southern Spain and Greece. Brandon reminds me of those.

I am drawn to him. I like his sunny disposition. I like how he makes me feel.

But if he desires someone else, I need to let him go. Maybe I need to find someone else. Even if I do not want anyone else.

"What's that look on your face?" Bran asks.

"I guess ... I guess I do not like the idea of you wanting a guy."

His eyebrows pull together. "Why not?"

"I am a little jealous," I admit.

"Jealous? Why would you be—"

There's a knock on the door, and Clay comes barging in. "Hey, what's up? I haven't seen you in a minute, Bran. Wanna watch a movie?"

Brandon shrugs. "Sure, why don't you join us. Is it my turn to pick or yours? Or should we let Steve?"

"Definitely let Steve," Clay says.

I do not like that Clay has interrupted my afternoon with Brandon. But at the same time, I am relieved, because it means I do not have to tell Brandon about my feelings. That would be painful, and there is no reason to do it if he is pursuing someone else.

13

BRANDON

"**S**o, what's going on between you and your roommate, Fernandez?" is how Clay greets me as he reaches my table at Mummy Mocha. This has become my go-to study spot. I've started talking with Tanner, the dude who always seems to be working here. Tanner works a lot of jobs, so he's struggling academically. Poor dude. I get it. If I didn't have my scholarship, I'd be in the same boat.

Clay sits down next to me, his bony, cold knee banging against mine.

"Things are kind of confusing, but we hang out now," I say happily. Thinking about Steve always makes my chest warm. I've found myself humming the song he wrote for me while I'm walking to and from class or in the shower. "He's actually supposed to be meeting me here soon for a study session. So I think he likes me—more than my other roommates did, anyhow."

"Good, but that's not what I meant. You guys seemed cozy last night. I think you have a crush on him, and the feeling is mutual."

I whip around and stare at him. "You ... you could tell he likes me? He told me he wants me." Or wants my soul.

"If I recall correctly, you're the one who was so oblivious to everyone wanting to bang you."

"I haven't banged anyone," I huff, keeping my voice low.

"Really?" Clay says. "You're a virgin?"

I give him side-eye. "*No*, I mean I haven't been with anyone since I've been here. You've dated like fifteen people in that time."

"That's so weird to me. You're ... you look like you." He gestures to me.

"Having the opportunity to have sex with people doesn't necessarily mean I want to do it. If someone wants me only because of my appearance, that's not very appealing."

"I understand that."

"And besides, it's not like I always looked like this. Because of my past, I don't place that much importance on looks," I say.

Clay's brows furrow. "What do you mean?"

"I went from being a pudgy kid to a teenager who weighed twice what I do now. Then I got so into water polo that you couldn't keep me out of the pool, and I dropped a bunch of weight." I shrug. "I like my body regardless of its size."

Clay purses his lips, tilts his head, and pauses before saying, "Huh."

I shrug. "In any case, this is what I look like now, and my crush on my roommate is getting bigger. Except I'm not sure if it's based on my own feelings or some nøkk bonding thing."

"What do you mean?"

"When I see Steve, I get butterflies in my stomach and my knees go weak. My heart races. I hang on every word he says. I come up with excuses to get close to him. To see him."

"That's a crush all right. So why do you think it's not coming from you?"

"Steve told me that when I gave him my blood, he cut his finger pulling the slide out of the bag, and our blood mingled, which is apparently the first step toward bonding. Then there's kissing and giving each other our hearts. I hope that last one's metaphorical. So do you think there's some kind of mystical force going on? Don't I have free will?"

"No idea. Hang on." Eyebrows raised, Clay pulls out his phone and looks up nøkk on Witchipedia again. "Huh."

"What do you mean, 'huh'?"

"Has he tried to drag you to the underground world?"

"No, although he said he wanted to. He said it involves a lot of paperwork."

"Really? Well, that's Europe for you."

"I'm pretty sure you can sign your soul away with paperwork just about anywhere."

"Yeah, maybe," Clay says, tapping on his phone. "Did you know that his scream causes drownings?"

"He mentioned that he's an omen of that."

"But it sounds like nøkks can *cause* drowning, not just predict it. Maybe it wasn't smart to put him on the water polo team."

I wave a hand. "What's he going to scream about? He's so quiet. And we all know how to swim."

"I dunno. Just be careful. Or ... don't. Do you still want to kiss him, given the bonding thing?" Clay studies me intently.

Do I want to risk bonding further? Most of me is saying hell yes, because it sounds exciting. I suppose I should be smarter than that, but what can I say? Something inside me has wanted him from the second I saw him—before I even gave him any gifts.

Contented resolve settles into place in my heart.

I nod, but before I can answer Clay in words, I hear "Brandon!"

Savannah is standing in the doorway to the coffee shop, waving at me. I give her a smile. Ever since I saw her at Brainz Liquor, I've been running into her everywhere, and she wants to meet all the time to study for monster history.

Before she even orders, she comes over to us. Her wings are rather large, and she accidentally nudges someone. "Oops, sorry," she says.

"Hola," I say, trying for enthusiasm. She's cool and all, but I'm getting the idea she likes me more than I like her. "How's it going?"

"Oh, you know. The usual. Say, what did you do with that last question in the homework?"

Behind her shoulder, I see Steve walking in. He cranes his head, looking for me, and I wave to him. I don't want to be rude to Savannah, though.

"I had trouble with it," I admit. I glance at Clay, who's watching me very carefully.

Savannah keeps talking, but Steve appears to have left. As soon as I can excuse myself, I text him emojis of a coffee mug, red question mark, fairy, hug, and troll with a walking stick.

He leaves me on read. He hasn't done that in a long time.

Finally, Savannah heads off to class, and Clay nudges me. "I think someone's jealous."

"I'm not jealous," I say.

"No, I think *Steve's* jealous of how Savannah is always hanging all over you."

I blink. "You're right. I think maybe he even started to say something like that last night, before you got there. I'll have to fix that."

But with classes, dinner, and Clay dragging me to a movie, I don't see Steve until late that night. I'm too tired to get into anything heavy, especially since we have to get up early for practice, so I just say good night and go to bed.

It feels weird to bring it up in the morning, too, all bleary-eyed and half-asleep. I decide I'll do it after practice. We'll go have coffee, and I'll lay it all out for him. How I feel and everything.

While I know that's the right thing to do, and I'm hopeful it will have a very good outcome, it also makes my nerves spike.

When Steve and I walk into the locker room, the team's standing around Phil. The barrel-chested Sasquatch is in his Speedo, exposing the tufts of hair that are growing everywhere on him. And I mean everywhere—the tops of his feet, his forehead, the backs of his hands, his shoulders.

So the team is helping him wax. Again. Since his Sasquatch hair magically grows back so fast, they have to do it right before he jumps in the pool, otherwise it's pointless; good thing the salt water apparently doesn't irritate his bare skin. He's in enough hurt from ripping out his fur. Diego and Nick are applying the sticky strips to Phil's body, then yanking them off as he yelps in pain.

"Why do you go through this week after week?" I ask, shaking my head and wincing in sympathy as I drop my lounge pants and shove them, along with my hoodie, into the locker. "I know you don't want the extra drag during games, but isn't the pain too much just for practice?"

Steve takes off his T-shirt and sweatpants and joins us, wear-

ing a new blue-and-green Speedo. He looks so good in it—I'm not sure why I didn't notice that before. "What are you doing?" he asks.

"Phil thinks he's too hairy," Nick says, "so he makes us do this because he can't reach all his spots."

Diego nods and grabs another wax strip. "It's a lot of work."

Phil shrugs, then shrieks as Nick rips off more of his hair. The skin underneath is tan, but reddened. "A Sasquatch looks terrible in a Speedo," he says defensively.

"Some people may think so. It's who you are, though. Why change it?" I ask. Given my history, I'm very pro letting people be in the body they are in. I glance at Steve, whose dark eyes are on me, and he seems to be taking in my every word.

"Swimmers always wax," Phil insists.

"Maybe before an important game," I acknowledge. "Every little advantage helps, and it can feel good to be all smooth in the water. But why bother when it's just us and just practice?"

Phil looks sheepish. "I dunno."

And I get it. He wants to fit in. What he needs to understand, though, is that him being a Sasquatch is fine. "I'm good with you not waxing," I say. "Not that my opinion matters. But I think everyone would be comfortable with you being your regular, hairy self. We like you how you are. Don't worry so much about it."

Phil looks around. The whole team is nodding at him.

Nick gives him a smile. "You really don't have to do this."

"Well, maybe just before important games, like you said," he says. "I have to admit, waxing hurts worse than getting a limb ripped off."

"Be your furry self," I say, clapping him on the back.

Phil bites his lip and nods.

A phone sounds inside one of the lockers, and Steve startles. "I think that is mine," he says, in a wary tone. "I don't receive many calls."

"Is it your father?" I ask.

He shrugs as he walks over to his locker. "It could be."

"If it is, you'd better answer it," I say. "It might be important."

He nods, opens his locker, looks at the phone, and sighs. But he answers, saying something in what I assume is Norwegian. His voice gets grumpy, and soon he's saying something very sharp.

I'm worried about him, but I'm not sure there's anything I can do to help. So I join the other guys and head out to practice.

On the pool deck, I set my towel on the bleachers and do dryland lunges and squats with the team. Then Coach starts us on intervals, where we do five laps, then get out for push-ups and sit-ups and repeat.

After my first set, I pop my head out of the water, but I don't see Steve. Should I go check on him? I get out of the pool and drip my way into the locker room.

Steve is still on the phone, and his dark eyes flash in my direction for a moment. I could swear his body almost shifts to his other form—gray and green. But it might've been a trick of the light.

"You okay?" I mouth.

He rolls his eyes and nods, then says something in Norwegian.

"Let me know if you need help," I whisper, and he nods again. I return to the pool and jump in feetfirst, with my hands at my sides. I need to do my laps and catch up with the rest of the team, who are back doing dryland exercises, but before I begin, I notice

Clay is still in the pool, over at the edge.

"Got a cramp," he says. "Had to take a breather. I think it's gone. Let's finish the laps. I'll join you."

A vibration is emanating from the locker room and suffusing the entire pool. It's Steve's voice, but it's amplified, and it's making the water tremble.

Clay stiffens. "Oh, that's not good."

"I know. I wonder what's going on. I hope he's okay."

"I didn't mean that," Clay says, "although yes, we should find out what's wrong. But if I'm not mistaken, Steve is getting close to screaming. You know what that means."

"Pfft." I wave a hand. "Like I said before, we all know how to swim. And that's not a scream. He's just pissed."

"Still. Be careful."

"I will," I say.

We do our first lap. When we're done, Steve's still not in the pool, and his voice sounds like it's taking over the whole indoor space. I wonder what's going on. He didn't say for sure he was talking with his dad. Maybe he has a best friend in Norway. Or a girlfriend. Or a ... boyfriend.

I don't like that idea. I mean, Steve can have *friends*, of course. But the idea of Steve in love? It gives me a funny feeling in my stomach.

Clay comes up next to me and gestures. "Race you?"

I notice everything's gone quiet. Steve must be off the phone. Everyone else is doing lunges. "Tell me when to start."

"One, two, go," Clay says, the little cheater.

But I push off the wall and swim fast, my body sliding through the water, my arms cutting the surface. I make it to the other end, but Clay is there ahead of me. Dammit.

"One more time," I say, panting.

He nods, and this time I take off before him.

Then there's an overpowering noise.

The biggest vibration yet passes through the pool, and I fight to keep moving forward. My chest goes tight, and I can't turn my head to breathe. Water rushes into my nose, and I swallow huge, salty gulps.

Darkness invades my brain.

And the world ceases.

I4

THE NØKK

N^{o.} No, no-no-no-no.

Not him. Not that sweet golden retriever of a man.

My limbs shake, and my heart threatens to explode. My vision whites out, and I just react.

I race toward Brandon, who is facedown in the water and sinking, and dive in next to him. Hooking my arm under his armpits, I pull him to the surface, then drag him to the side of the swimming pool, where the coach and Phil each grab one of his arms. "Get him out!" I say, trying not to scream again. My stomach is full of lead.

"Got him!" Phil yells, as they yank an unresponsive Brandon out of the pool while I push from the water. Clay comes up next to me and helps.

Together, we manage to get Bran lying on the coping, and I haul myself out of the water. Brandon's face is blue, his lips a dark purple.

Oh my monster gods.

I shut my eyes and pull myself together. I caused this. I need to fix it. I am well-versed in resuscitating humans, because when I learned what nøkk are capable of, I made sure to learn CPR. It is like an antidote for my flaw. I feared it would come in handy one day.

I have never had to do CPR on a real human being before. I've never had a nøkk scream burst out of me before—but I was just so frustrated with my father.

And now I have to do it on someone I care about.

"Move so I can start CPR," Coach orders, but I push in front of him, my body still shaking. I am barely hanging on to this form, but that does not matter right now. The possibility that Brandon could be permanently injured is so much more terrifying than the idea of people seeing me in my true form.

"I will do it," I say, my voice cracking. "You call emergency services." There are legs and bodies around us, but I do not look up to see who is present. I am focused entirely on Brandon.

Gently, I open his airway and check for breathing.

None. *Gods*.

With my hands positioned between his nipples, I begin chest compressions, hard and fast, although not as hard as I could, because I am worried about breaking his rib cage. I know that can be a side effect of CPR, and if I need to do it, I will. But I am hopeful that I am getting to him in time.

My lips lower to Brandon's for the rescue breaths. When our lips touch, my cool ones to his, which should not be cool, an overwhelming surge of power shoots through my body, the same way it did when our blood mingled.

The second step in bonding.

I cannot worry about that now.

I set the sensation aside and return my full attention to Brandon. I do another round of chest compressions, then more rescue breathing.

Come on, I start chanting in my head. *Come on, come on.*

His lips are cold. He is not breathing. I am beginning to panic, but I keep going ...

One more round. There are murmurs behind me.

Come on, Brandon. Please.

All of a sudden, Brandon lets out a huge cough, and water spurts out of his mouth and nose.

Thank the monster gods.

He starts retching, and I roll him onto his side so he can get the water out. His chest is heaving, and his stomach is doing weird rolls, but I think he is going to live. I could not handle it if he did not. Especially if I was the cause.

"He is breathing," I say, finally paying more attention to those surrounding us. "Take a step back."

Everyone does. "You heard Jobs," Coach says. Sirens squeal in the distance. "Give them space. Practice is canceled; be here bright and early tomorrow." Lowering his voice, he tells me, "I'll want to talk with you at some point, but we need to take care of Fernandez right now."

"Yes, Coach."

Most of the team leaves—seeming reluctant but obeying Coach—but Clay and Phil remain.

Finally, Brandon opens his big, brown eyes. He looks confused. For a moment, he simply takes labored breaths. I reach out, wanting to run my fingers over his jaw, through his hair, but I pull back. I am not worthy to touch him.

There is a lump in my throat, and my nose is running. I never should have joined the water polo team. I never should have answered my father's call when I was so close to a body of water. I should have ignored my jealous feelings about Brandon and his "baby girl." I should have controlled myself. I never should have put Brandon in danger.

He looks at me. "Wha-what happened?"

"Do not try to talk yet," I say. "Give yourself a moment to recover."

Brandon nods and closes his eyes again, still lying down.

Once his breathing gets more under control, he struggles to sit up, and I help him. Someone has brought a towel, and I drape it over Brandon's shoulders.

"What happened?" Bran repeats. His voice is raspy.

"It is all my fault," I whisper. "I screamed."

"So that isn't just a folktale? A nøkk scream really does cause drowning?"

"It is not a folktale. It is true. I have never screamed like that before. I am sorry I got so upset that I lost sight of the risks to the people around me." My words are utterly inadequate to express how horrible I feel.

Brandon gives me a weak smile. His dimples still flash. "It's okay. I'm okay. I just thought I was a stronger swimmer than that. I didn't think it would *cause* a drowning—I thought it was just, like, *foretelling* a drowning."

I shake my head slowly. Two EMTs arrive and come directly to Brandon. Coach briefly gets them caught up, and they begin to examine Bran.

"How does your chest feel?" one asks.

"Hurts."

I wince, and my stomach sinks to the ground. "I am sorry. I

was trying not to crack your ribs, but I needed to revive you."

Brandon nods, but he still looks wan. "I don't think you broke anything." He turns to the EMT. "I've broken bones before, and this isn't like that. It's just a little sore."

"Uh-huh," the medic says, getting out a large kit of equipment.

He continues to evaluate Brandon, asking questions and measuring his vitals, but—thankfully—it soon becomes apparent that Bran is out of immediate danger.

"He seems stable, but the health center can run more tests than we can," one of the EMTs eventually says.

"I'll take him there," I say. "Should we go right now, or can he get warmed up first?"

"He can take a shower," the other EMT says, packing up a bag, "if he feels up to it."

"I'm fine," Brandon says.

The EMTs leave, and everyone exhales.

"Get him to the health center as soon as you can," Coach says. "They'll evaluate him and make sure there's nothing going on that we can't see. Take tomorrow's practice off, too, so you can keep an eye on him."

"I'll be fine," Bran says.

I look around at the few people who remain. "I'm sorry," I repeat. "I will try to control my emotions better."

"Monster things happen," Phil says. "We understand."

They all nod, but I still feel horrible.

Brandon tries to stand, but he wavers on his feet, and I hurry to position myself under his arm so he can lean on me.

"I'll take care of him," I tell Coach. "I promise."

Brandon leans on me as we walk to the locker room. One of

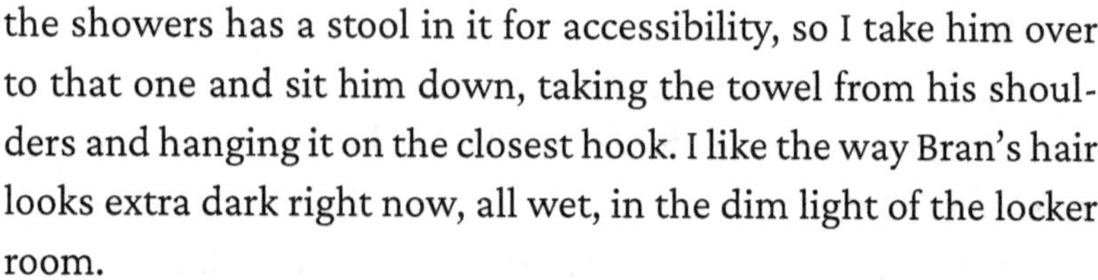

the showers has a stool in it for accessibility, so I take him over to that one and sit him down, taking the towel from his shoulders and hanging it on the closest hook. I like the way Bran's hair looks extra dark right now, all wet, in the dim light of the locker room.

"Let me help you," I say.

He gives me a weird grin. "I know how to shower."

"I do not want you to stand up right now. You just had a shock."

I turn on the shower, aiming the spray nozzle away from him while the water warms up. Then I tilt his head back carefully, not wanting to get water in his eyes.

"This is okay?" I whisper. This feels more intimate than I intended.

"Um, yeah," he says, his eyes closed and his voice hoarse.

I rinse him off to warm him up, then reach for the all-purpose hair and body wash the school provides. I squirt some into my hands and apply it to his hair. I have to step between his legs to do that, which puts my groin closer to his face than I intended.

This Speedo does not hide anything.

Oh well. I scrub his hair, sudsing it up to get the salt water out, and tilt his head back again to rinse.

Then I fidget until I come to a decision. "Can I get your shoulders and arms?"

"Um. Okay."

Not a ringing endorsement, but I imagine Brandon doesn't have a ton of energy. Nearly drowning can do that to a person.

When I apply the foamy soap to his shoulders and down his arms, I realize what a huge mistake I have made.

Because I am touching Brandon's soft, muscular skin. The

strong lines of his body are so sexy. I try to be clinical, but it is hard when he has such beautiful pecs. Tiny, peaked nips. I get on my knees and scrub his thighs, too. I ignore the parts covered by his Speedo.

As I wash him, he seems to relax and become closer to his normal self. I am hoping that since the drowning was magical, his recovery will be faster than it would be otherwise.

And now he is looking at me as if I am edible.

"Hey," he whispers. *Gods.*

He is getting hard, and so am I.

"Want me to—" I clear my throat. "Want me to get the rest of you?"

"No. I'm ... I'm good."

"Brandon," I say. "I had to kiss you to save you. I did not know what else to do. I did not want anyone else to touch you ... but now we are further bonded."

"That's okay. I've been wanting to kiss you, so I've already kind of dealt with the whole bonding concept. At least in my head."

"You have?" I am so confused.

"Yeah."

"I thought you were dating a girl."

Brandon frowns. "No, I'm not dating anyone."

"What about the one who calls you? The one you call baby girl?"

"My sister? Viviana?"

I am sure my eyes bug out. "That's your sister?"

"Yes. And before you say anything, no, I'm not interested in Savannah or anyone else. Just you. I meant to tell you that last night, actually, because it looked like you thought I was into her.

But I'm not. I'm into you."

A smile that I cannot stop spreads across my face.

Brandon goes to stand, and I think he should probably stay seated a bit longer, but I let him get up. "Um," he says. "So, can I … can I kiss you? I've never kissed a boy before, but I really want to kiss you. CPR doesn't count, dude."

"It might—"

"I really, um, like you," he continues. "And I know this could go badly, because we're roommates, and we have to see each other all the time … but I like you too much, and I'm willing to take the risk if you are." He gulps, his lips just a breath from mine. "Are you?"

"Yes," I whisper. "I am willing to take the risk with you."

My entire body clenches up in anticipation. As the warm water sprays over both of us, I lean in to kiss him, and unlike the rescue breaths earlier, Brandon's lips are warm and giving. He lines us up so that his cock is rubbing against mine, and he parts his lips, moaning into my mouth.

Gods, this is the most erotic thing I have ever done in my inexperienced life.

Fuck.

Our kiss goes wild, my tongue dipping into his mouth, his hands reaching around me to pull me to him. I want to never stop kissing him. I have felt that he was mine since the day we met, but now I think he really is.

Brandon blinks as if he has been under a spell. I don't think I have ensorcelled him. I think this is him kissing me voluntarily.

While my nøkk instincts urge me to take his soul, I have the strength to resist, because having him could only be satisfying if he wants me of his own free will.

Amazingly, it seems he might.

We continue making out, hungry for one another. A dam has burst, and now there is nothing but him and me.

I love it.

Eventually, our kisses slow, though we are both hard. We take long sips from each other's mouth. Finally, Brandon murmurs, "I think we need to get out of the shower before I turn into a prune."

"I think you need to see a medic or a nurse."

"I'm fine," he says. "Just get me to a bed."

I shake my head, thinking about the way Brandon looks with his dark hair splayed across his pillow. "If the situation were reversed, would you let me avoid getting medical care?"

He shakes his head and sighs. "Okay, fair. Let's go to the health center."

I kiss him again. Then I dry him off with a towel, doing my best not to further stoke his erection.

He shrugs. "Sorry. I, um. Yeah."

"It is all right," I say, not faring any better. We both get dressed, and we leave the pool complex, headed to the health center.

My brain is whirring. My first priority is to give Brandon protection so I do not accidentally drown him again. On one of my walks avoiding the dorm, I found a place in town that might have what I need. That is important, because I am too dangerous. He is going to get hurt if he stays around me.

But I want him. He is irresistible—the way his warm lips felt against mine. How eagerly he kissed me. I do not know if that is the way all kisses are, since I have never been kissed before.

Brandon is special. I want him to be all my firsts—and my

only. I want to do everything with him.

Bran reaches out and holds my hand as we walk. His palm is warm, both from the shower and because his body temperature is hotter than mine.

We have joined blood and kissed. That leaves our hearts. Where is his? Because I know where mine is headed.

R.I.P.

15

BRANDON

After a trip to the health center, where the nurse checks my blood oxygen, listens to my lungs, and inspects the bruises on my chest before pronouncing me mostly unharmed—although I'm told to take it easy and come back if I develop any trouble breathing or other symptoms—I take Steve's hand again as we walk across campus toward our dorm room. It's still morning, before most students have classes, although plenty are up and having breakfast.

Part of me can't believe we kissed. I don't know if it was a good idea or a bad one, but I know I liked it. I want to do it again.

While I am battered from the almost-drowning—okay, actual drowning—my spirit is light. I suppose a near-death experience will do that to a person.

I squeeze Steve's hand. I like holding it. His skin is cool, but not frozen like Clay's. I'm walking slower than usual; otherwise, I think I'll be back to normal soon. A day or two off from practice won't hurt, though. It might be nice to have some extra days to sleep in.

"I feel horrible," Steve says. "Again, I am very sorry I made you drown. Words are inadequate to express my sorrow—"

"It's not your fault," I say.

Steve looks at me, his eyes stricken and his mouth agape. "It absolutely is my fault. My scream causes drowning."

"But that's just your nature. It's like asking a vampire not to drink blood. It's who you are."

"I do not like who I am a lot of the time," Steve admits, and it makes my heart hurt.

"I like who you are all of the time," I say with a smile.

"Why are you like this?" he asks, his voice a mixture of annoyance and amazement.

"Like what?"

"Cheerful and forgiving. I almost killed you with my scream." His dark eyes are imploring.

"Ah, but you didn't. Just because you drowned me doesn't mean you killed me." I pat my belly. "See? Still here. All good. You're the one who said nøkk are omens of drowning, not death. We'll ignore the effects of a nøkk's scream."

Steve not-Steve shakes his head in disbelief.

"Who called and got you so upset?" I ask.

"My father. He is so hurtful sometimes. He tells me that I am not a proper nøkk. I got angry when he told me I needed to do things I do not want to do." Steve gives me a wan smile. "Like taking human souls."

"I'm so sorry, dude," I say. "I don't know much about nøkks other than what you've told me and I've read online, but if you're just talking about what's traditional, then you should be free to make your own choices. I'll support you."

"Thank you," he says quietly.

"Can I kiss you again?" I ask.

He stops in the middle of the quad. "What? Here?"

"Yeah." I pause. "Am I not supposed to want to kiss you? I do. Are you okay with that?"

Steve looks at me with a combination of affection and confusion. "Um. Yes. Okay. Or maybe ... over there?"

He points to a bench under a big tree, and we go to it and sit. When I kiss him this time, it's even better than in the shower. Definitely better than the CPR that I don't remember but apparently happened.

Steve parts his lips for me, and his cool tongue brushes against mine. I get the same shivers up and down my spine that I did when we first kissed.

"Yeah," I whisper, my voice turning husky. "I like that a lot."

"That—in the shower—was my first real kiss," Steve says.

I grin. "Oh yeah? It was my first kiss with a guy. And first kiss with a monster. Who happens to be sooo sexy."

My emo roommate has a smile on his face, and he looks dazed. He swallows hard and nods, then takes in our surroundings, tensing. More than one pair—or trio, or octet, or whatever, depending on the monster—of eyes are on us. Steve's expression changes to worry.

Does he not want to kiss me in public? Insecurity hits me in the gut. What does Steve think of me?

"Do you think I'm sexy?" I ask. Maybe I shouldn't have asked it so bluntly, but Steve's not choking on his tongue.

Then again, maybe he's getting used to me asking random questions all the time.

He closes his eyes, smiles, and shakes his head ... and my stomach drops. He doesn't?

Then he slides both hands behind my neck. "I cannot believe that you would ever think that was in question. Yes, Brandon. You are so sexy, I do not know how to be in the same room with you most of the time. That has been why I have been doing everything I can to stay away from you. It is because I have wanted you so, so badly."

He leans in for another kiss, but I hold him with both hands behind his neck, too, pulling him to me, and we meet in the middle with a kiss that shatters my world. Steve's cool mouth is plundering mine like he can't get enough of me. I can't get enough of him in turn.

I'm giddy. I could spend my life kissing Steve not-Steve.

"Yeah," I say, when we break apart. "I definitely like this kissing-boys thing. I should do more of it."

"With someone else?" he asks shakily.

"No, Steve. You're the only person I'm interested in. So I misspoke. It's not 'this kissing-boys thing.' It's a kissing-*you* thing. I hadn't realized before that I was into guys, but I'm very into you. Go on a date with me," I say, in a rush, as the idea occurs to me.

Although if this goes downhill, breaking up with my roommate would be a mess ...

Nah, I'll think positively.

"Sorry?" Steve says.

"Come out with me on a date. You know." I make a motion with my hands, but Steve looks like he's not sure what I'm indicating. "A date."

"What would you want to do on a date?"

"I'll come up with something. Do you want to go traditional, dinner and a movie? Or I could be more creative. We could go see a show in the city. Or go to a concert."

"I want to do anything with you," Steve says. "Because I always want to be with you. I don't care what we do or where we go. Or if we even go anywhere at all."

"Bowling?" I ask.

"I don't know how to bowl."

"You didn't know how to sing karaoke or play water polo, either, and look how good you are at both of those," I say.

He turns faintly pink, and it's adorable.

"I'll tell you the truth: I just want to spend time with you, too," I say. "But why don't we go out to dinner, for starters."

The grin Steve gives me is breathtaking. He's still a little fuzzy around the edges. Like he's on the verge of winking into his true form—what I wouldn't give to see that. But his smile comes across plainly. "Yes, okay. Good. That is acceptable. I would like to go on a date with you, Bran."

"Awesome. When do you want to go? Is tonight too soon?"

He shakes his head. "I would like to go on a date with you tonight."

I give him a wicked smile. "I know where to pick you up."

"Ha."

"Before we go on a date, though," Steve says, "I need to buy you some protection."

"I mean, that's a tad fast for me, but when it's time, I have condoms."

Steve coughs and tugs at his hoodie collar. It's sweet that he's flustered. "That is not what I meant. I am referring to protection from drowning. So that I will not cause you to drown, even if I accidentally scream again."

I frown. "What?"

He leans in and kisses me. "I will give you something you

must keep with you for your safety. Can you drive me into town?"

"Sure. After we clean up? Since we're ditching classes today?"

"That is fine. I will feel better knowing that you have what you need." He sags against me, and his outline goes wavy again. I love it when that happens. It's like he can relax around me.

"I wish you'd let me see your true form," I say.

Steve freezes. "No."

"Ouch," I say. "I can't know your true name. I can't see your true form. Am I entitled to any part of you if we're dating?" I'm playing it off like I'm kidding, but it hurts more than he knows.

But then Steve does something I don't expect. He puts a hand on his heart. "You can have this. If ... if you want to be bonded. Which you do not have to do."

I stare at him for a long moment. "You know, I can't decide if that's the sweetest or the cheesiest thing anyone's ever said to me. I'm going to choose to believe sweetest." I lean in for another kiss, and it takes us a long time to break apart.

He reddens. "It is true. That is the real me. You may have the real me. Should you choose to."

"I'd like to know *all* of the real you. I feel like you think I'm not going to like your true form, because I'm used to you being all Norwegian emo boy."

He huffs. "I *am* a Norwegian emo boy."

"You don't have to be scared of me not liking the way you really look," I say, cradling his face in my hands. "I'm good with it."

"I do not think you know what you are getting into."

I grin at him. "Try and stop me from doing it anyway."

He rolls his eyes, and I kiss him again. This time, I get a small grin from him, and that lights up my insides like nothing else. Seeing him happy makes my entire world better.

WHEN WE GET back to our room, I'm not sure what to do. I'm turned on, and I want to do something about it, but I don't want to pressure Steve into something he's not ready for.

Steve hangs up our towels on the hooks on the back of the door. I strip off my hoodie. "I have no idea what's happening to me," I say. "Are you bewitching me?"

Steve stiffens. "No! At least, not intentionally. I don't want to lure you to your death. I just want to kiss you."

"You are welcome to do that." I grin. "Or more."

"Gods," Steve whispers. "Okay. Um." He shuffles his feet.

I grab him by his T-shirt and pull him to me, widening my legs so he fits between them. Holding his chin with one hand, I lean forward and touch my lips to his. It's a sweet, gentle kiss.

His lips are cool and firm, and he hesitates for just a moment before opening to me, his cool tongue always a bit of a surprise against my own warm one.

Steve shivers, but it doesn't feel like the bad kind of shiver.

I pull back far enough to ask, "You good?"

"Yes." His voice has gone low and husky, and with his accent, it's super hot. In fact, now I want to know what his voice sounds like when he's doing more than kissing.

He leans toward me as if by instinct, and I have to kiss him again. He gasps into my mouth, and it's this innocent, sweet sound that makes me want to absolutely devour him.

I suck on his tongue, and he moves closer, his pelvis grinding against me.

It's not like I didn't feel his dick in the shower just a little bit ago. But feeling it now against my leg is another reminder that

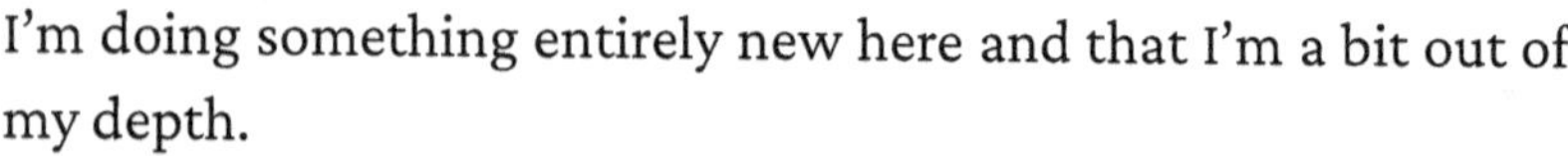

I'm doing something entirely new here and that I'm a bit out of my depth.

I don't want to stop, though.

"C'mere, you." I wrap my arms around him and tug him to me. He comes willingly, so now we're pelvis to pelvis, belly to belly, and my spread legs are cradling his thighs. The desk is hard against my ass.

I kiss his cute nose. His dark hair falls into his eyes. Then I bury my face in his neck. He shudders, and I wonder if he's been starved for touch. He's always seemed so alone and aloof. But sometimes those among us who are the prickliest are actually the ones who need cuddles the most.

"We're gonna go at your pace," I say.

"But what if that is too fast for you?" he asks.

"It won't be." I grin at him. "Are you saying you're ready for more?"

He turns pink and nods. His fingers pick at the hem of my shirt, so I grab the back of the collar and pull it over my head and off.

Steve licks his lips as he takes in my chest, maybe allowing himself to really look for the first time. I puff up a little, let's be honest. Because I do work out hard. These muscles didn't appear by accident.

He traces a lean finger up my arm, along the prominent vein that snakes its way from my wrist to my elbow. As he does, his form gets a little fuzzy—reminding me that he is, indeed, a shapeshifter. And that under the right circumstances, he can turn into something else entirely.

His cool hands then smooth over my chest—along my pecs, circling my nipples, running down the ridges of my abs.

"Man, you're torturing me. I swear. Kiss me and put me out of my misery," I whine.

Steve gives me another one of his fleeting smiles, and then he leans in and kisses me, and this kiss is not tentative at all. It's like he's satisfied himself that I'm flesh and blood and am not going anywhere, so now all systems are go. He kisses me hungrily and lets out a moan that sends my dick, which had been stirring this entire time, to full mast.

"Shit," I groan. "You're so hot."

For some reason, that makes him sad—I can tell by the mournful look in his eyes. "Hey," I say, grabbing his cheeks. "What did I ... Ohhh, because this isn't your true form."

He looks away. I put a finger under his chin and tilt it back toward me.

"I'm talking about who you are, not what you look like. The way you touch me is hot. And while, yes, in this form you're what most humans consider beautiful, you could have moss-covered teeth or pruny skin, or whatever it is that nøkks look like in their true form, and I'd still think you were sexy AF." I kiss him. "I'm attracted to the things you say and the sounds you make. The music you create and how shy and cute you are, but then how you get in the water and are free. I like who you are under that." I wave at him. "Not the surface. Trust me, there are plenty of hot people out there, but if their insides are trash, then I'm not gonna want them. I want you."

"I want to believe you," he whispers, like he's scared to break some kind of spell. "But I am not sure you are going to like who I really am—"

"Stop," I command. "I know what you show me when you think you aren't doing anything. I like that you're not arrogant, but you don't have to hide your talents. You can be yourself. Because yourself is amazing."

"Okay." His voice remains quiet. "Can I touch you—"

"Yes," I interrupt. "Please. Anywhere. Everywhere. I'm yours, Steve. My body is fucking yours." And the other parts, too.

That earns me a rare grin, and he kisses me, then tentatively touches the waistband of my pants.

"It's fine," I assure him.

He steps back, takes off his shirt, and strips off his pants and underwear in just a few seconds, and then he's standing before me, pale and sleek. I've seen him in his Speedo, of course, as well as glimpses when he changes clothes, but there's something super sexy about being able to stand and drink in the part of his hip that's normally covered up. That strip of flesh from just above his upper thigh to his waist—when it's uninterrupted by any clothing.

His cock is hard and ruddy, and it occurs to me that I haven't ever seen an erection that isn't my own before. Certainly not this close-up. (I'm ignoring porn; that doesn't count.) I hastily finish shedding my clothes.

Now we're both naked, and I step forward, grabbing his bare hips and instinctively brushing my cock against his.

"That feels good," I murmur, as his dick rubs the sensitive underside of my own. I like how his skin is cool—in Arizona, I'm always too hot, so having him around is kind of like having my own personal AC vent.

He smiles into my neck and then pulls back to kiss me. "Am I doing this right?"

"How do you feel?"

"Amazing," he whispers.

"Then yes, you're doing it right. I feel the same." I take hold of his erection and stroke it, noting that he's leaking precome like he's a fountain. It's pretty damn sexy, and I use it help my hand glide. We need to buy real lube, though. I don't have any, but I do have that suntan lotion, and with a few squeezes of that, we're in business.

"Come on," I say, pulling him over to my bed. I lie down on my back and invite him to straddle me so he's in charge.

With our dicks slicked, we kiss and reach for each other. "I really want to come," I moan.

"Me, too. Please. Please," he begs, and it's so fucking sweet and hot. "Please make me come."

"You got it, babe." I jack Steve off until his whole body stiffens and he starts shooting. When he climaxes, the outline of his body blurs again, and his skin gets greenish—like his true form wants to come out, but he's not letting go enough for that to happen.

Sometime I want to make him come so hard he forgets to be shy. I won't care.

But that will have to wait, since he's now making me come, and I release all over my own belly.

Steve leans down and kisses me sweetly. "That was ..."

"Yeah. Agreed," I say.

We kiss for a while, until the stickiness gets too gross, and then we get up and head for the en suite.

"I'm so excited you're going to go on a date with me!" I say as I turn the water on. My dick is already starting to harden again.

"Yes. I am, too. But let me buy you that protection first."

I'm really wondering what he's talking about.

I'm also wondering if he'll let me touch him again in the

shower.

He turns and kisses me, his soft cock rubbing against my interested one, and I get my answer fast.

16

The Nøkk

I cannot get enough of my roommate. Brandon seems to want me as much as I want him. Once we are in the shower, I use his body wash to repeat what we did in the locker room, only this time I do not avoid his most sensitive areas.

I start soaping up his gorgeous cock, which responds to my touch by getting thicker and thicker. I want to lick it. I want him to seduce me. Or maybe I will seduce him. I want to know every part of him.

I am watchful of the bruises on his torso from the resuscitation earlier. But he seems okay.

When he is fully hard, I drop to my knees and slide my soapy fingers over his taint. He groans. I take one of his balls in hand, then the other.

"Please," he whispers. "Please touch me."

The water is washing away the suds, leaving me with a very clean Brandon.

I give him a grin. "Okay." I open my mouth and suck his hardening cock down.

"Oh, shit," Brandon says in that quiet voice. "Oh, god, that feels so good."

I hum around him, wanting to get him off again. Wanting to give him pleasure. I do not know what I am doing, but this feels right.

But he tugs on my chin, urging me back. "What?" I ask. "Is something wrong?"

"I'm going to come."

"That is good."

"I want you to come, too."

I smile at him. "I will." I stand up and kiss him, my erection bouncing against my abs.

I cup his face and kiss him, then reach behind him, gripping his ass as I rut against him.

Brandon reaches out and squeezes some soap into one of his big hands, then uses it to jack both of us.

"I'm not going to last long," I say.

"Me neither." He grins. "I like this."

Brandon's rhythmic strokes get faster and faster until my body releases and I let go, spurting over his fist. Then I watch as he comes, his head thrown back and his lips parted. Ropes of his come land on my stomach and get washed away.

We keep kissing until his skin starts to get waterlogged—which is the way my true form is. It is the best I have felt in a long time.

ONCE WE GET dressed, I have Brandon drive me to a craft mall in Creelin. It's a large warehouse with booths staffed by many different makers selling pottery, visual art, wood products, textiles, glassware, foodstuffs, and more.

While I had been worried about aftereffects from Brandon's brush with drowning, he does not seem to have many. He is moving slower than usual, but that is it.

So maybe he is going to be all right. Regardless, that needs to not happen again.

Holding hands—which still sends a thrill through me—we walk up to a jewelry maker I had noticed before. On a display table is a curb chain necklace with links that are thick and chunky and have been flattened and twisted so they interlock tightly. The necklace clasps in a large O the size of an American quarter.

But the important part is that it is made of steel.

I gesture to it. "I want to get that for you."

"Um. Thanks, but you don't need to buy me—"

I look around. No one is paying attention to us. Nevertheless, I lower my voice. "It is steel. If you throw steel into the water where you are swimming, a nøkk's scream cannot drown you."

Brandon stares at me. "What the hell kind of lore is that?"

I shrug. "It is not lore. It is a fact. I want you to be safe around me. Will you wear this?"

He fingers the necklace, and I can tell he likes it. It's a modern design, edgy but subtle. "How does that work?"

"I do not know. With the nøkks like my uncle, who turn into boats, maybe the steel came from anchors? Or maybe it absorbs the vibrations from our scream?"

Bran smiles at me. *Dimples.* "I like learning about your culture. And yes, I can wear this around, and I'll love it." He gives me a quick kiss, and a thrill rushes through me. Then he bites his lip. "But I can't wear it in the pool. No jewelry during games."

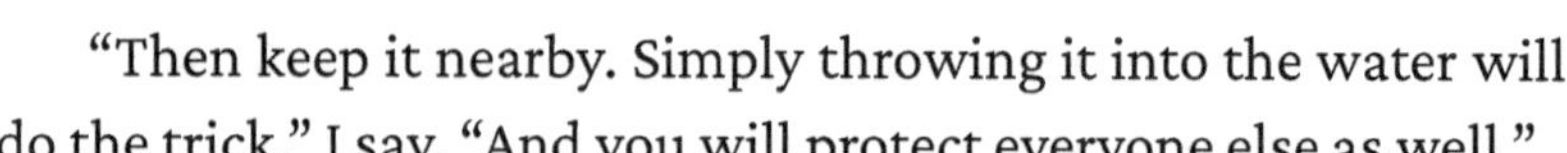

"Then keep it nearby. Simply throwing it into the water will do the trick," I say. "And you will protect everyone else as well."

"So I can toss it in before the game and let it sit on the bottom?"

I nod. "Yes, that is a plan. I am sorry I did not think of it earlier. Please keep it on you as much as you can when you are around me. It will protect you from drowning—at least from me causing it."

"Thank you." Bran's voice sounds scratchy, but I do not believe it is from any of today's activities. "This necklace is kind of punk, actually, and it feels very emo. Like you."

"So you like it? You will wear it?" I ask.

"Yes to both."

I pay for the necklace but do not touch it. I do not think touching it would harm me or diminish its protective properties, but I do not want to be careless. Brandon puts it on, and I admire it around his neck.

I swallow hard. "That looks good."

"Thanks. Can I kiss you while wearing it?"

"Yes. It just keeps you from drowning. It does not mean you cannot touch me."

"So. Interesting," Bran murmurs.

"It would go well with a see-through shirt," I say. "Or one of those mesh ones. Maybe in black. Just saying."

Brandon laughs, and it loosens everything inside me. "You're getting your perv on. I like it, Steve."

"Just wait until our date."

TONIGHT, I AM putting on my best shirt, a black button-down, and my nicest black pants. I could likely just wear jeans, but I wanted to show an effort for Brandon. I line my eyes with kohl a bit more carefully than usual.

He comes out of the bathroom wearing a soft sweater and dark jeans, and I know I chose well.

"I want to kiss you," I whisper.

"Then what's stopping you?"

I step into his arms, and he holds me tight. At first, the kiss is very soft, but then our lips part, and we're making out.

If we don't stop soon, we'll end up staying here and forget about dinner. And while I have no problem with that, Brandon seemed to want to take me out somewhere. I don't want to ruin his fun. I am dating an overaffectionate puppy.

I wish I could bring myself to hate it, but ... I can't. I like how Brandon throws his arms around me, smacking a kiss on my cheek. I love how he ruffles my hair and messes it up. I love how he is always touching me.

He did that even before we kissed, but today he can't seem to stop.

I don't want him to.

Brandon drives me to a restaurant in town that is owned by a coven of witches. The place is welcoming and friendly, and Kellie and Elaine had mentioned it, saying it has the best soups.

When we pick up the menus, the letters are enchanted so that they arrange themselves to show the dishes they think we will enjoy. So my menu looks different from Brandon's, and we compare notes. The witches rightly assume that I want fish and Bran wants spicier food, and we order accordingly.

We fall into easy chatter, and all I can think is how much I like being with him. How good it feels to be with someone it is so simple to talk with. Nothing is difficult with Brandon.

"If you could go anywhere in the world right now, where would you go?" Brandon asks.

Without hesitation, I say, "Creelin, Pennsylvania."

"That's convenient. Why?"

"Because you're here."

Bran's eyes melt. But it's the truth. I want to be near him.

"Where would you go?" I ask.

"Well, now I feel like I need to say something sweet and romantic. But the truth is, I want to see where you're from in Norway."

It's my turn to melt. He wants to learn more about me? That is as sweet as it gets.

"Maybe I can take you to the underground world sometime," I say slowly. "By your choice, and only for a visit. Not me forcing you to stay there forever."

"I'm in," Bran says. "Tell me more."

"In Scandinavia, there is an entire world where the spirits reside. It is ... under the ground."

"That doesn't make sense. The earth is solid."

"I suppose it exists in the space between worlds. I can access it from anywhere, but it is strongest there."

"That's so cool."

"If we went, I would need to protect you from having your soul stolen."

"How exactly does that work? I don't see how someone could steal something incorporeal."

"Fancy word." I raise an eyebrow.

"I know, right?" Bran looks pleased with himself.

"I don't actually know how it works," I admit, "since I've never done it. What I know is that nøkks are born without a soul, and the only way they can get one is through this process."

Brandon looks at me, and he's more serious than I've ever seen him. "I think you're doing just fine without a soul."

I raise an eyebrow skeptically.

"You don't have to agree with me. Do you want to talk about something else?"

I nod.

"What does the underground world look like?"

"Similar to this one—there are living spaces and so forth. But I have more powers there. Here, I am limited to controlling my shape. Oh, and water, of course. I can stop waterfalls and the like."

Bran holds up his fork. "Hold on. Stop waterfalls?" He pauses, then nods. "Yeah, I maybe remember something about that from Witchipedia, but at the time, I was mostly focused on how to get you to like me. But it's real? Like, big waterfalls?"

"Yes—"

"I've got to see this."

"I can show you after dinner. We can go to Lin Falls."

Brandon shakes his head incredulously. "Okay. Yes, let's do that." He takes another bite of his entrée. "So the underground world is a lot like this one?"

"Basically. We live in houses or caves. It's more magical than this world, and I can kind of make things how I want them to be. Although this world has plenty of magic if you just look for it."

"That's so cool. I want to learn more about your world. I want to know everything about you."

"No, you do not," I say.

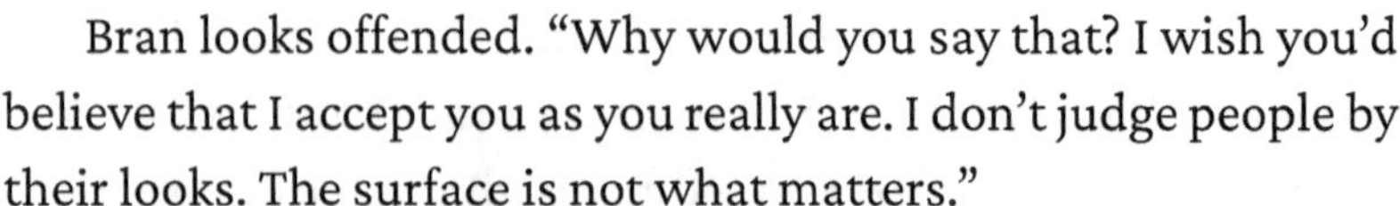

Bran looks offended. "Why would you say that? I wish you'd believe that I accept you as you really are. I don't judge people by their looks. The surface is not what matters."

I gesture at Brandon's beautiful body. "It's easy for you. Everyone wants you when you look like that."

Brandon's expression goes harsh—harsher than I've ever seen on him. "I didn't always look this way. And it's kind of insulting that you think no one could have liked me before."

I scrunch my nose. "I am sorry?"

"You should be." He still looks angry, but I cling to the affection in his tone. "You're right that some people are focused on the outside, but not all of them. Bottom line, I had to love my body as is—and you need to do the same thing."

The scoff that comes out of me is way too cynical. "What do you know about it?"

"Where do you think my stretch marks came from? I lost half my body size. But that happened because I fell in love with polo, not because I hated how I looked. I discovered the pool, and now you can't get me out of the water. But I couldn't put off accepting myself until I met some external standard. I had to be happy first. At any size, in any shape or condition. I look like this now because I exercise so much, and I like it. But in some ways, it doesn't matter to me. What matters is inside."

I swallow down a lump. "I never feel like anyone is going to accept me."

"That's because you don't accept yourself. I think you're wrong about how people see you—I like you a lot, and I bet a lot of other people do, too. But you'll never believe that until you get over this self-image issue. Gotta do that first, bruh."

While I want to roll my eyes, I am listening to what Brandon is saying. "It is hard for me to believe that you weren't always so beautiful and popular and athletic," I say.

"Every single person had to start somewhere. Sure, some people have natural talent, but even then, that doesn't tell the whole story. They still have to work to improve. For me, that meant extra weight room practices to build muscle. I took up running, even though I hated it, because it helped with my endurance in the pool. I changed my diet and started eating corn tortillas instead of flour, because it made me feel better. I stopped judging myself and started loving my own body. And little by little, my body changed. That became a virtuous cycle, because every time I felt better—felt stronger, felt like I could move faster in the water—I wanted to do more and more of what had made that possible." Brandon swallows hard. "It took a few years, but by the time I was a senior, I was one of the best on the team, because I worked harder than everyone else did. I put my reps in, as they say. At any rate, I very much sympathize with not feeling comfortable in your own body. I think a lot of people are in the same situation. Look at Phil, worrying about how hairy he is. We can be so hard on ourselves, and the thing is, so few people are happy with their bodies. Somewhere along the way, I decided I was going to buck the trend. My stretch marks are part of me, and I love them. So, when I tell you that I won't judge you for your true form, I mean it." He winks. "I think I'll find it cute."

I gape at him. "Only you could think that something as repulsive as a nøkk's true form is cute."

"Pretty sure I'm not the only one." Brandon digs out his mobile phone and starts scrolling, then finds a photo and holds it so I can see it. "Here. This is my 'before' picture." He shows me a photo of a much chubbier Brandon. Shorter hair. Braces.

Adorable.

"You are very handsome."

"Darn right." Brandon grins. "There was a time when I hated pictures of myself from back then. But now I can look at that kid and see someone I like. Someone I understand and care about." He looks me in the eye. "I'm not saying it's always easy. I hear all the same societal messages you do about how I can't possibly be happy if my teeth aren't straighter or I don't have the right shoes or whatever. But, even if I have to remind myself of it sometimes, I know deep down that it's the inside that counts."

I sigh. "But I have problems there, too," I say. "If I don't have a soul, then what do I have inside?"

"You have everything inside. You're a good guy—you're kind, you care about people. You are worthy, even if you don't have the same things inside that others do. Who cares if the way you're constructed is different?"

"Everyone does," I mutter.

"I'm not everyone," Brandon says.

"No," I admit. "You aren't."

17

Brandon

After dinner, I take Steve to Lin Falls. We park at the side of the road and have to hike a bit, but it's not too far. There's a full moon tonight, so we hear some werewolves. I'm not scared, but I hold Steve's hand as we walk through the woods. I want to touch him whenever I can.

The moon provides enough light that we can stay on the path without much difficulty. My new necklace is comfortable on my neck—not too heavy, but not insignificant. I pass my fingers across the skin-warmed metal.

The forest is eerie, and leaves rustle in the dark. I slip once on some loose gravel, but Steve catches me. He's stronger than I am. That's easy to forget, because he's so small, but he's got all those nøkk powers.

The waterfall comes into view, a roaring tower with a dark pool at the base. It isn't super tall or super wide, but there is a large amount of water feeding a pool that looks big enough to swim in. "I think it might be too cold tonight to go in," I say to Steve, before remembering that he's from Norway and he's mostly water anyway, so the cold likely doesn't faze him at all.

"Would you like me to ..." He gestures at the waterfall. "Stop it?"

I smile. "Absolutely."

He holds up his hands, and the waterfall halts.

I stare.

The water is just ... suspended. It's shiny in the moonlight. The river is still going past us, but the waterfall is waiting.

It's so gorgeous. A wall of stopped water.

"I can't believe I'm seeing this," I say, moved almost to tears.

Steve smiles and kisses me, then lets the waterfall go.

"The song you wrote for me—does it have words? Can you sing it?" I ask.

"It does not have words yet. At least, not words that you would understand. They are in Old Norse."

"Can you sing it anyway? The melody is so beautiful." I wrap my arms around him, and he kisses me again. The kiss goes a little wild.

Eventually we break apart, and Steve holds me close and begins singing to me in an ancient language. He's right, of course; I don't understand the words—but I understand what he's trying to communicate. He's telling me how he feels about me. He's the dark to my light and the monster to my human, and together we're much more than we are apart.

I am so happy when I'm with him.

Steve finishes singing.

"Even though I don't know what the words mean, I can tell the lyrics are about me," I say.

"How is that?"

"I can tell by the way you sing it. Like, I have all this energy.

And you're more sleepy hollows and caves and pools."

"That's right," he says.

We make out a bit more—quite a bit—by the river. "Do you want to go in?" I ask.

He looks at the water longingly.

"Do it," I say. "You can even shift into your true form if you like."

Steve shakes his head. "No, I don't think I can do that. Yet."

The *yet* makes my heart pound almost as much as the kissing.

Steve strips down to his underwear and jumps into the water, where he quickly dives out of sight, reemerges on the other side of the pool, and dives again. I stick my feet in, but I was right: It's too cold for me. After a little while—I think he gets out before he really wants to, so I'm not left waiting in the dark—Steve gets dressed again in his nice date outfit, going commando. I watch him the whole time, wanting him.

When we get back to our room, without thinking about it too hard, I gesture for Steve to crawl into bed with me. He holds me all night long. I don't know if he sleeps, but I know he's there for me.

THE NEXT DAY I argue that I'm well enough for practice, though I take it easy. After, we all head over to the cafeteria for breakfast, as usual. Steve begs off from eating, although he does have coffee. As usual.

When we're done, Steve sets out for his morning sociology class, and Clay and I head back to the dorms, taking a route past the sports fields.

"I was—we all were—really glad to see you this morning," Clay says when we get outside. "I texted you yesterday, but you didn't respond."

"You did?" I look at my phone and notice for the first time all the missed messages. "Sorry, guess I got busy." In a few senses of the word.

"And you're feeling okay? You almost drowned. It was scary as hell."

I finger my new necklace. "Yeah, it sucked, but it's over. I don't think it will happen again, either."

Clay raises his eyebrows. "How do you know?"

"I talked with Steve about it."

His voice goes quiet. "How is he? Is he feeling guilty? He seemed like he was panicking yesterday, but today everything was chill."

I think about what he looked like, naked in front of me. "He's good."

He gives me a knowing look. "What's going on?"

"We kissed," I admit. "Not the CPR kiss, real kisses. And more."

Clay pumps his fist. "OMG. Yes. That's awesome. Tell me more."

"I don't really want to kiss and tell." I shove my hands into my pockets. "Except I feel like I should be having more of a crisis than I'm having."

"Is there a certain minimum level of crisis that is acceptable?"

"I have no idea, but I feel like *none* isn't the right amount."

"Only you could be upset that you're not upset enough over your sexual identity," Clay says, chuckling.

"I suppose. But everything seems so easy with Steve. Well,

except the fact that I don't know his real name, what he looks like in his natural form, or for sure if he likes me for me or if all this is because I gave him my blood and that instituted some kind of supernatural bonding thing."

Clay pats my head like I'm twelve. "Pretty sure Steve likes you for you. First, as we've previously established, you're hot. Everyone wants to bang you. Second, you're a great dude. Why wouldn't he like you? All the other stuff—the ritual with the presents—he could just be a hoity-toity princeling and say 'Thanks, but no thanks.' Instead, he's saying 'Please let me suck your dick, oh hot one.'"

I smirk. "That's not quite the way he talks."

"Yeah, okay. I know. But he could have turned you down. Plain and simple. If he wasn't interested, he wouldn't have reacted so strongly."

"I guess." I pause. "Also, I was wondering ... I want to have sex with him. Or rather, more sex."

Clay trips over a patch of grass covered in leaves. He recovers quickly. "I thought you guys were having sex. At least, you implied that."

"Some kinds, yes. But not other kinds yet. And I want to. I can't get enough of him."

"I understand the feeling," Clay says wistfully.

"But I still don't know his name. Isn't that weird, if we're ... you know, doing all these intimate things together?"

"If it will kill him for you to use it, then no, it's not weird. I mean, it's definitely out of the ordinary, but it makes sense in the context of his life."

"I suppose. I guess I just never thought I'd have sex with someone and not know who they really are."

I'm distracted by the baseball team practicing to the side. We stop at the chain link fence surrounding the fields near a shorter dude who I think is a gorgon, judging by the snakes peeking out of his knit cap. I hook my fingers around the wires, watching the human pitcher toss the ball to the human catcher. Rumor has it that the Creelin team is going to finally do well this year because of those two. The gorgon's most definitely got his eyes—and maybe the eyes of his snakes—on the catcher.

After watching a few moments more, Clay and I take off again. When we're out of earshot, he says, "I dunno, Bran. I think you're getting to know who he really is. Steve talks to you, and he seems more alive when he's near you. I think you nourish his soul."

"Well, that's the thing. He says he has no soul."

"Oh, that's right. Okay, maybe he doesn't need one. I mean, isn't he worthy of love whether or not he has a soul?"

How is Clay so unintentionally brilliant? Sheesh. "That's what I'm going to tell him," I say. "You're so smart."

"Um. Thanks. I think." Clay looks at me hard. "You like him, don't you?"

I nod. "Uh, yeah. Isn't that what we've been talking about?"

"That's so cute. You're falling for the little Norwegian dude."

"I'm fine with you thinking it's cute. But thanks for reminding me that he doesn't live here permanently. What's going to happen when he goes back to Norway?"

"Oh, you'll figure that out. Long distance is a thing. People also do actually stay longer in places than they realize. And people move. If you really like each other, you'll figure something out."

I huff, annoyed at where this conversation has gone. An-

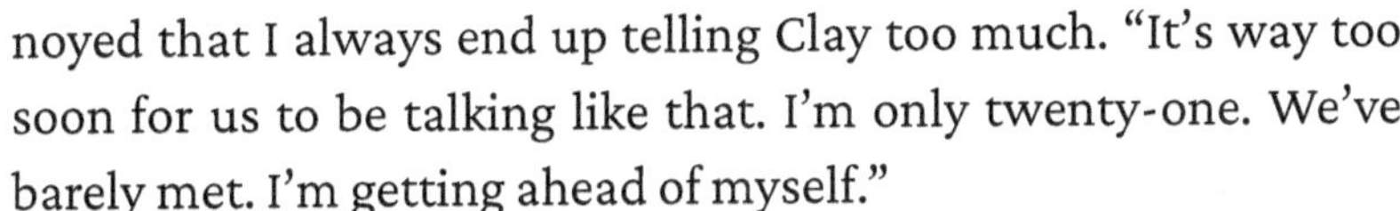

noyed that I always end up telling Clay too much. "It's way too soon for us to be talking like that. I'm only twenty-one. We've barely met. I'm getting ahead of myself."

"But he's done something, hasn't he? He's gone into your soul, even if he hasn't stolen it."

"That's kind of ironic. He's all worried about taking my soul. But I'd like to be at the point where I can just give it to him."

"But not your ass yet."

I shove him.

Clay laughs. "Don't forget to ask him to the Halloween Ball. It's tradition."

"That's weeks away still."

"I think he'd want to be asked."

"Fair enough."

"You should know," Clay says, "there's a blood moon on the night of the Halloween Ball. That's one of those times when shifters can't control their shifts. So be aware that things may be quite a bit different that night."

I grin. "It will be fun." Then I think of something. "But Steve doesn't like anyone to see him in his true form."

"It's Halloween, dude. He can wear a costume if he wants."

I GO TO CLASS, and all I can think about is Steve's face. It's funny, because I know his face is a mask he wears, and I want to see who he really is. I've formed a mental image based on the glimpses I've caught when Steve's human form buzzes out and for a second there's something different in its place. I think his true form has the same eyes, but more-webbed feet and hands. And I think his true form is more ... nature-y. Green-gray and mossy. More like the deep lakes and fast rivers he's from. Since I think that suits him, I worry. His mother must've done a number on him for him to think he's unworthy of love because of the way he looks.

Love.

Is that what I'm feeling toward Steve? I'm not sure. I'm irresistibly attracted to him. I want to know everything about him. And I care about him. I want him to be safe and happy and ... and loved.

I know I need to keep my grades up to keep my scholarship, but I'm useless today. I stare out the window, thinking about what it feels like to be with Steve intimately. Thinking about his voice and the way he treats me. How carefully he holds me.

He doesn't make me feel like I'm too much. On the contrary, I can be the true me when I'm around him: curious and enthusiastic and into things, even if they aren't for everyone—like karaoke and eighties movies.

I let Steve in, and he didn't flinch. He's the first. He might be the only, for all I know.

What we do together is more than sex. More than getting off. I don't mean to be emo about it, but ... something has happened over the period between when he moved in, when we hung out, when we first kissed, and now. Something that makes me want to be near him always. That probably isn't healthy, but I'm not sure I care. I feel more reckless than I've been in my entire life. Like I'm free.

My world is rocked, and I don't know what to do. Part of me wants to run away, because this is too much. Part of me wants to go find him and beg him to do more sex things. All of me is confused. Except all of me does know one thing: I am into Steve. And

I want a lot more.

A little voice in the back of my head is asking if this is all driven by some monster power—if I caused this by giving him my blood.

Except I felt an insistent tug toward him before he ever opened that paper bag. I just need to trust him. Period.

AFTER DINNER, Steve and I head out to walk along the river. Fall is truly here, and the yellow, red, orange, and brown leaves cascading like confetti onto the neat lawns are unlike anything I've seen before.

"I want to jump in a pile of leaves," I say, gesturing to where the zombie gardeners have gathered them in enormous heaps.

Steve looks at me like I have leaves coming out of my head. "Sorry?"

"I know I shouldn't, but this is the first time I've been in a place where the leaves turn colors. There are seasons in Arizona, but they're subtler, and it's not like there are maple trees among the cacti. If I'd grown up here, I'd have made such a mess every year."

He chuckles, and it sounds like a singing brook. "You are like a child sometimes."

"Just because I want to have fun? I know how to control my impulses."

"That is true. You do. And no, I do not think only children can have fun."

"Speaking of fun, do you want to go to the Halloween Ball with me?" I blurt.

Steve tilts his head. "The dance?"

"Yes. Fair warning, I hear it's on the night of the blood moon. Clay told me about that."

Steve's face falls. "Oh."

"I was thinking that you could wear a costume when you're outside, if that would make you more comfortable. Not," I hasten to add, "because I want you to hide. It's the total opposite. But what I care most about is that you're comfortable and happy. The second priority is going to a dance with my ... my ... *you*. So do you want to go?"

A brilliant smile takes over his face. "Absolutely, yes. I would like to go to the dance with you. We can sort out a costume." He leans over and kisses me.

"Cool." A giddy feeling courses through me, and I yip out a cheer. A few zombies look at me.

I shouldn't.

I really shouldn't.

I take a running leap and dive into the closest pile of leaves, scattering them everywhere. A few poke into my hoodie, and some get shoved down my pants.

Steve's hand flies to his mouth as he starts laughing. "You're going to make the work harder for them."

"I clean up my messes. I just believe in having fun and living for today." I pick a leaf out of my hair and grab a rake from a nearby shed. "I'll fix it."

Steve helps, and together we gather the leaves back into order.

"It's too tempting," I say, eyeing the neat pile we just made. "I want to jump in again."

Steve smiles. "You're incorrigible."

"It was worth it. And I'm so happy you're going with me to the dance." I lean in and kiss him. "So should I jump in the pile of leaves or leave it. Get it? *Leave* it?"

Steve closes his eyes and shakes his head, then reaches out and wraps his cool fingers around mine. "Let's go where the leaves cease to cast their spell on you."

18

The Nøkk

While at the beginning of the year I would go to class early and dawdle before leaving so I did not have to see Bran in our room, these days I am rushing into the lecture hall seconds before the professor begins and heading back first thing so I can have as much time with him as possible.

Brandon is cuddled with me on my bed, under the duvet. We normally use his bed, but we got it a little messy. Ahem.

So now his sheets are in the laundry, and we are lying in my bed. Bran keeps playing with my hair, pressing it under my nose so it looks like I have a mustache, then wrapping it around his finger.

He has *me* wrapped around his finger. And I love it.

"No one in my life has ever treated me the way you do," I say.

"No one? I'm so sorry, babe. Twenty years? You're twenty, right?"

I nod and decide to tell him about my family.

"When the Halloween Wave hit, my father changed into a nøkk, but my mother remained human. She was pregnant with me at the time, and I was born a nøkk. We are born in our true form. I am told that she took one look at me and screamed in horror."

Brandon's face falls, and he touches my shoulder comfortingly. "That's terrible. Where is she now?"

"She wanted to divorce my father, but he dragged her to the underground world and took her soul."

"God, babe. That sucks. No wonder you're all skittish about your true form. But I promise you it will be okay with me." Brandon hugs me. "What class do you have next?"

"Jazz ensemble, but it's not for a couple of hours."

"Do you need to practice?"

I stiffen. "I don't want to accidentally enchant you."

"That's awesome that you worry about it, but I'm already enchanted. Don't worry about it getting worse."

"Are you sure?" I really could stand to practice. And I like playing for Brandon.

"Very."

"Okay." I get off the bed, pull out my electric guitar, and plug it into my mini amp.

Then I start playing.

I lose myself in the music. In the way it feels to pluck the strings, to hear the music coming out. The smooth guitar under my skin and the notes surrounding us. It feels right.

As I play and play, I notice that Brandon's enthralled. He's not enchanted, though, which is a good thing. Instead, he's just … *into it*. When I finish the song, he claps.

"You're so good at that. I don't know why your dad doesn't want you to play what you want to play."

"It's because the violin is what nøkk are supposed to play."

"This totally suits you, and you look so hot, babe. I want to start keeping track of things we do together. Stay right here, holding the guitar." He pulls out his phone and takes a photo of me, then shows it to me. I look happy in it.

I open my arms, and he steps into them, putting his phone back in his pocket. My hands go to his ass and pull him closer to me, and our mouths meet in a sweet kiss.

Our kisses soon get a little bit more spicy, with a lot more tongue, and soon we're making out on my bed. First he's on top, then I flip him, and he laughs. He draws a hand down my face. "It's not your looks I'm drawn to," he says. "It's *you*. I see you. You get me?"

While I do sometimes overstate the amount of English that I understand—and idioms can be particularly challenging—the truth is, yes, I get him. Bran is telling me that he accepts me exactly the way I am. That's the best feeling in the world. If only I were brave enough to show him every part of me. I don't know if I'm ever going to be comfortable showing him my nøkk form. But if there is a human on the planet I would voluntarily show it to, it would be him.

We make out some more, but we keep our clothes on. We laugh. We kiss. While we could get more hot and heavy, sometimes I like to hold back. I like cuddling with him. I like being with him.

Face pressed to my skin, he asks, "Can we tell the team about us?"

I flinch. We've only been together a short while. "There is an us?" I ask, even though I know I'm being insecure. On some level, I do not believe it's possible that the most handsome guy on campus—the one everyone desires—is mine. He's going to be the best thing in my life … or the thing that brings about my ruin.

"Of course there's an us," Bran says. "You're my person. We're boyfriends. Right?"

An effervescent thrill courses through my body. I have a boyfriend. The *best* boyfriend. "Yes, absolutely. From now on, that is what we are."

"I kind of thought we already were boyfriends. I mean, I don't usually go around touching other guys' co—"

"Okay, Brandon. I get the idea." I look at him, feeling vulnerable. "But are you sure you want to be exclusive? Are you not interested in dating anyone else? Of any gender? Or species?"

He gathers me in his arms and kisses me. "Nope. Just you."

That makes me grin despite myself. This human *is* mine.

The next day, after a game, Brandon kisses me in front of the whole team, and there's a chorus of whoops and whistles.

"We knew you two were together!" Phil yelps.

My cheeks are warm, and I want to bury my face in Brandon's neck—by his steel necklace—but he stands with his shoulders back, as if he's proud to be with me.

"Yep. I'm dating Steve." He's all smiles. This man is something else. I love that he wants to show me off in front of other people. That he is not ashamed to be near me.

He is going to have my heart. I have never given it away before, but Bran can have it. In fact, I think it is already his.

AS WE GET DEEPER into fall, my days are filled with classes, music, water polo, and—most important—Brandon. We have moved our beds together and sleep side by side every night.

Well, he sleeps. And so do I, sometimes. Other times, when I am sure he is asleep, I let myself change into my true form. I watch him, cuddling him and making sure he's safe, until shortly before it is time for him to wake up. I occasionally look at the little slide that holds our blood, knowing that I'm not imagining the power binding us together. With every kiss we share, it gets stronger.

Every night, I get braver and braver, wanting to be closer and closer to Brandon. Wanting him to see the real me in a way no one else has.

Similarly, Brandon is opening up to me. While his family does not have the funds for all of them to fly out here for a visit, he calls them frequently, and recently he's been calling them on video and including me.

The first time he did it, he took a deep breath, then hit call. A cute teenage girl with Brandon's eyes and nose answered. "Bran!"

"Baby girl!"

"Hi! How are you? Who is that behind you?"

"I'm great, and Viviana, this is my roommate, Steve. He's a nøkk. He's also my boyfriend. Steve, this is my baby sister, Viviana."

"Ooh, you have a boyfriend?" Her voice is excited, not teasing.

Bran puffs up his chest. "I do." He slings an arm around me and kisses my cheek.

I wave, feeling foolish. "Hi."

"Are you the one from Norway?"

"Yes, I am from near Bergen," I say.

"OMG, Bran, you're right, he does have the cutest accent."

I turn to him. "You think my accent is cute?"

Bran gives me his adorable smile. *Dimples.* "I really do."

Two older humans show up on the screen. "Hi, Mom, Dad," Bran says. "This is Steve. He's my roommate, and also my boyfriend."

To their credit, Bran's parents take this announcement with ease. "Oh, Bran, we didn't know that you were into boys."

"Neither did I." Bran's hands shake the camera slightly. It warms my heart. My boyfriend is braver inside than he lets on. Things get to him more than the happy-go-lucky persona he wears like a costume.

"We're so happy to meet you, Steve," his mom says. "I hope you'll come visit us in Arizona sometime. Maybe at Christmas, if you're staying in the US for the holidays."

"I am, and that would be fun, yes, if Brandon finds it acceptable," I say.

"Of course," Bran says. "I bet Christmas in Arizona is a lot different from what you're used to in Norway. There's no snow."

"Yes, that will be very different."

"Then it's settled."

"Thank you," I say. "I am very grateful for the invitation." I want to tell them how I do not feel welcome in Norway and would prefer to only go back there on my own terms. How I have never felt better than when I am in Brandon's arms. But I suppose those are things that I should keep between me and him. "I would love to see some more of the United States."

We chat for a bit with his family, and after we hang up, he throws the phone onto the mattress.

"You just came out to your parents," I say.

"Oh. Huh. Yeah, I guess I did. They didn't seem too surprised," he says. His lower lip trembles slightly, and he seems relieved.

"It seems they are just as open and accepting as you are."

"The world is better when you accept people as is." He smiles. "I'm not saying you shouldn't work to change things that aren't right. But when we're talking about people being who they are born to be—that should be accepted and celebrated."

"Agreed." I open my arms to him, and he snuggles into me. I kiss the top of his head. "Even though you're human, I think you're secretly a monster."

"What kind?"

"You're a snuggle monster," I say.

He laughs. "Speaking of different kinds of monsters, what do you want to wear to the Halloween Ball? Have you thought about a costume?"

I look down at my body. "I do not know. I have never dressed up for Halloween before."

Bran's eyes go wide, and his eyebrows shoot up. "OMG, I have the best idea! You'll look hot, and it will mostly cover your face, so you'll feel comfortable until we get back inside."

"Yes, okay." I am swept along by his enthusiasm.

"Let's go into town and go shopping. What do you want me to wear? A costume? A tux?"

Brandon Fernandez, my human, in black tie. "Please, will you wear a tuxedo?"

"Since you asked so nicely, absolutely." He's grabbing his keys and wallet, his usual bundle of energy. "C'mon, I don't want to miss out on all the good costumes. All I can think of is how sexy you're going to look in what I want you to wear."

"Whatever," I huff. Except I think I'm starting to believe that he actually wants to be with me.

19

BRANDON

Cool, salty water splashes in my face, but I laugh it off and pass the ball to Clay, then hustle my way to the other side of the pool, where Ren's tending goal.

Clay passes to Steve, who is being defended by Phil. We can't wear goggles, for safety reasons, so sometimes it can be tough to tell what's going on, but when I pop my head up from doing the fastest crawl stroke I can, I learn that Steve's scored. Again.

I've always loved playing polo, but now I have my boyfriend in the pool with me, which makes practice even more fun. It also makes me more aware of how tight my Speedo is.

I've been wearing my steel necklace in the pool ever since Steve gave it to me. Coach said he had no problem with it during practice, although it's gotten tugged a few times what with all our roughhousing. Polo can be brutal, especially under the water, where we all end up kicking each other a bit too much—even on the same team.

After a few weeks of playing, Steve's gotten used to how the game works, and he's turning into a star. Definitely no longer a provisional team member. His natural grace and speed in the water make up for his lack of experience.

I'm treading water in the middle of the pool when Coach blows his whistle. We all look up at him.

"Jobs," Coach calls. "Tend goal."

Steve tilts his head. "Me, Coach?"

"Yes, you. Switch places with Ren. I want to try something. Everyone, get in a line and take shots on the nøkk. I wanna see how Jobs does in goal."

Steve's never tended goal before, but I have faith in him. Dutifully, we all swim over and get in a line. Steve looks warily at us, and his deep, dark eyes seem to be taking in the size of the goal. I know from experience that if you're trying to score it feels too small. If you're defending it, though, it's the size of a small country.

Ashton is first in line and dribbles the ball—you bounce it off your chest in polo—then picks it up and dongs it with all his strength at the upper left corner of the goal.

In a flash, Steve is there and deflects it.

We all murmur. Ashton's one of our best players.

Next up is Clay, who aims for a different area, but Steve's there with the save.

Over and over, Steve tends goal. When it's my turn, I look at Coach. In his human form, he doesn't have tusks, but his teeth are tending that way, and I've never seen him grin wider.

I can do this.

I palm the ball, then lift it up, hoping I can fake Steve out. I turn my head to the left as I throw to the right as hard as I can.

But Steve turns in time, and the tips of his fingers tap the ball enough to deflect it from going in.

"Guys, I think we have a new goalie," Coach says.

"Nick and Ren are terrific," Clay says. "But Steve seems unstoppable."

"You're gonna be our secret weapon," Coach says. Steve smiles shyly and looks away, but he seems pleased. Coach blows his whistle. "Gather round."

We all swim over to the side of the pool.

"There's a rumor that Shuford may be planning some kind of sabotage. Keep your wits about you, okay? I don't know if it's only gossip or if there's truth to it. But with those jackasses—" Coach shakes his head. "Better to be safe than sorry."

"Yes, Coach," we all say. I wonder what they could do. It seems like we're more dangerous than they are, since we have Steve and his nøkk scream.

Coach claps. "Okay, guys. Do your laps, and then I'll see you on Friday for the game. Good practice. "

We all take off, racing across the pool and back a few times, because Coach says ending strong is just as important as beginning strong.

Panting, I haul myself out of the water and drip my way to the locker room. I try not to eye Steve's ass too much, but when he's walking around in that tiny scrap of fabric, it's hard not to.

Still, I don't want to make our teammates—or him—feel awkward. I dry off and pull on my sweats, then wait for Steve so we can head back to our dorm.

"What do you think about being goalie?" I ask as we make our way across the quad. Water drips down Steve's face from his wet hair, and he looks like a model in some perfume or underwear ad.

"It is making me anxious, because it's a lot of responsibility," he admits. "But I think I can do it."

"I know you can do it, dude. You got this. Let's shower and then get coffee?"

"Sounds good."

The moment the door to our room is shut, I attack Steve. There's no other word for it. Grabbing him by the ass, I haul him to me and kiss him. His towel and gym bag thud to the floor. "Oof," he says against my lips, but he's kissing me back just as hard, his hands holding my face to his.

I love the way his cool skin feels against me—it's staticky, too. Like there's a burst of energy pulsing through him.

Steve wraps his arms around me and backs me against the wall, his erection pressing against mine. I'm freeballing it in my plaid pajama pants and pitching such a tent it's embarrassing. Steve's basically wearing the same thing, and together we get his hoodie off, then mine.

Then he's back on me, kissing me hard, his hands on either side of my head, his knee pressing between my legs.

He's got me boxed in against the wall, and I don't know why that turns me on, but it does. We're close to the same size—he's slightly smaller than me, and he told me his monster size is about the same—and it feels like a battle for dominance. He'd win, though. He's immovable. I like it. He could push me around. He just chooses not to.

Major turn-on.

I grin against his lips and kiss him some more, then start kissing down his neck and collarbone. His erection is as obvious as mine.

And I want to try something. I drop to my knees.

"What are you doing?" Steve whispers.

I pause with my hands on his waistband. "Giving you a blow job."

"Are you sure?" He sounds like he can't quite believe this is happening to him.

"I am." I want to encourage him to take his pleasure. I want him to use me. I love seeing him get off. I get off on it.

"Okay."

"I've never done this before, so you're going to have to guide me as to what you like. I can guess it's the same as what I like, but let me know."

He nods vigorously, and I shove down his pants and take his hard cock in my hand. His form blips a little bit, and I take that as a good sign. I lick all the way up his length and suck on the cushiony, velvety tip.

He groans loudly, and his knees shake. I guess I'm doing a decent job. I love how salty he is—and I don't think it's from the pool. He's just part water.

I suck more and more, getting into a rhythm, and it's really fun. It's like sucking a lollipop. A big one.

I almost giggle, and Steve gives me a sharp look. My brain goes weird places when I suck cock, it seems.

I pull off him so I can say, "I love doing this."

Steve looks down at me with so much affection, I can hardly stand it.

I love doing this to my boyfriend. I love that I have a boyfriend. I love that this makes me feel powerful.

"Are you going to come on my face?" I ask. "Or down my throat?"

"Wow," he whispers. "This is so fucking sexy."

I pause. "I don't think I've heard you swear before, and that's a turn-on."

He bites his lip, his black eyes full of desire.

"Do what you like," I say. "I want you to come."

Ngh. I want to be kissing him and getting off with him all the time.

"I will come in your mouth, then," Steve whispers, and I suck him harder. He's gentle at first, but at a certain point, he loses control. He sometimes lets out a monstrous roar when he comes—different from his nøkk scream.

He's headed to a tipping point, and soon he lets go, his warm spurts of release sliding down my throat. I've never swallowed this much come before (I tasted my own, once, but only a drop), but if this is what it's like, Steve can have me sucking his dick any time he wants, no questions asked. I'm good with this.

Before I can do anything, Steve is hauling me up by my armpits, kissing me hard. He pushes down my pants, which I kick off so I'm as naked as he is. Then, with a wink, he gracefully drops to his knees and starts returning the favor.

It's so hot. Or, rather, his *cool* tongue wraps around my dick, and the pressure and wetness and suction are unbelievable.

I'm so close to blowing anyway, it's not long before the pleasure takes over and I'm shooting down his throat, so, so happy that I get to do this. So happy that I have him in my life.

I walk him back to my bed and tackle him, our heads landing on the pillows with an oomph.

He laughs. I never knew such a melancholy creature could have such a warm laugh, but he does.

"I think we need to do that more often," I say, holding him as tightly as he's holding me.

He nods, his shiny dark hair splayed across his face. I love the way he smells—like fresh air and clean water. Things that might not have a strong, distinctive scent, but when you're near them, you know.

We make out until we're both breathless, then lie back, taking a break but unable to keep our hands off each other.

I grin at him. "You want to go do something? I don't have class until later. Wanna watch a movie or go swimming or go for a run or ..."

"I've got homework," he says regretfully.

"Then let's go study. Where do you want to go? The library?"

"Yeah, okay. Sure."

We get cleaned up—sharing more kisses in the shower—and dressed, then pack up our backpacks with our laptops and study materials and head outside.

Steve and I walk out of the room, holding hands, and run into Savannah. She startles, looking at our joined fingers. Then she tilts her head. "Are you two ... together?"

I let go of Steve's hand, and he stiffens for a moment, perhaps thinking that I'm going to betray him. But I sling an arm around his shoulders and kiss him on the side of his mouth. Even Steve can't contain his grin.

"Yep," I say. "We're dating."

Steve curls into me, and while there was never any question about my being willing to claim him in public—at least not on my part—I hadn't counted on coming out again and again. But I'll do it as many times as it takes. He's my boyfriend. I want to be with him. And I know he can be scared of how the world sees him, but I will defend him with everything I have.

"That's cool," she says, sounding wistful. "I guess I'll see you around."

When she's gone, Steve whispers, "I was jealous of her. I thought you were dating her. Before we got together, that is."

"Nope. No one but you."

We arrive at the library, grab some Mummy Mocha coffee (saying hi to Tanner and Seth), and then climb the stairs to a quieter area. It's been harder to focus on studying, now that I'm so into my roommate, but today, at least, I'm able to get some work done. Though I'm also enjoying sitting next to him and watching him scrunch up his nose as he works on his laptop and reads.

He's so cute.

I'm in trouble, aren't I? He's going to be the end of me.

But that's okay. I'm good with it. I think I've wanted him from the moment I met him.

And now he's mine.

FRIDAY, WE HAVE a game against a team from Ohio. It's the first real game where a team of humans and monsters have played against an all-monster team.

We don't get our asses handed to us, which I'd half expected would happen. I'm not a pessimist, but we humans simply don't have the same abilities as the monsters.

But what we do have is strong team intuition. Apparently eating breakfast together, going to karaoke together, and hanging out watching movies—on top of practicing all the time—pays off, because we're better able to predict where each other is going to be and pass the ball more efficiently.

Also, the Ohio team is not as awful as some—cough, Shuford, cough—in the area of cheating by kicking under the water. They do it, sure, but it's a normal amount.

As goalie, Steve's just about unstoppable, but we have to rotate players, and Ren lets in a few goals. Still, the final score's 4–3, with us on top, and the entire team goes out afterward to celebrate. We had something to prove, and we did it.

I hadn't realized how much of a risk Creelin was taking by encouraging humans to play, but we're showing that we're valuable members of the team.

We all pile into booths at Scareoke again, and this time, when Steve sings, I go up there with him. He commands the attention of the entire room, and at the end, when he kisses me, we bring down the house. Today has been a very good day.

Brandon falls asleep wearing only his underwear and his necklace, sated after our usual bedtime play. More and more often, once he's asleep, and in the safety of the darkened room, I have been letting myself change. I just make sure to get up early, so I'm back in my human form before he wakes.

But I always let out a sigh of relief when I can curl up behind him with my skin its true dark green/mottled gray. I wish I could be brave enough to show him who I really am.

As I lie next to him, I think about how my life is going. For the most part, I love it here at Creelin. In terms of my studies, things are going well. I am taking a composition class, and I have felt very inspired to write. Perhaps that is because of the new set-ting—this beautiful campus in the USA. Or perhaps it is because I am away from my father, so I have more freedom than ever be-fore. But I know much of it is attributable to Brandon. Thanks to him, I am experiencing all sorts of emotions I have never felt be-fore. They are uncomfortable in their newness, but they are good emotions, like joy and happiness, sexiness and lust, and even contentment.

All my life, I have been told that I am defective because I do not have a soul. Bran is starting to make me believe that I may be worthy without one.

In other words, I do not have to be like everyone else to be valid.

He shows me this every time he wraps an arm around me. Takes a selfie with me. Goes hiking with me. Sits with me in the library and studies. Watches movies with me and Clay. I am beginning to feel that I am okay as I am, even if my monster form is still not something I can share with others.

And being welcomed onto the team is amazing, too. I drift and doze through the dark hours of the night with these comforting thoughts floating in my head.

As the sky outside begins to turn gray, I shift into my human form and kiss Bran. "Ready for practice?" I ask.

He nods sleepily and tugs me closer. I never want to leave his arms.

In the locker room, the team is buzzing about the upcoming dance.

"It's gonna be wild," Clay says. "'Cause of the blood moon."

I have never felt a forced blood moon shift before, because when I am with the nøkk I never have to shift. This will be the first one I've experienced when I am around humans.

"It is only if you are outside, correct?" I ask.

"Correct." Nick smiles.

"Are you gonna finally let us see your true nøkk form?" Phil asks.

I shake my head. "No. I am planning on wearing a costume."

"That's cool," Nick says. "But you know we'd be good either

way."

I am still anxious, and the costume Bran suggested does not cover me completely. But it is better than nothing.

Brandon slings an arm over my shoulders as we walk back to the dorm. "I wish you could believe that I'll like whatever your true form is. You don't need to hide from me."

"I hear your words, but I am scared," I admit. "Because that has not been my experience."

"Your mom," Brandon says. It's not a question.

"Yes."

"I can understand why her behavior caused you to doubt yourself, but I hope you know I'll support you in moving past it." He gives me a shy smile. "I don't want to feed your insecurities. I want you to feel comfortable. And I wanna go to the dance with you. I can't wait to see you in your costume." He gives me an exaggerated leer. "And out of it."

"Yes, that sounds good," I say.

He glances around the quad. "I have a feeling that we're going to see a lot of interesting forms on Halloween. All the werebears and hellhounds and Wampus cats and whatever else ... they're gonna be having a lot of fun."

My heart seizes with a new fear. "Will you be safe?" I am now imagining my human getting attacked by dragon shifters and lindworms. And whatever else shows up on Halloween night.

"Of course. They're all registered with the OME. They wouldn't be allowed on campus if they were going to hurt humans." He kisses my cheek. "Don't worry so much."

THE NIGHT of the ball, Brandon is in the bathroom, refusing to come out until he's dressed. I am already wearing my shirt and pants. I cover my hair with the black cloth, then affix the mask across my eyes. While the costume usually shows more skin, I am tying the shirtfront up when I am outside, and my mask is bigger than the one the character wore in the movie. I intend to get to the ball without Brandon seeing me fully in shifted form.

I look in the mirror and adjust my sleeves. My eyes are deep and dark as usual, but I look ... happy, for once, despite my worries about shifting.

The door opens, and Brandon appears behind me. Strong arms come around my waist, and he kisses the back of my neck. I'm not sure if I'll ever get used to this casual affection from him—a human. I hope I never do. I hope it's always as special as it feels now.

I turn in his arms and suck in a breath. Brandon's wearing a classic black tuxedo, the crisp white shirt popping against his tan skin and his dark hair. "Wow, you look stunning!"

Brandon smirks, his dimples appearing. "So do you. The Dread Pirate Steve!" He leans in to kiss me, and I kiss him hard. He kisses me back equally hard.

Now we're both hard, and I think we may not be going anywhere if we keep this up. I am okay with that.

Brandon seems to have realized the same thing. He pulls back, panting. "We ... we really should get to the dance."

"We don't have to," I whisper.

"Yes, we do. Our friends are all going to be there. If we don't show up, they'll come looking for us."

I sigh. "I suppose." I can imagine Clay pounding on our door and barging in. I put on my gloves, finish tying the mask, and pronounce myself as good as it's going to get. I'm still in my human form, but that is not going to last much longer tonight.

We gather our phones, wallets, and keys—and my big jacket—and join hands as we walk down the hall. Before we get too far, Brandon stops short and pulls out a phone. "Let's take a selfie." I nod. He gets in the shot, and we take a photo together—me in a black mask, him with dimples and a tuxedo.

I wish I could take off the mask.

Through the windows, I see chaos. Monsters are everywhere: climbing trees, running across the lawns, flying. I can feel my body start to shift, and I'm tempted to hide, but I do not want to let Brandon go out by himself. My hands are inside my gloves. My jacket will cover my chest, and the mask covers most of my face.

I tremble slightly but take a deep breath.

We step out into the brisk October night, and I shudder. I can feel my skin changing into my true form.

So this is what a forced shift feels like.

I consider running back into the dorm, but I need to be brave.

Brandon does not hesitate to hold my gloved hand. But he will not want to see my face. It would put him off me for the rest of his life ... just when I thought I had a mate.

When we step inside the building where the ball is being held, I exhale and return to my usual human form.

"You good?" Bran asks.

I nod. In truth, I am somewhat shaken up. It is one thing for me to shift by choice. It is quite another for nature to take over. I take off the bigger mask and put on the smaller one. Now I am Westley from *The Princess Bride*, with my all-black ensemble: billowy lace-up shirt, gloves, tight pants, boots, sash, head covering, and mask. I skipped the sword.

Inside the venue, the decor is orange and black. The banquet hall is decorated with ornate candelabras everywhere, and it has the proper spooky but fancy atmosphere. Monsters and humans alike are dancing, drinking punch, and chatting at maximum volume in order to be heard over the music.

It is fun.

I do not see anyone we know when we walk in, but Brandon tugs me to him. "Dance with me?" he murmurs, his soft lips against my cheek.

All I can do is nod.

Brandon pulls me into his strong, suited arms and walks me to the dance floor. With one hand on my hip and the fingers of his other twined with mine, he holds me close as we sway to the slow song. Being with him like this in public feels unusually intimate, energy passing between us. I kiss him, and he smiles against my lips the way he always does. When I pull back, his dimples are flashing, making my heart expand. What I wouldn't do for those dimples ...

Around the room are individuals and couples, some of whom I recognize from classes or just passing by on campus. Many are unfamiliar. I think one might be a dryad, who might be dating Tanner from the coffee shop. The mummy is also here, surrounded by men. I wave to Kentley, who is across the room with a guy I don't know.

We keep dancing, and if I had a soul, I would give it to Brandon. I am ready to give him my heart.

After dancing for a few songs, we take a break and talk with Clay and Phil. Clay is sipping blood, while Phil towers over most of us dressed as Chewbacca.

"Nice," Bran says to Phil, gesturing at his getup. He turns to Clay. "You decided to go full-on classic vampire?"

Clay looks down at his black cape, white shirt with ruffles, and black trousers. His makeup highlights his cheekbones and eyebrows. "Figured it would be fun to try it."

"It's cool, dude."

"How did the forced shift go?" Clay asks me. "Are you all right?"

His gentle concern reminds me that Bran is not my only friend here. I have friends on the water polo team, too. I have friends from class, like Kentley. I have friends in town, like Kellie and Elaine. Friends who seem to watch out for me.

"I did not like the feeling," I admit. "But I am okay. This costume helps."

"You look great. Is Bran Buttercup? Or is he the Six-Fingered Man?"

"Neither, dude. I'm just hot," Bran says.

Clay chokes. "At least you're finally admitting it."

While I know Brandon is teasing Clay, no truer words could be spoken. Bran really is gorgeous in that tuxedo. And he seems to have eyes for no one but me, which I'm starting to get used to.

The song changes to one Brandon likes, and he drags me back to the dance floor. After a few more dances, he murmurs in my ear, his voice seductive, "Let's get out of here."

"Yes," I whisper, and we walk to the coatroom. I retrieve my coat, make sure my mask and gloves are on, and hold my breath. Time to be forced to shift again.

I glance out the windows. Shifters are climbing trees and slithering on the ground. Dragons are flying by, and a phoenix rises.

"Are you okay?" Brandon asks.

"I am not sure."

"Do you want to stay inside?"

I shake my head. "I just have to make it back to the dorm. That is not very far."

Bran smiles, and his dimples distract me. "We can run, if you want." Holding my hand, he pulls me outside, and my true form comes out immediately in the red moonlight.

A goblin zooms past us, cackling.

I remind myself that I am okay. My face is mostly covered by the mask, and the scarf over my hair also helps.

A centaur gallops with a minotaur, and two griffins are vaping near a grove of trees.

It is not that far to the dorms. We can make it. Brandon and I start walking toward Karloff Hall, but a werewolf, hydra, and merman appear in front of us, blocking our way. The hydra, a dragon with multiple heads, circles us while the werewolf leers at Brandon.

"You're on the water polo team," the werewolf says.

"Yeah, so?" Brandon says, a hand on his hip. But I can tell his adrenaline is surging, because mine is, too. No one threatens my mate.

The merman hisses, "You should never have won that scrimmage. Watch your back in the game. We're coming for you. One by one."

Brandon scoffs. "Whatever."

They turn to me. "Is this the nøkk?" the werewolf taunts. "You look different than you did in the pool. Uglier."

"Fuck off," Brandon snaps. "Don't make fun of him."

"Why not?" The werewolf snatches the scarf from my head

and the mask from my face. "He's disgusting."

Tremors hit my body as my knees weaken. My biggest fear, showing Brandon my hideous form, is coming true, and I cannot stop it. I try to hide the tears in my eyes and cover my face, but then I see the hydra cornering Brandon, who takes a step back. The hydra's jaws are snapping, and the werewolf joins him, claws out, while the merman blocks my way.

No. My muscles quiver, and I bare my teeth. My nostrils flare, and my lips curl.

They will not harm my human in any way.

No one will ever hurt him while I live.

I shove the merman to the side with my full monster strength, and he falls to the cement. He must not have been expecting me to fight, and he pauses a moment before getting up. I stalk to the werewolf and grab him by the back of his neck. He scrabbles at my arms, but I'm too quick for him, and my sharp nails make him bleed. He gets some scratches in, but my body is not processing pain for now. I feel edgy. Twitchy.

We are attracting a crowd, and a cyclops I don't know steps in to help me, keeping the merman down.

"Fuck you," the werewolf says, spitting.

"No." My pulse speeds, my heart pounding. I have tunnel vision, wanting these threats to my human to be gone. A scream escapes from me—no one will drown; we're not near water—but it still overpowers the wolf, sending him crumpling to the ground. The vibrations shatter the glass in the lamps overhead, which rains down on us, leaving only moonlight to see by.

"Get the fuck away from me," Bran snarls at the hydra.

It seems the hydra is preparing to spit venom at him. I race over and tackle Bran, putting my body between him and his attacker. There's a pounding in my ears, and my hands shake.

"Do not fucking hurt him," I growl. I gather my enchantment powers and let them loose. "Leave. Now."

The hydra freezes, finally affected by my power. With the werewolf and merman down and the hydra stabilized, I take a step back and boom, *"You will leave now."*

Thankfully, the enchantment works, and all three of them scramble away. The crowd hisses at them. I put my hands on my hips, breathing heavily, watching them weave their way past the other monsters.

When my breathing stabilizes, I realize what I've done.

Brandon has seen my true form.

I cover my face with my hands and flee to the river.

BRANDON

Steve's taken off running in the direction of the river. I race after him in the dark, passing all kinds of shifted monsters frolicking around—and an idle thought has me wondering if any of them are in my classes and I just don't recognize them. Then I slip and decide I need to focus on my footing, since my slick tux shoes are doing me no favors.

That was fucking scary. I knew Shuford were a bunch of dicks, but I didn't think they'd actually come to CU to, what, intimidate us?

On the other hand, it was hot AF to see Steve go ballistic.

Poor Steve. He doesn't realize that I've caught plenty of glimpses of him in his true form by now. I wish he'd let me see it more. I'd like to take it in, study it.

I plow through underbrush, shielding my face from random twigs, as I slip-slide my way down to the river. When I reach the bank, Steve's already splashing in the water, his body obscured by low-hanging branches that dip down to the surface of the river. Even in the shadows, though, the moon sheds enough light that I can make him out.

"Steve!" I bellow.

"Leave me alone," he yells back.

"No," I call, my voice breaking. "I need you. Come out, and come back to the room with me."

"I can't," he roars.

He's got his back to me, and for once his outline isn't shimmering. His dark shirt clings to his body, and I can't see his face.

I dive into the river, and I hear a yelp. "Brandon! No!"

But I don't listen. I swim over to him, even though the water is damn cold and my rented tux is likely ruined. I'll have to cut back on the nights out at Scareoke to pay for it.

When I reach my boyfriend, he turns away from me. He could easily elude me in the water, but he seems to have given up.

"Don't look at me like this," he whispers, covering his face with his hands.

"What makes you think that I won't like your true form?"

"Because it's ... ugly."

I'm treading water, but I manage to put a hand on my hip and sigh. "Let me see."

"No."

"Steve. Stop hiding from me. Let me see you."

"You're going to hate me. You'll be repulsed. You'll never want to touch me again."

I reach out and put my hand on his arm. His skin is cool, but it's always cool.

Finally, he faces me, and I am shocked. But not for the reason he thinks.

Yes, he looks like a monster. His eyes are the same—entirely black, like a seal's, and his teeth are broken and yellow, with gray spots. His lips are gray-green, and he's got all kinds of mossy debris hanging off him. He's got long, gray nails on spindly fingers, and his palms seem waterlogged. His hair is longer in this form, and it lies in hanks across his shoulders and down his back. His skin is mottled greenish and dark gray, and his skin is rippled and pruney. His tongue darts out, and it's green-black. I'm amazed how clearly I can see him in the moonlight.

But I don't think he's ugly. Not by any means. His true form has a natural beauty all its own.

"Hey," I say quietly. "I like you in any form. This one, too."

He scoffs.

"Listen to me." I tug him closer, and despite his supernatural strength, he lets me. I like the way my skin looks against his. Like we're both part of nature. And I like the way he feels next to me, solid and cool.

We go toward the shallows where we can both stand. He's stopped trying to hide and is instead looking at me defiantly, like he's daring me to find something good about him. "You're just so damned cute," I say, and pull him to me for a kiss.

A surprised kiss, since this is clearly not what Steve had been thinking we were going to do. But he gets the hang of it soon enough, kissing me back with fervor.

He smells like Steve. This is my boyfriend. My true boyfriend.

My boyfriend with a green-onyx tongue.

When we break apart, Steve's gasping. "What the ... Why did you do that?"

"Because I like you a whole damn lot, silly. No matter what form you're in. You don't have to be that emo Norwegian kid. You can just be you. I like *you*, not your body. Or, rather, I like that you can change it, but I like how it is originally, too. Don't worry so much, okay?"

He stares at me. "It's hard for me to believe you."

"I know, babe. But do me a favor. Just try."

Steve tilts his head. "Try?"

"Try believing me. I can't know your name. At least let me enjoy what you really look like. Because I think it's awesome."

He swallows hard and looks away, shaking his head, and my heart breaks for him. If only he could see what I see—that he's spectacular just the way he is.

"Try," I repeat.

Finally, he sighs. "All right, I will try. It just—I'm so used to people running away and screaming when they see me in my true form."

"Well, then they have no sense of decency or adventure." Steve rolls his eyes, but I ignore him. "When you're recharged, how about coming back and joining me in our bedroom. I need you."

"Ha ha," he says bitterly, but then he catches my expression. "You are serious."

"I am so fucking serious, boyfriend." I kiss him again. "I like you this way better, I think. Because I know it's the real you."

"I do not understand how that is possible."

"Stop the negative talk. Who is to say who is beautiful and who isn't? I think you're gorgeous inside and out. Why can't I be attracted to a monster? Especially one as kind and sweet and talented as you? Why?" I demand.

And before he can answer, I'm kissing him again.

Also ...

I think we may be bound. Because somewhere, somehow, during some interaction, I gave him my heart. And I'm pretty sure he gave me his.

Well, if we're going to be bound, I need to know more about him.

"Hey," I say. "Will you teach me Norwegian?"

He stiffens at the non sequitur. "Why?"

"So I can talk with you in your native language, obviously."

"But that will take a long time."

"I want to be with you for a long time. Are you okay with that?"

He shrugs, which morphs into a nod, then a grin. "I'm very okay with that." He leans in and kisses me, this time less tentative. And, sure, he's mossy and has weird skin. But I love him. So what's the big deal?

He stares at me. "I ... let us get back to the dorms."

One more kiss. "You got it. Just do me a favor and don't try to shift back."

Steve nods.

WE'RE SOAKED, and it's damn cold, so we race back to the dorms past all the other frolicking students. When we get inside our room, I shove off my wet tuxedo and strip down fast, but Steve is still standing there in his Dread Pirate Roberts costume, looking away from me. He must be reacting to the artificial lights, which don't hide anything.

Naked, I move toward him carefully, not wanting to spook him. He looks me up and down with visible hunger.

"Baby," I say, "come take a shower with me."

He bites his lip. I wrap him in my arms and hold him close.

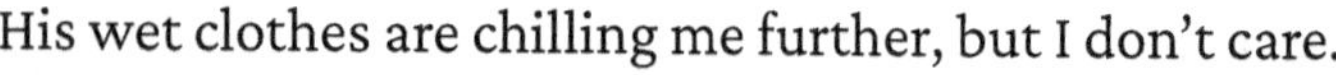

His wet clothes are chilling me further, but I don't care.

Like he can't help himself, he grabs me by the ass and grips me tightly to him, his body shaking and shuddering. He's crying.

Oh, my heart.

"Steve," I whisper against his neck. "I will never willingly hurt you."

He sobs harder.

"There's something else I need to tell you. I love you. I am totally in love with you."

Steve's sobs turn into hiccups, and I begin taking off his wet costume. I start with the jacket, and then he helps me remove his boots. Half of the Lin River spills out on our floor, but it will dry.

When I get to the laces of his black shirt, I pause and look at his face. His monster-cute face. His sweet, natural coloring, complete with wrinkles and moss.

"Yeah. I love you," I say. Then I get his shirt off.

"I want to tell you my real name," he blurts. My heartbeat picks up.

"Yeah?" I get excited, but then I ask, "Wait, will it hurt you? Because there's no way I'm using your name if it's going to hurt you."

His cheeks go a darker shade of green. "If you use it when you're in love—when you're bonded—it won't. It's only if you use it with the intent to hurt someone that it can kill."

"Are you telling me ..."

"That I love you? Yes. That we are bonded, because we have given each other our hearts? Yes."

I exhale. "Good. I think I fell in love with you sometime between the first time I saw your dark eyes and when you sang to me, so it's nice to know it's mutual." He kisses me. Then he takes a big breath, but I hold out my hand to stop him, saying, "I still don't like the idea of having that kind of power."

"I trust you."

He trusts me. I need to trust him, and maybe myself.

I nod and swallow hard. "Then I'm honored you're telling me."

"My real name is Calder Hemming. Calder means rough water. Hemming means shapeshifter."

Something inside me relaxes. "That's *such* a better name for you than Steve. You are not a Steve."

"I know."

I gulp. "I'm still scared to say it. I don't want to kill you."

"My love," Steve—Calder—says, "we are bonded. You have my heart, and I have yours, no?"

"You do."

"Then you can do it safely."

"Calder," I whisper, and he leans over and kisses me. A power like I have never felt zings through me at our kiss.

"Yes, Bran."

"I love you, Calder Hemming."

"And I love you, Brandon Fernandez. You now have power over me, but I like that you have it."

"But 'Steve' is safer," I insist.

"Yes, when we are in public."

"I like knowing the real you. All of you."

22

THE NØKK

I look into the eyes of my sweet lover, Brandon, as I hold him against my green-gray, waterlogged chest with my webbed hands. My teeth are yellow, my tongue is green-black, and my hair is a mess. My instincts tell me to run and hide. To change.

But then Bran smiles at me.

He leans in and kisses me passionately. His mouth is making love to me.

Startled, I need a second to recover. Then I kiss him back, clutching his face. As he stands naked before me, I strip off the remainder of my wet costume. Then I push him toward my bed.

Brandon falls onto his back, and I settle between his legs, and we're kissing hard. "Don't ever leave me again. I need you with me," he says between kisses.

"I couldn't help it."

"But you hid from me. You ran away, because you thought I wouldn't like you like this. You're wrong," he mutters. "You're so wrong. I love you. And now that I can see who you really are, I love you even more. Don't hide from me. I love all of you. All of you. Do you hear me?"

As if Brandon knows what I'm thinking, he starts kissing me again, only this time it's not just my mouth, it's everywhere. He kisses the webs between my fingers. He kisses my black nails and wrinkled skin. He runs his lips down my mottled arm. He makes me shiver.

"If you need to shapeshift into a human form to feel more comfortable when you're out in public, I will support you. But when we're alone, promise you won't hide from me anymore. I can't stand it if you don't think you can be who you really are."

"I love you," I say. "So much. No one else has ever treated me the way you do."

He hugs me tight. His grip around my body makes me feel safe. *Brandon* makes me feel safe.

I kiss him. He doesn't seem to be put off by my black tongue and my mossy skin. He seems to enjoy them. Revel in them.

I am so in love with him, I don't know what to do with myself.

"Come on, let's shower off the river water," Bran says, and I get up and follow him into the bathroom.

Warm, soapy hands slide all over my body. Bran spends time touching me everywhere—even places that don't really get dirty. He washes my balls as if they're fine china.

That image makes me laugh. I tell him, and we both double over.

"You're mine," he whispers. "Mine to take care of."

"It's the other way around. You're mine."

"Then maybe we belong together."

"There's no maybe about it," I say. "You belong to me. I'm never letting you go."

"Good."

He bites his lip. "Calder," he whispers. And I melt. I'd already melted for him, but now I'm gone.

"Brandon."

When we've dried off, our skin warm, we go to his bed. Brandon settles on top of me, his legs between mine, and plays with my hair. He seems to love my hair.

"Can we, um, do it?" he asks, kissing my neck.

"Do what?"

His cheeks go red. "You know. Have sex. Make love. Fuck."

A shiver runs through me. I've wanted to be as close to Brandon as possible. Inside him, or him inside me. I do not care which. All I know is that he is my lover, and I want to show him how much I want to worship his body.

I try to remain calm and collected, when in reality my heart is going at double speed or more.

"Sure," I say, attempting to be nonchalant. "How do you want to do that?"

"You inside me. Or do you want me to be inside you?"

"I don't know," I whisper. "I've never done it."

"Me neither. Not like this." We look at each other a moment, and then Brandon says, "I really want to try bottoming. I've been watching porn and wondering how it feels. The guys seem to like it."

"Okay. We can do that." My heart skips a beat, and I almost shift into my human form. But no. Brandon wants me like this.

"I think I need to prep." Brandon bites his lip. "Witchipedia says we need to use a lot of lube and stretch me a lot."

"You Boo-gled it?"

"You can find everything there," Brandon says.

I kiss him. I can't not kiss him. My skin is buzzing, and I'm aflame with the desire to possess this man. To make him mine.

I want to make this good for him. I believe it will hurt if I go too fast, and I want to be sure that I never hurt him, this fragile human.

Fragile human who's done what I thought was impossible: accepted me as I am, for who I am.

As I dip my tongue into his mouth, Brandon lets out a low moan that's the neediest sound I've ever heard. I run my cool hands all over him. He's so warm and full of sunshine. He reminds me of a summer meadow bursting with golden flowers.

I don't want to stop kissing him, but I grab the lube and squirt some into my hand so I can take care of his erection, which is jutting up and hitting me in the hip.

Now it's my turn to groan. "Do you understand how beautiful you are?" I ask.

He smiles at me and kisses me harder, grabbing my ass so he can grind his cock against mine. He's kneading my back. I'm thrusting against him, but I'm going to have to go slowly or else I'm going to come fast.

"I'm not entirely sure what I'm doing, but ..." I pat his hip. "Get on your stomach and let me prep you. I think I can figure this out."

He hastens to obey, and I pick up the lube bottle again. When I drip some along his ass crack, he shivers. "Oh my god, that's cold and ... lubey."

I snort. "Lubey? Is that a word?"

"I have no idea."

I gather some of the liquid on my fingertips and gently circle his hole, then press inside.

He hisses and stiffens. "Oh, monster gods. That's a weird feeling. It's full. I guess the doctor's done it before, but wow, that's different."

"Want me to stop?" I kiss his shoulder.

"No. Keep going. I want to experience this. I want to experience everything with you."

Once he seems more relaxed, I wiggle a second finger into him, and he starts to loosen up. I'm so hard I could probably saw down a tree with my dick.

But eventually his body accepts my fingers easily. Meanwhile, I'm kissing every bit of his skin that I can. His ass, his gorgeous back. I'm whispering how beautiful he is.

Brandon turns to look at me, and his eyes are red. I go still, trying not to panic. "Are you okay?"

"Yeah," he says. "I like it when you're talking all nice to me."

"I've wanted you since the moment I saw you," I admit.

"Want as in to have sex? Or want as in to drag me to your nøkk world."

"Both, but also just to get to know you. You're so kind and full of life."

He chuckles, which turns into a pleasured hiss. "What's that?"

"I think I found your prostate," I say, satisfied.

"I ... I can deal with that. Can you do it again?"

I gently press against the soft flesh, and he hisses again. "Oh my god, keep that up and I'll see stars."

"Do you want me to use a condom?" I ask. "Nøkk don't get human conditions, so I can't pass anything to you—and I haven't been with anyone anyway—but if it would make you feel better, I'll wear one. It would probably also be less messy that way."

"It's fine without," he says. "I haven't been with anyone since

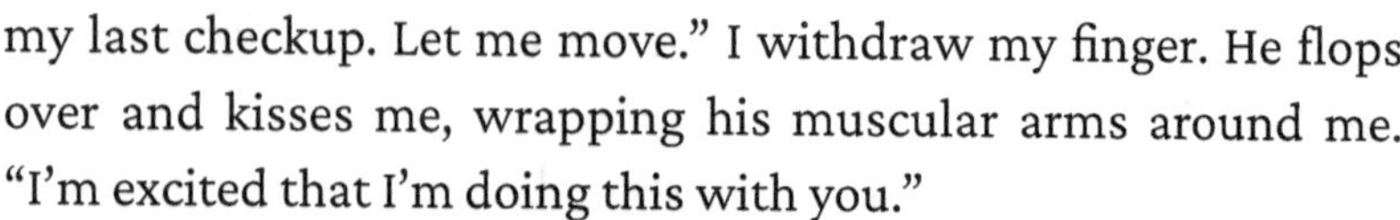

my last checkup. Let me move." I withdraw my finger. He flops over and kisses me, wrapping his muscular arms around me. "I'm excited that I'm doing this with you."

"How do you want to … I mean, what position?" I ask.

"Um, I think it might be easier if I'm on my hands and knees," he says. "Or," he adds with a wink, "we can experiment."

Brandon kneels forward on the bed, and I take a moment to drink him in as he looks over his shoulder. He's perfect. His soft, warm, tan skin. His athletic muscles. His messy dark hair. His sweet eyes and pouty mouth. His smooth, gorgeous ass.

"Fuck, I need you," I groan and line up behind him. Deciding I need even more lube, I drizzle a ton on me and then start pressing in.

It's more difficult than I expect. I bounce back out at first and have to press harder.

Brandon inhales sharply, and I freeze. "What's wrong?"

"It burns. Stings."

"Want me to pull out?"

"No. Hang on. Just … I read about this. It will take a moment, but my body should accept you."

"I don't want to hurt you."

He insists on continuing, though, and at a nod from him, I press in farther.

"Oh, god," he groans.

"Is that good or bad?"

"Both."

"I'm getting worried that we should stop," I admit.

"No. Keep going."

I do, little by little, until I'm all the way inside him, my hips pressed against his perfect ass.

We both stay there a moment, panting.

"Oh my monster gods, this is the strangest feeling ever," he says.

"Do you like it?"

He bites his lip and nods. "Weirdly, yeah. It's ... Fuck, I like it, but it kind of hurts, and I kind of need you to move."

"Whatever you say," I whisper. "I'll do anything you ask."

I pull out and thrust back in, little movements, not wanting to slip out, because it feels like it would be hard to get back inside.

I needn't have worried, though, because after a moment, I get into a rhythm.

Fuck, yes. I bite the muscle of his shoulder, gently, and he growls.

I reach around to stroke his cock, but it's softened. "Are you okay?" I whisper. "Tell me."

"Yeah. I like this. I, oh, damn, that feels good."

I must've got his prostate right. I do the same move again and again, and his cock starts to recover.

Good.

"Brandon, love. You look amazing like this. And you feel even better."

"Give me more cock," he says. "More cock, less talk."

I giggle. "Okay."

I can't do that and stroke him at the same time, so I brace my hands on his hips and really start fucking him. I thrust over and over, mesmerized by the way his hole swallows my cock. The way the muscles in his back flex and move. The way his ass cheeks jiggle when I slap them with my body or my hand. The way his damp curls stick to his temples and the back of his neck.

The way I'm dripping sweat on him, and he's panting, stroking himself with one hand.

"I've dreamt of this so many times," I tell him. "The first night I was here, I had a wet dream about you. Like a teenager."

"Is that why your sheets were stripped that morning?"

"Yes."

"Awesome. Fuck, that's sexy. Also, I might come without you touching me," he says, breathless, letting go of his cock and bracing himself on the bed. "If you keep this up."

"Then yes, let's do that."

Both of us are weary and kiss-stung. Brandon's got a bite mark on his shoulder. I'm single-mindedly determined to make him come. So I keep going, the same angle and intensity, listening to him moan and wail, listening to him pant and beg for more, and giving it to him over and over and over again.

At last his body seizes, and he holds his breath, puts his face in the mattress, and comes with a buried shout.

It's a thing of beauty. *He's* a thing of beauty.

Then I'm coming inside him, and I've never experienced bliss like this before in my life.

"I love you, Calder," he says, and I collapse against him, holding him tight to me.

This is my human.

23

Brandon

I'm pancaked on the bed, mind blown from having sex with Calder, my boyfriend and love.

"Yeah, okay. I like that," I say, turning and holding out my arms. "Sex, I like the sex thing. I like the way it feels when you're all up in my business."

He cuddles into me, breathless. "I do, too."

"I want to do it again. I am foreseeing that I'm going to be the neediest bottom who ever bottomed."

"Is that true?" Calder murmurs.

"Yes. OMG. I love the way it feels to have your dick up my ass. I want it up my ass all the time."

That gets a full-on laugh. "I think you're going to have to go to class once in a while."

"I can't get out of it by saying I want Calder to ream me?"

"No."

"Huh. Too bad." I snicker. Then I sigh, wrapping my legs around his body, clinging to him like a koala. "Today was eventful."

"Yes, it was, Brandon-love."

"I like how it ended, though."

"Me, too."

I drift to sleep wrapped around Calder, reliving the sensation of his body inside mine. His strong hips thrusting into me. The way he focused on me, giving me all his attention. The way his cool hands always feel on my bare skin. The way I now know he's got a little wiggle in his hips that hits the right parts inside me.

The way he makes me come undone.

I never knew that having a lover could feel like this. All-encompassing. Like he's hijacked my body, spirit, and mind.

I don't want to lose myself, but I want to lose myself in him.

The next day is Sunday, and we spend it in bed, only going out to pick up coffee and accept a pizza delivery. It's one of the best days of my life.

ON MONDAY, Calder has a choice to make: Go to class in his true form or in his shifted form.

"It's up to you," I say as he tugs a shirt on over his green skin. "But you look adorable." I don't want to influence him too much. This should be up to him. Just because I'm loving having him be his true self with me doesn't mean he's going to be comfortable around other people.

But I might push him a little bit. Gently. Because if he looked around at all on Halloween night, he should know that he isn't alone at Creelin. There are monsters of every shape and size— and humans, too. And we can all be self-conscious about the way we look. I used to feel that way about my stretch marks, until I decided that they were a badge of honor. They're a reminder to love my body as it is, at any weight. Regardless of my physical shape, I am worthy of respect and love.

And so is he.

Old habits die hard, and he's going to take some convincing, but he's starting to not flinch when I kiss him. He's lolling around in our room unselfconsciously.

I know what I think he should do, but I don't want to force it on him.

When he steps outside in his true form, I tackle him in a hug. "I'm so proud of you."

Later, he reports to me that in his performance class, he is playing a quartet with his friends, and that no one batted an eye when he walked in.

Just as I suspected.

But at the end of the day, he comes back to our room and collapses into me, holding me tight.

"I'm proud of you," I whisper against his hair. "Sometimes showing the world who we really are is the bravest thing we can ever do."

He snuffles into my chest and nods.

A WEEK LATER, it's time for the big game against Shuford.

"Proud of you for playing in your true form," I tell Calder, as we stride into the crowded pool area suited up in our Speedos. The noise level in the pool is overwhelming, with a lot of the school having shown up to cheer us on. Despite the audience seated on bleachers to each side, I slap his cute ass.

"It is so I can focus my energy on playing, not on maintaining my shift," Calder says, rubbing his butt and dropping his towel with the team gear. I do the same.

"Whatever. I'm just glad you're doing it. That you're being yourself. And I really want to get those bastards."

His toothy grin is crooked and makes my blood warm. "Me, too."

"Good luck, babe," I say. "Or, I mean, Steve."

He leans in and whispers, "Use my real name."

"No!" I hiss, glancing to either side. "Isn't it too dangerous?"

"Just whisper it."

I pull him close and breathe in his ear, "Good luck, Calder Hemming."

He closes his eyes and smiles again. "Good luck, Brandon." He gives me a quick kiss, and we jump in the water.

As I do at every game, I carefully put the steel necklace in a corner of the pool that's blocked off for players to wait their turn, because while I can wear it in practice, I wouldn't put it past any of those sleazeballs to yank on it and choke me. And I wouldn't put it past Calder to get pissed and go all nøkk-scream on them.

We swim a few laps to warm up, and then the starting players—including Calder and me—take our positions, holding on to the edge of the pool.

"CREELIN!" our team shouts as one.

I study the opposing team, all wearing their swim caps.

There's the jerk of a werewolf. There's the asshole merman. There's the shithead hydra.

We got this.

There's a bit of a disturbance in the bleachers, and I look up to see a monster—unmistakably a nøkk—taking a seat. He's gray, like Calder.

It has to be his father. Calder looks at him, then looks again. But then he gets his glare on and takes his position in the goal.

The official drops the ball into the designated spot in the middle of the pool, and we take off swimming. Phil gets there fastest. He waxed this morning for the first time in weeks, so he has to be feeling extra fast in the water. He passes the ball to Clay, who throws it to me. The hydra tries to grab me, but I dodge and pass to Nick, who sends it to Ashton. Back to me. And I dong it into the net.

I think that's the fastest we've scored yet.

Buoyed by the quick point, we settle down and dig in. We're gonna beat Shuford. That's what we've been working toward all year. We didn't want to let these bastards get away with anything.

But Shuford has the next possession, and they're down near Calder and the goal in a heartbeat. A troll takes a shot on goal, which Calder blocks. Then the werewolf, and Calder blocks again. Nick fouls the merman—I'm not grumpy about that—and the merman gets a penalty shot.

It zings past Calder's head, and now we're tied.

"No worries!" I call to my boyfriend, and he nods, looking determined. He glances up at his father, who is watching him intently.

Now we have possession, and Phil's dribbling the ball fast toward the Shuford goal. Instead of shooting, he fakes them out and passes to me, lightning fast. I shove it into the upper left corner.

Goal!

Fuck yes.

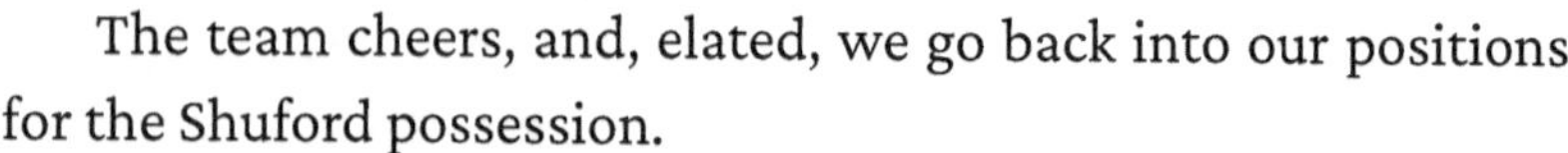

The team cheers, and, elated, we go back into our positions for the Shuford possession.

Point after point, we score, they tie it up. We score, they tie it up. We just can't get a solid lead. Coach rotates players in and out. Nick tends goal for a while, as does Ren. But Calder's back for the final few minutes of the game.

That jerk of a werewolf is dribbling toward him, and I swim as fast as I can to block the shot. While I miss—though Calder makes the save—I do land a satisfying kick to the werewolf's chest. It genuinely was an accident, but I smirk as he howls.

The ref didn't see it.

"Well done, Brandon," Calder yells. "Nice one."

Whipping his head toward my boyfriend, the werewolf sneers, "Fuck you, Calder Hemming."

Calder's body goes still and begins to sink to the bottom of the pool.

For the second time in my life, the world ends.

"No!" I scream and dive under, avoiding the legs of players who haven't figured out what's going on.

Panic lances through me as the water fights my movements, but I kick my way down to Calder, who is lying on the bottom of the pool.

He cannot be dead. *He cannot be dead.* He just needs CPR.

Must get to the surface.

Must save him.

But Calder's a literal dead weight, and it's a struggle for me to bring him up. I'm not sure how much more my lungs can take.

Must save him.

As I'm about to pass out from holding my breath, there's a burst of energy near me, and Nick—in full Loch Ness Monster shift—appears, his snakelike body curving to support Calder's weight like a sling. I help get Calder cradled on Nick's back. Then Nick heaves them both out of the water, leaving a mass of bubbles behind.

At the surface, I gasp for air, but there's no time to do anything but focus on saving the love of my life. I haul myself out of the pool, and Ren and I gently roll Calder off Nick's back to the coping. Coach has raced over, and the refs have clearly stopped play.

I look up, and Calder's father is running to us.

"They said his real name!" I yell, gesturing to Calder. "Save him!"

With a stricken look, Calder's father says, "I cannot. You are his mate. You are the only one who can."

I don't ask. I just do. I lean down and kiss Calder as he lies on the side of the pool, water spreading all around him.

His chest remains unmoving.

"No!" I scream, shaking Calder's chest and kissing his cold lips again. What the fuck? Why isn't it working?

I start CPR—quick chest compressions and rescue breathing.

Doesn't a true love's kiss fix everything?

Some rotten voice inside me tells me it didn't in *Frozen*. That Disney princess needed her sister. Who can save Calder if I can't and his father can't?

Commotion behind me makes it clear that someone has called emergency medical services.

But how can they bring him back? This is a magical death.

I'm counting out breaths and compressions.

His father crouches next to me, wringing his hands. "I do not understand why you are not bringing him back. I can see your bonds. They are visible to any nøkk."

I'm barely registering what he is saying, sweat pouring from my brow as I try to revive my boyfriend.

The EMTs come over with an AED, setting it on the pool coping and placing the electrode pads on Calder's body.

"Son, let us do this. You need to step back from the electrical pulse," one says to me.

I don't want to let Calder go, but what I'm doing isn't working.

With one last kiss, I step back, too stunned even to cry. The entire pool complex is silent as everyone holds their breath, waiting.

With a few more moves, the EMTs set the AED to go, and it zaps Calder. His body convulses and then lies still.

Not breathing. He's not breathing. There's no chest movement.

"The AED will analyze him and tell us what to do next," the EMT says. Another one is readying a stretcher for when it's safe to move him.

I feel useless. Helpless. Someone has taken my soul and stomped on it.

"Stand back," the machine says, telling us it's going to zap him again.

Calder's father starts to sing. His voice is haunting. It's got the same qualities as Calder's but is even sadder.

I start humming the song that Calder wrote for me. My birthday tune. The one that is in part the payment for my gift of blood, Spidey, and vodka.

The machine zaps Calder.

He remains motionless.

Someone—Clay—comes up behind me and puts my steel necklace on me. The one Calder gave me to protect me from him.

I feel a surge of some kind of power. I don't know if it's from the necklace or his dad's singing or my humming.

"Perform chest-only CPR," the machine says.

The EMT leans in to do so, but before he can move, I yell, "Let me. He's my mate. We're bonded."

"No, I'm a professional—"

I shove him out of the way with strength that comes from somewhere down deep.

"Chest only," he says, sounding resigned, as I straddle Calder again.

I do chest compressions, desperately humming his song through my tears.

"Come on, baby," I'm chanting. "Come on."

Calder's lips are parted, and I feel the overwhelming need to kiss him again. I lean in, and the EMT yells, "No!"

I make a shooing movement, tilting Calder's head back. "Let me kiss him! He's my mate!" I touch his lips, wearing his necklace, and concentrate on our bonds.

That moment I first met him, and it seemed like electricity coursed between us.

The sight of his eyes lighting up when I bring him coffee.

Every emoji he's ever texted me.

His unbridled joy when he swims in the river.

How he can stop a waterfall.

What he looks like when he kisses me.

How he's mine. All mine.

This time, when I give him a rescue breath, a spark dances between us. I hope it's not just from the AED. A surge of power races through me, and ... I can see *them.*

Our bonds.

I can see what his dad was talking about. Strings of light, like bright strings of hot glass, are connecting Calder's heart to me.

I can feel them.

I'm connected to him. He is a part of me, and I'm a part of him.

The bond is pulsing on my end, the end that's coming from my chest.

From my heart.

Using all my concentration, I send that pulse down the string of light.

"Come on, my love," I mutter. "You can have my heart. You can have every part of me. I'm yours. Take my soul, even. It's all yours."

I dig deep for every ounce of energy I can summon, pushing my love along our bonds and into Calder.

His back arches, and he starts to cough.

I burst out crying.

Hurriedly, I get off of him, giving him space to breathe.

There's murmuring in the crowd around us while I start sobbing for real, clutching at his shoulders.

"What a relief," the EMT says. "Son, you need to step back."

I shake my head, but Clay puts his hand on my shoulder. "Good job, Fernandez. You saved him. Let them do their job."

THE NEXT HOUR or so is a blur.

The EMTs take Calder out on a stretcher, even though he now

seems out of danger. I want to go with him in the ambulance, but they point out that I'm dripping wet and wearing only a swimsuit, so Calder's dad goes instead. I return to the pool complex, intending to change and join them as fast as I can.

But before I do, Coach approaches me. "What in the name of the monster gods just happened?"

"Shuford's werewolf used our goalie's true name with bad intent. And it killed him," I say, my lip trembling.

Coach's whole body puffs up with anger. He stomps over to the referees, and I can see him throwing up his hands as he yells at them. It's hard to hear him over the loud voices talking everywhere.

"How did that werewolf know Steve's real name?" Clay asks. "And how did they know it would hurt him?"

"I don't know. I whispered it before the game," I say. "He told me to. I thought I was almost silent, but they must've heard it."

"Werewolves do have superior hearing."

"Fuck! I feel so fucking guilty." I rub my eyes. "I should've known not to do it." I pause, thinking. "You know, Shuford was there when Steve and I were Speedo shopping and he told me that knowing his name would kill him. Fuck. Now I want to kill *them*."

"That won't solve anything," Clay says. "Although I understand the sentiment. They need to be thrown in jail."

Now that Calder is safe, I'm taking in what's going on around me. The Shuford team is huddled off to the side, towels over their shoulders. Most of our team is hovering nearby. One of the referees is on his phone. He hangs up, talks with the other ref, and blows a whistle, beckoning the teams to gather around.

The pool complex goes quiet.

"We have a few announcements," one of the referees says. "First, we are appalled by the Shuford team's lack of ethics. There will be a thorough investigation, but based on what we just witnessed and the information Coach Rosmarus has provided, we are going to recommend to the governing board that Shuford be banned from water polo for five years."

There's a gasp from the audience, and Shuford's team looks mutinous, but it's what they deserve.

No, they deserve worse.

"In addition, of course, law enforcement will be taking the individuals involved in for questioning," the ref continues, and as if on cue, two of the campus security zombies appear, approaching the Shuford team.

The werewolf finally looks caged.

"Finally, Shuford forfeits the game. Creelin wins."

We were up one point anyway, but we'll take the win.

I'm so tired, I don't even know what to think. Along with the rest of the team, I head into the locker room to change. I have a boyfriend to go find.

Before I can leave, though, Coach calls us together. "What Shuford did today was criminal," he says, "and I will do everything I can to see that they are properly punished for it. I am furious about what happened."

We all nod.

"Fernandez and MacGregor, good work. You saved Jobs's life."

There's a smattering of applause from my teammates. I don't feel like clapping. All I feel is exhaustion coupled with relief.

"Clearly, a player's safety is inordinately more important than any game. But since it appears Jobs is going to be all right,

I want to take a moment to say that before Shuford's disgusting attack on him, you all were playing the game of your lives, and I am so proud of you all," he says, his walrus tusks popping out. "There were those who questioned the OME opening Creelin to humans. But from day one, all of you, human and monster, have worked together to achieve this result. Congratulations. You've proven you all deserve to be here."

The team does a group cheer, but it's not as enthusiastic as usual. We've been through something major, and it's going to take a little while before we're back in our regular mode.

When Coach releases us, I race to my car and drive to the hospital in town. I find out Calder's room number and skid in there.

He's sitting in a hospital bed, dressed in a flimsy gown, with a blood pressure cuff around his arm, but otherwise he looks unharmed.

In fact, he looks downright normal. Must be because he was in the water?

I carefully put my arms around him. "Babe," I say, my chest heaving. "You're okay!" I kiss the top of his head.

"I am." He gives me a small smile. "Thanks to you."

Carefully taking a seat on the side of his bed, I make him go through everything that happened since he woke up. It sounds like he's mostly fine, his monster strength returned.

"But you died," I say, tears forming in my eyes.

"And you saved me." He tilts his face up to mine. I drop a light kiss on his lips, still wary of hurting him.

"Is that going to happen again?" I ask. "Is it dangerous for you to be on campus now? How many people heard your name?"

Calder shrugs. "I don't know. I suppose it is a risk. But I think what you did might insulate me from more harm." He rubs his

chest. "My heart is beating now because of you."

That makes me kiss him harder.

AFTER A LITTLE while, a nurse bustles in and checks his vitals. I look around, realizing I haven't seen Calder's father since I got here. "Where's your dad?" I ask. "Did you know he was coming to the game?"

"I did not know he was coming. I have not talked with him in ... a while. A few weeks? I guess he wanted to check up on me. I asked him to give me some privacy and to wait for me outside."

"Do you want me to go with you to talk with him?"

"Um. Yes?" Calder looks at me in surprise.

"If you don't want me to, I won't," I say, taking a step back.

"I do want you to. Of course. I am ... not used to having someone supporting me, particularly when he is around."

"Well, now you have me."

"Then, yes. I would like that, and if you are willing, you should properly meet him. You matter to me."

We wait for the results of some tests, but eventually the doctors pronounce Calder magically healed and say he doesn't need to stay the night.

I give him his clothes, which I brought with me, and he gets dressed and signs the discharge papers "Steve Jobs."

Mr. Hemming is waiting at the entrance to the hospital.

"Pappa, hei," Calder says, stepping out of the wheelchair as soon as the orderly says it's allowed. "I hope you are well."

"Son," Mr. Hemming says, his face taut with fear. "I was so worried about you."

"You were?" Calder sounds so genuinely bewildered I want to hug him.

"Of course I was."

Calder's gaze falls to the ground, and he kicks at the concrete.

Mr. Hemming looks at me. "Thank you for saving my son. And you are?"

"This is my boyfriend, Pappa. Brandon Fernandez."

I hold out my hand. "It's nice to meet you, sir." I'm not sure whether I can use Mr. Hemming's real name, so I'm going to err on the side of caution.

"It is nice to meet you, too, Brandon. I do not know how I can ever thank you enough."

"You don't have to thank me, sir," I say. "I'm in love with your son. It wasn't a question of whether I would do everything in my power to save him."

"Yes. I love him, too." Calder takes my hand and squeezes it.

"Hmm." Mr. Hemming rubs the back of his neck. "I had come here to remind my son to engage in more traditional nøkk activities. To not forget where he came from. Or who he is."

"I think you'll find that he is all nøkk," I say, leaning into Calder.

Mr. Hemming nods. "It seems so. I was not expecting to see my son in unshifted form ... or bonded to a human."

"I'm not taking his soul, Pappa," Calder says.

He is worthy of love just as he is.

I kiss his cheek, not caring that his dad is watching.

"Hmm."

"Is there any way you can give Mamma back her soul?" Calder looks as if he's expecting to be chastised for the question—or worse. I think it's incredibly brave of him to ask anyway.

His father opens his mouth and closes it. He shakes his head. "Once it is taken, it is not replaceable. You, by contrast, have what I have been looking for all these years: a true bond. I am jealous," he admits. "But I can be glad that my son is well bonded."

Calder nods a few times. "Let us drive back to campus, Pappa. And then, if you like, I will give you a tour."

"That would be acceptable, yes," Mr. Hemming says. I'm amused—though not surprised, I suppose—that he has the same reticent personality as Calder. I'm not happy with how he treated his son in the past, but I'm proud that Calder has figured out a way he can be himself rather than focusing on the need to please others.

24

THE NØKK

Brandon and I show my father around the Creelin campus, passing by maintenance ghosts and zombies who are readying the school for winter.

"This is a very nice facility," my father says when I show him the music rooms. I play him a song I wrote for the guitar, and he nods.

I don't need his permission to do anything anymore, but part of me wanted it, at least somewhat. Something inside me eases at his proud nod.

I was shocked to see my father here in Pennsylvania, and I'm even more shocked that he approves of what I'm doing. I guess seeing me out in public in my true form meant something to him. He thought I was embarrassed about being a nøkk. And I was, I think.

Now, though, I walk across the quad with my green skin on display, holding my boyfriend's hand.

So maybe I am finding my own way within the parameters of the form I've been given. I could be resentful of the Halloween

Wave changing me in my mother's womb. But instead, I'm learning to be content with who I am.

Once we have finished the tour, my father tells me he is going to go back to his hotel, but he will visit me again before he leaves town. Apparently he is planning to see some of the USA while he is here.

Brandon and I drop Pappa off at his hotel, and then Bran drives the two of us back to campus. He looks at me, grinning. "When you first got to Creelin, I wanted to charm you. I wanted to make sure I wouldn't have to deal with another roommate who hated me or who would never let me into the room because he was always having sex."

"You did charm me," I say. "But I think you should definitely be in the room for the sex."

"Good idea," Brandon says, and I laugh as he steps on the gas.

AFTER WE MAKE love, we lie in bed. It's started raining, and soon the weather will turn even colder. That feels like home to me. Although being with Brandon feels that way, too.

"What would you be doing if you could do anything?" Brandon asks, his fingers tracing a pattern on my chest. "Big picture, and you can't say you'd be lying in bed with me."

The answer is easy. "I'd start a band and play guitar in it."

"Do you have some friends who could play with you?"

"I ... I don't know. I can ask the other students."

"Why don't you put out a call for auditions? See if you can find a drummer and a bassist—at a minimum—if that's the kind of music you want to play. Or do you want violins?"

My mind starts working hard, thinking of all the music I want to play. "I want it all. Do you think anyone would respond?"

"I do."

We put up a flyer online and in the music department, and a week later, Professor Lopez lets me use a studio for tryouts.

A djinn appears, and he plays the bass. We get along immediately, because he's got a cool soul. Then a group of vampires playing trombones. I wasn't planning on a horn section, but I decide that I'll think about it. A shifter—I'm not sure what kind—is amazing at the drums. After hearing a bunch of drummers, I know she's the one I'm going to want to call back.

And I'm pumped. Excited. I know that this could work.

Two days later, my new band has a meeting. "So, do we want to try writing our own music, or do we want to play covers?" the djinn asks.

"I want to play original music," I say. "Is that all right? I can sing for you the sort of thing I'm thinking about."

I plug in my guitar, tune it quickly, and start strumming, singing along quietly. They get the idea, and soon they're mesmerized. I don't think it's because I'm enchanting them—I'm actively trying not to. I think it's because they're the right ones.

The drummer starts tapping out the rhythm, and the bassist picks out a tune, harmonizing with me. Then we're all jamming together.

I'm smiling. Since I met Brandon, I've smiled more than I did in my entire life before. But this is exceptional smiling. And it's all because of Bran. Without his encouragement, it would never have occurred to me to put myself out there. But now I'm thinking that this is what I truly want to be doing with my life.

Playing my music. With, possibly, new friends.

I don't even care if we do well financially, though I suppose the other band members may have opinions about that. But what's important to me is that I love the sounds we're making. Maybe, together, we can make other people's lives better.

Rather than dragging them down, I want to lift them up.

This may be my life's work.

OUR FINALS are done—both Brandon and I did well—and now it's Christmastime. We're in the cool Arizona desert. Brandon's fussing about me getting dehydrated, and he insists on us jumping in a saltwater pool a few times a day.

I love him for it.

I have met Brandon's boisterous family, who generally seem to be accepting that Bran is dating—soul-mated with—a monster. Apparently his older brother is dating an elf, so perhaps that helps.

Brandon's parents are both teachers, so they have the winter break off and are happy to show me around this region that is very unlike anything I am used to. I do not think I would want to live here year-round. But I love the flavors of the new foods they offer me to try—so different from the fish I grew up with. And I love the way everyone in this family is cheerful and encouraging.

My English continues to improve, now that I have been in this country for several months. But when we all sit down to watch movies, Brandon makes sure to put on Norwegian subtitles, just in case. We watch many Christmas movies from the eighties, and I listen to stories about Brandon's abuelo.

About the Author

Leslie McAdam is a California girl who loves romance and well-defined abs. She lives in a drafty old farmhouse on a small orange tree farm in Southern California with her husband and two children. Leslie's first published book, *The Sun and the Moon*, won a 2015 Watty, which is the world's largest online writing competition. She's gone on to receive additional literary awards and has been featured in multiple publications, including Cosmopolitan.com. Her books have been Top 100 Bestsellers on both Amazon and Apple Books. Leslie is employed by day but spends her nights writing about the men of your fantasies.

Website: https://www.lesliemcadamauthor.com

M/M-only newsletter: http://eepurl.com/hD9a4r

low Creepin U authors for making it fun!

Heather Roberts for always helping.

Whimsical Reverie Design for the cover.

My family for letting me write.

I traveled to Norway, Sweden, and Denmark last year, which served as inspiration. A fairytale book called *Vaesen* by Johan Egerkrans was particularly helpful.

Acknowledgments

Thank you to:

My younger child, who brainstormed plot points with me on our trips to and from their water polo practice. (No, they aren't allowed to read this book, but I will acknowledge their contribution in coming up with the idea of an inverse fake ID in addition to helping me with water polo terminology and more.)

My sister-in-law Katie for helping me with the airport scene—just after she returned from living in Sweden.

Kristy Lin Billuni, Mary Carr, Lex Martin, J.E. Birk, and Rachel Ember for helping me with the concept of this book.

Katy Cuthbertson, Megan Dischinger, and Susann Husfloen for beta reading.

Alicia Z. Ramos for careful editing. (Which never includes acknowledgments, so grammatical errors are all on me.)

Jerica MacMillian and Virginia Tesi Carey for proofreading. (But not this page.)

My new street team for being amazing.

C.D. Rachels for including me in his project. Thank you to my fel-

home."

Brandon walks with me to the house where I grew up. It is definitely shadowy, compared to the bingo hall.

"This is more what I expected," he says, pointing at the harp and fiddle in the corner of the dark home.

"Sometimes unexpected things can be amazing, though," I say.

"Absolutely." He grins. "Play me my birthday song, my nøkk. Please?"

"Anything for you."

THANKS FOR reading *The Nøkk and the Jock*. Be sure to read all of the Creepin U: MM Monster romance series!

When the tree spirit reunites with his childhood friend, seeds of attract that were never uprooted begin to blossom. Check out book 2, *Dryad, Try Again*, by C.D. Rachels.

When the gorgon has to tutor the star of the baseball team, the two of them discover that humans and monsters have plenty in common. Check out book 3, *Vexing the Viper*, by Ashley Rayne.

When the human volunteers to be the feeder of the hunky incubus, platonic research goes out the window. Check out book 4, *Penn and Incubus*, by Essie Sloane.

When the basilisk shifter is paired with a human pianist for a concert, he isn't sure if the man will be his downfall or his destiny. Check out book5, *Surviving His Gaze*, by Rorie Kage.

with room to spare. I had no idea there were that many nøkks in the world."

"The largest community lives here."

Brandon peers at the tables. "Those bingo cards ... what are they made out of? It doesn't look like paper or plastic."

"They are made of souls," I say.

Brandon spins on his heel to face me. "Wait, what?"

"Nøkk play bingo using the souls of the humans we have dragged down here."

"That's kind of horrifying."

"You see why it was so important that I resist you. I did not want you to be turned into a bingo card."

"Wow. I don't mean to judge," Bran says, "but this is strange."

"I can imagine. While I am used to it, it can take a bit to sort out, mentally."

"Thank you for not turning me into a bingo card."

"You're welcome." I kiss him. "I told you there was too much paperwork involved with taking a soul. And bingo cards aren't the only way we can take your soul. I could've put it in that jar you gave me the spider in. Remember?"

"Seriously?"

I nod.

"This place is ... interesting." Brandon's eyes are trying to take everything in, but it's clear it's too much for him.

"I should clarify, this isn't all there is to the underground world. There are places that are shadowy, too."

"Then lead on, boyfriend, and show me all the weird and wonderful ways of the nøkk." He takes a deep breath. "I ... I would still give you it. If you wanted it."

"I don't need it." I kiss him. "Come on. Let me show you my

"Basically, yes."

With a few more steps, I transport us to the entrance to the underground kingdom. The underground world isn't run by the same laws of physics that apply above. We can travel vast distances instantly.

We step inside, and Bran looks around.

"Whoa."

We're on a street. Instead of direct sunlight, the rippling water around our protective bubble provides filtered light for us to see. There are houses and caves and places for nøkk to sleep, work, and play.

I grin. "Come on. Let me show you where they take the souls. I don't think it is going to be what you are expecting."

We walk a short distance and then turn toward the main part of our settlement. There is a large, central hall where most of the nøkk gather. We step inside and are met by the chatter of voices speaking Old Norse.

No one pays us any mind, but Brandon's eyes are bigger than I've ever seen them. "Is this ... a bingo hall?"

"Yes. We love our bingo halls."

He shakes his head. "This is not at all what I pictured."

"What did you picture?"

"I thought it would be, you know, like nature. Shadowy. Caves. That there would be a lot of rivers and, I don't know, maybe fires burning in torches along passageways. Not, like, fluorescent lights and tables covered with bingo cards."

"Those aren't fluorescent—they're phosphorescent."

He looks more closely at the lights and around the room. "Oh, wow. This place is as big as those convention centers where they hold car shows. I bet they could have a thousand nøkks in here

"I do not want to take your soul from you," I protest. Though, while that desire has been banked since we bonded, I admit it still exists. But there are more important things, like making him happy.

He smiles. "I'm serious. Anything of me you need, you can have. I feel like you've given me all of you."

My heart pings. "I love you."

"And I love you."

We spend the day exploring. While we have reserved a hotel for our time in Norway, part of me wants to take him to my true home.

"Do you want to see the underground realm?" I ask.

Bran's eyes shine with excitement. "Yes! Is there anything special I need to do?"

I shake my head. "We're bonded. You can come visit with me and then return to your regular life."

"Will I be able to breathe there?"

I smile at him and nod. "Yes. Everything will be fine."

We walk to a large river on the edge of town. I need a body of water in order to access the realm. First, I transform into my true self. Then, holding Brandon's hand, we wade into the water.

I use my powers to create a protective bubble of air around us so we can breathe and our clothes won't get wet. It's a version of the same manipulation I can use to stop waterfalls. I don't need the bubble, but Brandon does.

Brandon watches the water swirling around us as we sink deeper and deeper into the river.

"This feels really weird," he says, reaching out a finger to touch the water. "Is this what it's like when you swim? Like you can just move the water? Cut through it?"

BONUS SCENE

THE UNDERGROUND REALM

The Nøkk

I'm walking down a street in Bergen, holding Brandon's hand. I'm in my human form, because I'm still more comfortable in public like this. I'm a shapeshifter, and taking on other forms is a part of who I am. I'm learning to accept that.

Bergen's rainy, and today's no exception, no matter that it's summer. I've made sure that Bran's comfortable and dry with a Nordic jacket and sturdy umbrella.

We make our way through the old merchant area. The buildings here are twisted, almost zigzag. Some of them are built from trees—full trunks, instead of milled wood.

Brandon's dark eyes are wide as he tries to take in everything. The waterfront activity. The tourists. And how Bergen is a gateway to the wild fjords beyond.

"You know that if you wanted it, I'd give you my soul," Brandon says.

I blink at him. "What?"

He raises his eyebrows.

Even though I am in the desert, as far away from my home as I can be, this is where I belong: wherever Brandon is.

Also by Leslie McAdam

IOU Series (lower angst m/m)

*Ambiguous** (audio narrated by Hamish Long and Kirt Graves)
*Studious** (audio narrated by Declan Winters)
*Delicious** (short story)
*Oblivious**
*Curious**
Notorious
Ferocious (coming soon)
* Also available in German

Creepin U: A Monster Romance Series (shared-world m/m)

The Nøkk and the Jock

With J.E. Birk and Rachel Ember (holiday m/m/m)

ILYBSM
TMI

FASTER series (shared-world sports m/m) (coming soon in Spanish)

Off Track

Sarina Bowen's World of True North (shared-world m/m)

Undone (audio narrated by Iggy Toma and Tim Paige)
Unmanageable (audio narrated by Jacob Morgan and Teddy Hamilton)

Albrecht College Series (college m/m)

Mixed Motives (short story)

All American Boy Series (shared-world m/f)

Boy on a Train (audio narrated by Desiree Ketchum and James Cavenaugh)

Romantic comedies with Lex Martin (m/f)

All About the D (audio narrated by Stephen Dexter and Ava Erickson)
Surprise, Baby! (audio narrated by Jacob Morgan and Muffy Newton)

The Giving You … series (m/f)

The Sun and the Moon (audio narrated by Tor Thom and Charley Ongel)
The Stars in the Sky

All the Waters of the Earth
The Ground Beneath Our Feet (audio narrated by Tor Thom and Charley Ongel)

Love in Translation series (m/f) (also available in Hebrew)

Sol
Sombra

Stand-alone novella (m/f)

Lumbersexual (audio narrated by Tor Thom and Charley Ongel)